To my husband.
Thank you for taking care of our home and its many inhabitants
while I follow this silly dream of mine.

DESCRIPTION

One dead. One risen. One caught in between.

For more than thirteen years, Winter Black has believed her little brother is dead—kidnapped and murdered by the same lunatic who killed her parents. The news of a lead into Justin's whereabouts brings her out of her hiatus and back to work at the Richmond FBI office. And face to face with the co-workers she's been avoiding.

Winter can't avoid them for long because a body is discovered in a fifty-five-gallon drum, and the team soon realizes that they aren't hunting your typical serial killer. Whoever killed this man isn't just a murderer—they are a skilled surgeon, and John Doe is just one of many. And now, the killer is after her friend, Autumn.

Welcome to book four of Mary Stone's debut crime fiction series. If you love a throat-clutching thriller with unexpected villains and riveting mystery, Winter's Rise will keep you turning pages until the end.

Grab your copy of Winter's Rise and discover that evil doesn't just hide in the dark.

1

As the haze thinned from Jensen's thoughts, he opened his eyes a slit. Though he could see a tinge of white light at the edge of his vision, the remainder of the room was cloaked in shadow. At the other end of the space was a door, and from the light of the narrow window, he could see a dim hallway. None of it was familiar.

Where was he?

How had he gotten here?

The recollection trickled back to him as his eyelids drooped closed. He could picture the parking lot of the bar, neon lights from the signs in the windows glinting off the damp asphalt.

Though he might have had a touch too much to drink last night—*was it last night?*—he had pushed aside the concern and reminded himself of his plan. A couple blocks away was a restaurant that served breakfast twenty-four hours a day, and *that* had been where he was headed. After a meal and a couple cups of coffee, he'd planned to return to his car to drive home.

Was he home?

No. This sterile room wasn't part of the house he and his wife had owned for the past ten years.

Grating his teeth, he forced himself to focus on the fuzzy memory of his trip to the diner. He vaguely remembered walking down the sidewalk, his attention focused on the screen of his smartphone instead of his surroundings.

In the midst of typing an "I love you" text message to his wife, Faith Leary, the world had gone black.

That wasn't where the memory ended, though. At least he didn't think so. He was sure he had stepped into the restaurant, could swear he had taken a moment to bask in the aroma of roasting coffee and frying bacon as he walked through the familiar double doors.

He had walked through those doors, hadn't he?

No, he hadn't. As soon as the realization crossed his mind, his eyes snapped open. The world had gone black before he hit the sidewalk, but he knew he hadn't been drunk enough to blackout.

He had been drugged. Not in the bar, but right there at the edge of the damn parking lot. A light sting in the back of his neck had given way to utter nothingness.

When he awoke the first time, his aching head had rested on a pillow, and he almost tricked himself into believing he had made it home. As he'd shifted on the hard surface beneath the light blanket, however, he wondered if he had fallen asleep on the floor *beside* the bed he shared with his wife.

Then, he'd opened his eyes.

He remembered how golden sunlight highlighted a square hatch in the ceiling at the other end of the narrow room. Room? He'd known right away that he'd been in an unfamiliar room.

Flinging off the sheets, a surge of adrenaline had pushed away the ache in his head as he'd leapt to his feet. In the meager illumination, he'd felt along the walls and hoped, even prayed, that he would find a door handle. Instead, he'd been greeted with nothing more than cool, smooth metal.

His movements had been fervent and soon bordered on panicked. One question had screamed over and over in his mind—*where the hell was he?* Even now, as he thought back, he wasn't sure.

Once his sight had adjusted to the low light, he saw it, snapping his mind back to another memory. The dark shape of a bubble in the far corner of the ceiling. A camera. Wherever in the hell he was, someone knew he was there. Someone was *watching* him.

When the hatch opened, the daylight that spilled through had seemed as bright as a supernova, and he'd been forced to raise a hand to block out the hellish illumination.

"Who are you?" His voice had been hoarse as he addressed the figure descending into the space. As best as he could, he squared his shoulders.

Jensen had intended to fight.

He had grown up in a working-class neighborhood in Philadelphia. He knew how to defend himself, and this wasn't the first time he had been in peril during his thirty-one years of life. But as the figure had approached him, the two tours in Afghanistan felt like they might as well have occurred in an alternate dimension.

The resurgence of the headache and weariness had closed in on him at the same pace as the dark figure, and the determination had drained from his disciplined fighting stance. Whatever he had been dosed with the night before had only been temporarily defeated by the flood of adrenaline, and he could have sworn the other man knew how rapidly the energy would melt from Jensen's tired muscles.

After another sting, the world had gone black again.

And now, he was here, in a room that felt like a forgotten throwback to a 1960s asylum.

"You're awake," a voice called out from behind him.

He tried to turn to face the source, but his head was fixed in place by a contraption he couldn't see.

"Who…" It was the only word he could manage. His throat felt raw, and his mouth was as dry as the distant Afghani desert. "Who are you?" The short question felt like a monumental task.

"Oh, you know me," the woman chuckled. Even her mirth felt like ice.

He blinked, tried to focus. Tried to remember. "N-no, I d-don't." He hated how nervous he sounded.

Try as he might, he couldn't place her voice. In the ensuing silence, he raked through memories of any woman with whom he had crossed paths in recent memory. None of them sounded like her. He didn't know why she thought she knew him.

"You've got the wrong person," he managed. The words were small and weak, but even the minimal effort to speak was exhausting.

"No, Jensen. I've got exactly who I want." There was no doubt in her tone, no room for debate.

A metallic whir followed her statement. What the hell was that? Was that a *drill*? A *saw*?

The marked increase in his pulse made the pounding in his head more pronounced. Eyes squeezed shut like he was a grade school kid trying to hide from imaginary monsters in the dark corners of his bedroom, Jensen swallowed against the rise of bile in the back of his throat.

"I'm not going to kill you, Jensen."

Her calm words cut through his haphazard thoughts, but he wished they hadn't.

"In fact, you might be the lucky one. When we're done

here, you might come out of this even better than you were before. Just relax. I've done this plenty of times, and I know what I'm doing. You're in good hands."

He didn't believe her attempt to placate his mounting anxiety.

As the metallic sound grew louder, he pictured his wife. For thirteen years, Faith had been at his side. For every celebration, every bump in the road, every new journey, he had always been able to count on her bright smile and that sparkle in her gold-flecked eyes.

This was it.

For some reason he couldn't fathom, he was about to die, and he hadn't even been able to send the text message to tell his beautiful wife how much he loved her.

2

W ith a smile and a five-dollar bill, Bree Stafford bade farewell to the driver of the sleek, black sedan. As she stepped onto the sidewalk, she couldn't help the reflexive glance to the edge of the building.

Three months earlier, around that same corner, Douglas Kilroy—The Preacher, as the press loved to call him—had knocked her unconscious with a fast-acting sedative. The bastard had then loaded her into the back of a white panel van to drive to the outskirts of a little Virginia town called McCook.

Maybe the brush with such a notorious killer should have left a definitive mark on her psyche, but when she looked to the dim corner, she could find no semblance of trepidation. After all, Douglas Kilroy was dead, and the man joining her at the bar tonight was responsible for the fatal shot.

As grateful as she was to have been saved so quickly, Bree knew with a certainty she didn't fully understand that she would have made it out of Kilroy's grasp unscathed, one way or another. That night at the dilapidated church wasn't the first time she had been taken captive, but she hoped it would be the last.

She turned her attention to a flicker of movement amidst a series of benches and tables to the side of the entryway. The glow of Noah Dalton's smartphone glinted off the whites of his eyes as he locked the screen to pocket the device.

When he was outside the office, Bree thought there were few who would have guessed he was an FBI agent. Between the plaid flannel over his gray t-shirt, his worn jeans and dusty work boots, he looked more like he'd just finished up his workday as a contractor.

As she glanced down to her white button-down shirt and slim-fitting black pants, Bree felt overdressed. "What are you doing in the smoking section?" Raising her brows to offer him a questioning glance, she pulled open one of the double doors and waved him forward.

"You're such a gentleman, Bree." Noah Dalton flashed her one of his patented, disarming grins as he made his way into the bar. "I was playing Mahjong, not smoking, by the way. My sister always told me that the coolest people at the bar were in the smokers' section. So far, I think I agree. It might smell worse than shit, but I've met some pretty cool cats in smoking sections."

Bree couldn't hide her surprise. "Your sister?"

The black-clad bouncer beside the doorway didn't rise from his stool to ask for their IDs. Glancing up from his smartphone, he smiled and nodded. He knew them well.

"Yeah, my sister," Noah replied.

"Are you guys not close? I don't think I've ever even heard you say that you *had* a sister."

He lifted one of his broad shoulders. "No, we are. We're both just busy, I guess. Plus, she's all the way out in Austin. She owns a tattoo shop out there, and word's been getting out about how talented she is, so she's been pretty swamped for the last year or two." He lifted the shoulder again.

"So, she's there and you're here," Bree prodded, hoping for more information on this interesting man. If she'd been straight, she thought he might be her type. If nothing else, she knew he was the type to be in her corner.

He winked. "Nice detective work, Bree. Yep. I'm here, and we've been, well…maybe not swamped, but you know what I mean." As his smile faded, a flicker of despondency passed behind his green eyes.

That sadness was no small part of the reason for Bree's proposed outing on a Thursday night. Aside from a call a few days earlier to tell Winter about the lead they'd found into her brother's disappearance, no one in their office had heard a single word from the woman.

Though Noah made a valiant effort to conceal the dark cloud in his demeanor, Bree had worked alongside the tall man for long enough to know that Winter's absence weighed on him, and she had seen enough of his and Winter's interactions to know he blamed himself for their inability to locate Justin Black.

Bree's reminders that he'd made the right decision to shoot Douglas Kilroy had been gentle at first, but in recent weeks, they had become more pointed.

If he hadn't fired that shot at that precise moment, Winter would be dead. That was it. That was the end of the story.

Bree had been front and center for the entire series of events, and the only reason *she* hadn't fired the killing shot was because she was worried the larger caliber round would have pierced through Kilroy and hit Winter.

Winter was smart, and Bree had assured Noah that even if she had harbored a sense of ill will for Kilroy's untimely death, she would have let the misgivings go by now. Whether he didn't believe her or he'd decided to shoulder the guilt for an unrelated reason, Bree wasn't sure.

"Your sister sounds cool." Bree offered him a smile, thinking of her fiancée and how talented she was. She leapt on the change of subject like a drowning woman to a raft. "Shelby's a fantastic artist. You know that painting in our living room, right? The one above the couch?"

Bree watched Noah's eyes move as he scanned his memory. "The water lilies and the gator? That one?"

"Yeah, that one. Shelby painted that. She grew up in Louisiana, so it's like her little piece of home."

"Really?" Noah scratched at the stubble darkening his chin. "Wow, that thing's really good. It's like a Bob Ross painting or something. Do you guys have any of her other paintings hanging up?"

"A couple." Bree nodded, unable to keep the pride from shining through her words. "I use one of the bedrooms as an office, and she uses one of them as a studio. Her job has been busy lately, so she hasn't had as much time for painting. But I'm sure as soon as it slows down, she'll be back at it. You want me to give her a request for you?"

As they neared the bar, he thrust his hands into his pockets and nodded. "The décor in my place is still, I mean, it's nonexistent. Might be nice to add a little bit of color somewhere. I can pay her for it."

Waving a dismissive hand, Bree shook her head. "No need. You're our friend. It's a labor of love."

"I'll come up with something to repay you guys." His grin widened as he glanced back to her. "I've been teaching myself to cook, and I've gotten pretty good at it. I can just come over and make you guys food for a week or something."

"Hey, don't say stuff like that unless you mean it, okay?" Bree laughed. "You might not be able to guess, but Shelby's appetite is a little insane. She's a swimmer, and that seems to be the norm for them."

"Lucky for her, my momma only ever taught me how to cook for an army. I don't even know how to cook meals for one person, which is why I pretty much never used to cook for myself."

"Shelby can eat like an army, so that's good news." As Bree chuckled, she turned to offer a quick wave to the woman behind the bar.

With an easy smile, Noah followed suit. "Do you know her?"

The redhead returned the gesture before she made her way to greet a couple who had arrived a few minutes after Bree and Noah.

"Sort of," Bree answered with a shrug. "Shelby loves her. A few months ago, I had to leave early one night for work, and Shelby just sat up at the bar and talked to her for hours. Now, whenever Shelby sees her, she has to give her a hug. Honestly, it's pretty adorable."

As they took a seat at what had become their favored booth, Noah looked thoughtful. "Huh, I guess that makes sense then."

"What?" Bree furrowed her eyebrows. "I think you left off the first part of that, friend."

"Oh, right, yeah. She's the one who pointed out your friends that night that…well…you know." He left the sentiment unfinished and flashed her a hapless look.

"Oh…" Bree lifted both eyebrows. "The night Kilroy nabbed me? Yeah, I remember that night."

There was a hint of self-deprecation in Noah's chuckle as he reached for a menu.

"It's fine, Dalton." She laughed. "That's not even the first time I've been kidnapped. I used to work in organized crime, remember? Way back in the day, back when you were probably still in grade school."

"Really?" He glanced up from the menu. "You've never mentioned that. Looks like we're learning all sorts of new stuff about each other tonight."

"I guess so." Bree snickered. "I'll make you a deal. You tell me more about your tattoo artist sister, and I'll tell you about some of the crazy shit that happened when I worked in organized crime in Baltimore."

"Baltimore?"

"I told you, it was forever ago. Twenty years, my friend. I was in Maryland for about five years, and then I came here. And let me tell you, organized crime is something else. Completely different animal, and definitely not for the faint of heart."

He gave her a "you've got to be shitting me" look.

Bree laughed. "Not that any of what we do is for the faint of heart, but the work from organized crime can follow you home if you're not careful. I never went undercover or anything, but I knew some people who did. That work, that's either something you're cut out for, or you're not. There's not really any middle ground."

"All right, I hope you know what I have to do now." With a clack, he tapped his menu against the polished tabletop. "I'll have to start making jokes about *The Wire* when we're at work."

As she laughed, Bree didn't bother to conceal the disbelief from her tone. "You've seen *The Wire*? That doesn't really strike me as your type of show."

"I'm not sure how to take that." He paused to feign a contemplative look, which made him look even younger. "But, to answer your question, of course I've seen *The Wire*. It's the best show of all time. Why? What did you *think* I watched?"

She thought about it for a good ten seconds. "Honestly, I've got no idea." Bree's smile widened as she spread her hands. "Like you said, we're learning all sorts of new stuff about one another tonight."

As she watched him laugh yet again, Bree figured she would give him a rundown of her entire FBI career as long as it kept his thoughts away from the desolate rut in which he had been stuck for the last few months.

❄

THE RICHMOND FBI office was sparsely populated at the evening hour, and the only person SSA Aiden Parrish passed on his way to Max Osbourne's office was Sun Ming. Even three months after she had taken a bullet to the shoulder, one of her arms still rested in a blue sling.

She and one other agent from their office had responded to the request for aid on the night Douglas Kilroy was shot and killed. Their assistance hadn't been requested in the rundown church outside McCook, but at the site of a mass shooting turned hostage situation.

One of the two assailants had been shot and wounded in the firefight, but not until after he fired off a round that hit Sun's left shoulder. Cop shows on television made gunshot wounds to the shoulder seem superficial, but complete recoveries were rare, and quick recoveries were rarer still. Even after extensive physical therapy, Sun would be lucky to regain full use of her arm.

Between Sun's injury and Winter's absence, he hadn't been able to shake the feeling that they would never recover from that fateful night.

For the past three months, he and Noah Dalton had set aside their differences to search for any trace of Justin Black's whereabouts. The investigation had been tedious, but at the beginning of the week, their diligence finally paid off.

They'd been given a tip just a few days ago, and it was exactly the break they'd been needing. A new grandmother who had been out of the country for the past six months to stay with her daughter and new grandbaby remembered seeing Douglas Kilroy at the same storage building they utilized.

After finally gaining entrance to the storage site, they scoured The Preacher's meager possessions. They hadn't found much, but they'd discovered an indication that a high school aged boy had been under Kilroy's care for an unspecified number of years. Aside from the fact that the kid existed, they had pitiful little else to go on, but Aiden had become so accustomed to uncovering nothing that the vague piece of information seemed monumental.

Max Osbourne's door was open as Aiden approached, and he paused to rap his knuckles against the metal frame. The Special Agent in Charge of the Richmond Violent Crimes Task Force's eyes snapped away from his two computer monitors and up to Aiden. "Parrish. Come in."

SAC Osbourne tapped a couple keys before he turned to face the set of chairs in front of his desk. Both elbows propped atop the matte black surface, he scooted forward.

As Aiden sat, Max's gaze never wavered. "To what do I owe the pleasure, SSA Parrish?"

The skepticism in his voice was plain to hear. Aiden and Max didn't cross paths often, and he could already tell his request for a meeting had piqued the older man's suspicions.

"It's been three days since Noah Dalton contacted Winter Black. Why the hell hasn't she shown up yet? We can't move forward in this investigation without her."

Aiden figured an upfront query would be less likely to put Max on edge. He didn't know the seasoned SAC well, but in each dealing he had with his boss, he had gathered that the man appreciated a direct approach.

"You know I can't tell you that, Parrish." Max's voice was flat, almost as if he had expected the question from the get-go.

"Since when are you bound to secrecy about situations like this?" He made his best effort to match the unimpressed tone, but Aiden doubted that anyone could exude quite the same blasé air as Max.

"When my agents take a personal leave of absence, I keep their reasons to myself. It's not your business unless Agent Black wants it to be your business, Parrish. If you want to know why she's gone, maybe you should ask her."

Aiden barely managed to keep from rolling his eyes. "I tried. She won't answer any of our calls. Not mine, not Dalton's, not even Agent Stafford's."

"Did you stop to think that maybe she's got a good reason for that? You're a smart guy, Parrish. Head of the damn Behavioral Analysis Unit, so I figure out of all the people here, you'd be able to come up with a reason someone might need a break from their friends and coworkers."

Aiden cleared his throat, pissed at the taunt and doing his best not to show it. "There are many reasons someone would isolate themselves, but at this point, it's interfering with an ongoing investigation."

The statement was true, but the need to uncover a new lead wasn't the main driving force behind his adamancy to bring Winter back to Richmond. He clenched his jaw at the thought and forced himself to pay attention to Osbourne's movements.

"Then do what you'd do with any other witness." Shrugging, Max leaned back in his oversized chair.

"You want me to get a court order to make a federal agent

come back to work?" Aiden surmised, narrowing his eyes at the flicker of amusement on Max's face.

"You do what you need to do, Parrish. I trust your instincts. If you think that's what you've got to do to get ahold of Agent Black, then you know where the courthouse is. I won't stop you."

In the silence that descended on the room, it took all of Aiden's self-control not to dive over the desk and wrap his hands around Max's throat.

A day or two after Kilroy's death, Winter had been officially moved back to Violent Crimes. By the time he'd realized she had no plans to return to work for the foreseeable future, her personnel records were already under Max's lock and key.

Though Aiden harbored no real malice toward Max Osbourne, he forced himself to bite back a handful of irritable observations at the man's unabashed stonewalling. He might as well have been talking to an actual chunk of granite.

"Damn it, Osbourne," Aiden nearly growled. "You can't just tell me when she's going to be back?"

"If I thought it'd get you out of my office, it would've been the first thing I said," Max replied. "Because I was just about to leave, and my wife made lasagna for dinner. Maybe that doesn't mean much to you, but that's just because you've never had Amy's lasagna. If that lasagna gets cold before I can eat it, I'm going to hold you personally responsible."

"For god's sake," Aiden muttered.

"That's a no, by the way. No, I won't tell you when she plans to be back. No, I won't tell you why she's gone. Think of it this way. Back when you were a field agent, if you had something personal come up that necessitated a leave of absence, would you want your superior telling all his or her colleagues about it? And if they did, would you ever trust them again afterward?" Max leaned forward, pinning Aiden with a hard stare. "If you answer yes to either one of those questions, then I'm going to call bullshit."

He was right.

"Fine," Aiden ground out as he pushed himself out of the chair. "I'll make sure I tell Winter what a great job you did protecting her personal information."

"You do that," Max replied, looking satisfied as he linked his hands behind his head. "See you tomorrow."

"Yeah. Good night, Osbourne."

"One more thing, Parrish."

Aiden had just reached the doorway, and he paused, turning back to face the SAC.

"Winter Black's a damn fine agent, and I've never seen her waver in her commitment to this department. I don't know what kind of shit you pulled to get her reassigned to BAU or to pull her into the Kilroy investigation, but if you ever do it again, we're going to have a much bigger problem than cold lasagna."

Aiden bristled. "I—"

Max stood, his knuckles taking his weight on the desk as he leaned forward and bulldozed on. "I don't know what kind of personal interest you've got in her, but you need to check that shit at the door. You're a leader now, Parrish, not a fucking babysitter. Winter Black is her own person, and she's capable of making her own decisions."

"I realize—"

Max held up a hand. "I don't care if you did any of that underhanded shit in the interest of keeping her behind a desk so she'd be safe. Honestly, if that was your logic, then it's a little chauvinistic, don't you think? You're not her keeper. Winter Black is a grown woman, and she doesn't need a protector. If you keep trying to protect her, you'll only stifle her. She's going to do good work here, and you can either hold her back, or you can get out of her way."

3

As he took a seat at the bar, Noah waved goodbye to Bree and her fiancée, Shelby. Upon Shelby's arrival, she had wasted no time before she made her way to wrap the bartender in a bear hug. True to Bree's word, the scene had been adorable.

Now, Shelby and Bree had decided to head home, but the return to his sparsely decorated apartment still didn't seem appealing. He knew once he was there that he would check his phone once every two minutes to ensure he hadn't missed a text message or even a damn email from Winter.

For the millionth time, he would walk through the last night he had seen her, from the morning briefing about Douglas Kilroy to the awkward kiss in Winter's kitchen. From the discovery of the Polaroid of Bree to the way the work light had glinted off the spatter of blood as Douglas Kilroy's lifeless body dropped to the dusty floor.

If Noah was by himself, not working or socializing, that damned night was the only place his thoughts ever ventured. Some called it rumination, others called it anxiety, but the feeling that weighed on him like a suit of lead was more simple. It was regret.

Regret that he hadn't taken a non-fatal shot at Douglas Kilroy. Regret that he had held back when he voiced his affection for Winter. He hadn't wanted to make her feel uncomfortable, but if he had known the encounter in the little galley kitchen was the last time they would be alone together, he would have done *something* differently.

Maybe he should have kept the thoughts to himself. Maybe he shouldn't have even gone to visit her in the first place.

Was that the last time he would ever see her? Had she decided to move herself and her grandparents across the country, or to a different country? She'd said she would return to Richmond to help the investigation to find her brother, but in the three days since they spoke, there had been radio silence.

With one hand, he stifled a resigned sigh as he forced himself back to the present.

A flicker of movement in the corner of his eye drew his attention to the bartender. As she arched an eyebrow, he didn't miss the shadow of concern in her bright eyes.

Shit, how much of the anxious thoughts had been written on his face?

Damn it, you're in public. Tone it down a little.

"You all right, man?" she asked. The query wasn't tinged with condescension or skepticism but had been spoken with the same sincerity he would expect from an old friend.

Even as he thought to lie and answer in the affirmative, he couldn't bring the words to his lips. Her question was genuine, and so was the hint of worry.

Rather than a verbal response, he shrugged.

"I hear that," she replied, the concern still evident in her expression. "Can I get you anything? You're Shelby and

Bree's friend, so it's on the house. Just the first one, though. Not to sound like a jerk, I just like to be upfront with my terms and conditions."

His chortle sounded closer to a cough, but he nodded his understanding. "I appreciate it. And I don't know. There's something like a hundred different beer taps behind you, and I've never seen half of them."

"Microbrews." Waving at the row of levers, she tucked a white towel into the back pocket of her dark jeans. "This half, the ones closest to me, they rotate seasonally. The other ones are pretty static."

"I hate to be 'that guy,' but you got any recommendations?"

"I do, but I doubt you'll like it. No one ever does." She feigned a weary sigh.

"All right, I like a challenge. Give me one of those, then."

"It's an IPA." The statement sounded like a warning.

"IPAs are all right."

The dim light caught the pint glass as she filled it from an unassuming tap. Producing a coaster from her back pocket, she set the dark amber beer down in front of him. He could feel her gaze as he picked up the glass to take a tentative sip.

Though there may have been a flavor beyond the bitterness of the hops, he couldn't place it. Lips pursed, he wrinkled his nose as he glanced up at her.

"I told you," she huffed, crossing her arms.

"How do you drink this?" Despite the criticism, he took another pull. "Good lord, what is this? Was it brewed in a dirty sock somewhere?"

"Okay, first." Rolling her green eyes, she raised a finger. "That's rude, Agent Mulder. I don't come into your bar and make fun of your favorite beer, do I?"

"Your favorite?" he echoed with a laugh. "It tastes like battery acid, darlin'."

"You drink battery acid often? You know, for the sake of accurate comparison." As she fixed him with an expectant look, the corner of her mouth turned up in a smile.

"I don't, but with this around, I don't know why I'd ever need to." For the second time, he followed his complaint with another drink.

"Whatever, dude," she chortled. "You might want to slow down on it, though. It's nine-percent alcohol."

"Damn, woman," he said with a laugh. "Is that why it's your favorite?"

"It might be." With a shrug, she leaned against the counter at her back. "So, what brings you out to The Lift on a Thursday, Agent Mulder?"

"I have a name, you know." He flashed her a matter-of-fact look as he sipped at the bitter IPA.

"How was I supposed to know that?"

"That I have a name? I mean, doesn't everyone?" He grinned and held out a hand. "Noah Dalton, not Mulder."

"You're just lucky I've never really seen much of *The X-Files*, or I'd be asking you all kinds of weird shit about aliens and UFOs. I'm Autumn Trent. Pleasure to make your acquaintance, Agent Dalton, not Mulder."

Her amused smile faded as her palm brushed against his. The look only lasted for a split-second, but he didn't miss the pang of melancholy.

"Are you...you sure you're all right?" The volume of her voice was lowered, and she kept her emerald eyes on his as she returned her arm to her side. She spoke with the same concern, the same sincerity with which she had first addressed him.

If he had not been so sure her worry was real, he might have brushed off the question.

Before he could answer, she laughed and waved a dismissive hand. "I'm sorry, I'm being weird, aren't I? It's just, I'm a doctorate student studying clinical psychology. So, sometimes when I see someone who looks a little bummed out, I guess I trip all over myself trying to be helpful."

Though the abrupt change threw him off-balance, he returned her smile. "There're worse ways to be awkward, I'd imagine. Being awkwardly nice isn't so bad."

"Spoken like a person who's never been awkward a day in their life. Awkward niceness comes across as being a creep most of the time."

"Well, you don't *look* like a creep," he offered with a shrug.

She grinned. "Spoken like a creep."

He laughed at her seamless sarcasm, and for the next forty-five minutes, he nursed the bitter IPA, chasing it with a glass of water. The weekday crowd had all but dispersed, and aside from the occasional patron who stopped by to pay their tab or order a refill, he and Autumn were the only two occupants of the bar.

As far as conversational partners went, he figured he couldn't have done much better than Autumn Trent. She was quick with a joke and a smile, and she employed as much sarcasm in her dialogue as anyone he knew.

He was sure Winter would love her.

While he and Autumn exchanged stories about their respective hometowns, he could almost push the anxiety over Winter out of his head altogether.

He learned that Autumn—what the hell was with women and their seasonal names?—had been born and raised in Minnetonka, Minnesota and that she had moved to Virginia for graduate school. As a transplant from the Lone Star State, he could sympathize, though the change in climate had come as much less of a shock to him.

"Don't get me wrong, it's mostly good." A small smile played on her pretty face. "The beach is pretty close, and unlike the beaches in Minnesota, it's, well, it's a real beach.

Not just one that's responsible for ten feet of lake effect snow every winter. But I don't know. I miss the cold sometimes."

"I don't think I've ever heard anyone say that before."

"It sounded a little weird when it came out of my mouth," she agreed, and disappeared into an office at the other end of the shelves of liquor bottles, then shrugged into a light gray canvas jacket as she made her way out from behind the bar.

"Anyway, my aunt is here 'til close if you need anything else. She's not actually my aunt, but she's my adopted mom's best friend, so I call her my aunt. It's been a long week, and since I don't have class or anything tomorrow, I'm going to go home and sleep for sixteen hours straight."

"I have no idea how anyone can do that." With a quiet chuckle, he hopped down from the stool. "I sleep for more than nine hours, and I feel like a slug. You're like a cat. Cats sleep for sixteen hours a day."

"Cats have it made," Autumn replied. "If reincarnation is real, I hope I come back as a pampered house cat. A dog would be okay too. My dog has a pretty cushy life. He just has to listen to me bitch about geeky stuff like statistical power and a slow internet connection."

Noah laughed. "A slow internet connection can turn even a lady as nice as my grandma into the Incredible Hulk. And that woman is one of the nicest people I think I've ever met, ever, and that's not just because she's my grandma. She fosters kittens, and I don't think you get a lot nicer than someone who fosters kittens."

At the thought of Eileen Dalton and her penchant for rescuing and caring for stray animals, Noah wished he was back home. The only other time he had been so far away from his family was during two deployments to the Middle East. Until he moved to Virginia, he had always been able to count on a visit to his grandma to help him through the darker points in his life.

Aside from words of wisdom, she provided encouragement, no matter the life path he walked. He could quit his job at the FBI to become a full-time rodeo clown, and Grandma Eileen would still encourage him if she knew it made him happy.

"You all right?"

Autumn's voice snapped him away from the reverie and back to the sparsely populated bar. Forcing the twinge of sadness off his face, he glanced at her and nodded.

"Sorry, that's the third time I've asked you that." Shouldering a black handbag, she offered a strained smile. "I should go before I start asking you to look at gray blobs and tell me what you see."

"Do you need a ride home?"

He blurted out the question before he could think it through. Despite the hour of lighthearted banter, he was still a stranger to this pretty redhead. FBI agent or not, a man's offer to drive a single woman home was only likely to be interpreted one way.

But was he so sure he didn't mean it that way? The unmistakable sting of guilt clawed at his stomach as he mulled over the idea. Autumn Trent was funny and kind, and even in a worn band t-shirt, dark jeans, and motorcycle boots, her good looks were undeniable.

He and Winter were not in a relationship, he reminded himself. Not even close. They'd had one drunk kiss and one awkward sober kiss, and that was it.

And then, without a word, she had disappeared. Dropped off the face of the planet without so much as a text message to explain her absence.

Didn't he have a right to be upset?

Hell, since he and Winter had become friends, this wouldn't even be the first time he had dated or slept with another woman. Though his two-week fling with a server named Jessie felt like it had occurred in another lifetime. He was only a little over six months removed from the fleeting relationship.

He'd told Winter that Jessie had dumped him for the bartender at the restaurant where she worked, but the confession wasn't entirely true. Jessie had broken up with him, but not just because she wanted to date her bartender friend. According to her, Noah's interest was quite clearly in another woman. He'd seen no reason to deny the observation, so he had merely agreed to an amicable breakup.

"A ride?" Autumn echoed. The grin had vanished from her lips, and he wondered how long they had stood in silence. "I'm fine. I drove myself."

"You just told me that you like your new apartment because you can walk to work when it's nice outside. The high today was seventy-five."

He didn't know why he chose to defend his choice, but like the question itself, the words left his mouth before he could think to stop them.

"I'm from Minnesota," she started, her tone one step below haughty. "Maybe seventy-five is too warm."

"I seriously doubt that." He couldn't seem to keep himself from talking. "Seventy-five is about perfect for anyone."

"Dude, you're being a creep." The statement was as flat as a worn-out couch cushion.

"I am, aren't I?" He sighed as he raised a hand to rub his eyes.

"Little bit, yeah." She opened her stance and faced him head-on. "Tell you what. I'll just shoot straight with you. I'm not interested in that, like, at all. This whole dynamic, the whole picking up someone at the bar, it's not my thing. No offense if it's yours, to each their own."

Noah felt like an ass. "Shit. Sorry, I—"

She held up a finger. "It's not you, I promise. This August,

I'll be defending my dissertation, and I've barely even started writing it. I've been too damn busy trying to get in all the practicum hours humanly possible, but now that those are almost over with, I've got to write a two-hundred-page research paper in the span of something like five months."

Noah straightened. "Damn, that's a lot of work."

She nodded, seeming to relax a little. "It sounds doable, but when you factor in trying to help my aunt out here at the bar and squeezing in the rest of those practicum hours, it gets a little fucking stressful."

He wanted to reach out and give her shoulder a friendly squeeze, but he kept his hands to his damn self. "I'm sure it is."

Her face fell, and she pushed a hand through her hair. "Damn it, I'm sorry. I didn't mean to ramble on about my life story, but there you go. I'm also about seven months removed from a really nasty breakup, so I'll call that icing on the cake."

He scratched his chin. "Damn, I'm the dumbass here, so why does it feel like you're apologizing to *me*?"

"Honestly?" She fiddled with the silver zipper of her jacket as her green eyes darted back up to meet his. "I've had guys say some pretty nasty shit to me after I turned them down. Anymore, I just try to cover all my bases and get ahead of it, so none of them decide to follow me home. Which *has* happened before."

"Wow." He cleared his throat. "Now, I definitely want to give you a ride home, but more as a form of hazard pay, you know? Police escort back to your place so no creeps follow you."

With a laugh that sounded more like a snort, she shook her head. "I go to Krav Maga lessons twice a week. I'll be all right."

"Okay, well, I'll be honest now." Though he made an effort

to give her a matter-of-fact smile, he was sure the look came across as more wistful than sarcastic. "I don't know why I said that. That was stupid, and I'm sorry. I'm not fit to deal with any of that shit right now, either. It's just, it feels like I'm a million miles away from home, and my best friend, she's going through some shit that I don't even know about. I don't know about it because she dropped off the face of the planet, and now I've got no idea what the hell is going on. All I know is that I can't fix it, and I think I'm losing my mind a little."

Her expression softened, and he could almost hear the tension leave her body.

"A compromise, then," she said as she stuck out her hand. "Because I could seriously use a friend that isn't another Ph.D. student working on their own dissertation. Plus, you're Shelby and Bree's friend, so you've already got that going for you."

Noah placed a hand over his heart. "Your trust brings me honor."

Autumn rolled her eyes, but the smile got a little bit bigger. "I'll accept that ride home, but I'm going to ask for one favor. There's this Mexican place a few blocks away that's open twenty-four hours a day, Alonso's, and they've got a drive-thru. If you could swing through there so I can buy myself some food, I'll even throw in a burrito."

As Noah accepted her handshake, he nodded and grinned. "I could go for a chimichanga."

"Chimichanga eating contest, then," she proclaimed, raising her arm for a high-five.

"Winner pays the bill?"

She snorted. "Oh, hell no. I'm a graduate student, dude. I don't have bottomless chimichanga money."

4

The scent of wet asphalt followed Winter as she pushed open a set of tinted glass double doors to make her way into the building. A recent storm had left the summer air heavy and damp, and even now, a new mass of leaden clouds pushed in to obscure the morning sunlight. She was almost half an hour early, but apparently, she wasn't the only agent in Violent Crimes who'd thought to get a head start on their day.

Fortunately, the only greeting Sun Ming offered was a half-smile and a slight nod. As Winter returned the gesture, she found for the first time that she was glad for Sun's stand-offish persona.

With Sun, she didn't have to worry about a barrage of questions regarding her whereabouts over the last few months, or an interrogation into the reason she'd taken more than two weeks to come to the office after she received Noah's phone call.

Sun wanted to have the conversation as much as Winter did, and this morning, that suited Winter just fine.

After she retrieved a bottle of water and a steaming mug

of coffee that could double as paint thinner, Winter slunk out of the break area and to her cubicle. Her movements were hurried, and she figured she looked more like a jewel thief than an agent on her first day back at work.

Instead of laser alarm systems and security cameras, Winter sought to avoid friends.

She knew she couldn't avoid them forever, but she told herself she at least needed a little time to settle in, to let the caffeine work its way through her system. With a tentative sip from the mug of battery acid, she logged in to the computer to sift through the emails she had missed during her absence.

Though she clicked and scrolled like a person who was paying attention to the screen, her thoughts wandered. To the best of her knowledge, the only person in the entire building who knew the reason for her sudden departure was her boss, Max Osbourne.

Max had been thoroughly unimpressed by her involvement in the Douglas Kilroy investigation, but the mass shooting a few hours outside McCook had created more than enough work to divert his attention. Aside from a pointed, "What the hell were you thinking," he had brushed past the topic altogether. Even if the SAC had been angry with her, she knew he wouldn't betray the trust of any of the agents under his command.

The day after Noah's phone call, she and her grandmother had taken Grampa Jack to the hospital after he experienced a spike in lower back pain. Though neither Winter nor Beth would admit it, they were prepared for the worst.

For hours, they sat in the waiting room beneath a blanket of silence.

When the doctor had pushed her way through the double doors beside the reception desk, Winter and Gramma Beth had leapt to their feet. The woman's smile had warmed at the anxious movement, and the kind expression was one Winter was sure she would never forget.

After a series of tests, the doctor determined that Grampa Jack was in the midst of a flare-up brought on by an autoimmune disorder. Though lupus was more common in women than men, the doctor had established that it was the cause of Jack's chronic pain. The condition didn't have a cure, but treatment with corticosteroids and anti-inflammatory medication could manage flare-ups.

Due in part to Jack's age, the doctor recommended he stay in the hospital for a couple days to ensure his kidneys hadn't suffered permanent damage. A week and a half later, when Winter was satisfied that there was no secondary disease beneath the lupus, she'd finally felt comfortable enough to head to Richmond.

The explanation she had given Gramma Beth about the request for her return to the office was vague. She didn't want to elevate Beth's hope just to return a week later to advise they had hit a dead end. Hell, she didn't even want to raise her own hopes.

As she took another sip from her half-emptied mug, Winter grimaced. Her sleep the night before had been fretful, and she reminded herself that she needed the caffeine boost.

"Agent Black," a gravelly voice called.

Wordlessly, she turned in her chair to face the SAC of Violent Crimes. Max Osbourne's gray buzz cut and his scrutinizing gaze were just the same as when she left.

"Sir," she greeted, her voice quiet but filled with purpose.

His features didn't change. "Conference room in ten minutes."

Winter nodded. As her boss disappeared around the corner, she returned her vacant stare to the computer monitor. She could hear her pulse as it rushed in her ears, and she didn't think the mug of gasoline was responsible for the churning weight in her stomach.

With a resigned sigh, she planted both palms on the desk and pushed herself out of the chair. She thought she could handle an awkward reunion with her coworkers and friends or a meeting about her brother's whereabouts, but she wasn't so sure she was ready to deal with both in one sitting.

By the time she stepped through the doorway to the small room, she was ready to turn around, throw up, or both.

White light glinted off Noah's eyes as he looked up from the laptop. Shadows moved along his scruffy face as he clenched his jaw and snapped his attention back to the screen.

"Long time no see," he muttered. "Glad you could make it."

At the flat sarcasm, she felt the first pinpricks of adrenaline on the back of her neck.

She deserved the sardonic greeting, but the tone still took her aback. Rather than offer a rebuttal, Winter was silent as she dropped down to sit beside Bree Stafford. Though Bree's smile was warm, the comforting look did little to ease the sting of Noah's offhand remark.

A flicker of movement in the doorway drew both Bree and Winter's attention, but as soon as she looked up at the tall figure, she wished she hadn't.

"Oh, you're here." Aiden's voice was as flat and unimpressed as Noah's.

Though she wanted to crawl beneath the table to avoid their scrutiny, Winter straightened in her chair and crossed both arms over her chest.

"Get it out of your systems," she ordered. "We've got work to do."

Aiden rolled his eyes as he eased the glass and metal door closed behind himself. "Right. Work."

From where he sat in the shadows off to the side, Max cleared his throat. "Dalton, Parrish, stop acting like a couple pissy teenagers and get to it. I've got a meeting in fifteen minutes."

Winter had to stop herself from jumping at the sudden disturbance. She'd been so preoccupied with Noah's sarcastic greeting that she hadn't even noticed her boss.

"Roger that," Noah grumbled.

"What did you find?" Bree's calm demeanor was a stark contrast from the tension that permeated every other square inch of the damn room.

Glancing from Bree to Winter and then back, Aiden took a seat in the chair beside Noah's.

"A month and a half ago," Noah bit out, his gaze fixed on the glowing screen, "we ran a picture of Justin Black through a new age progression software prototype to generate an image of what he'd look like now. The program is clearly new and still in beta, but its algorithms let you add photos of family members to make the image more accurate. Its primary use will be in missing persons cases and to generate images of fugitives who've been on the run for years at a time."

Winter wanted to ask what he meant when he said "we" ran the picture through age progression software, wanted to ask why they hadn't thought to make use of the program sooner, but every word coming from her brain got caught in her throat as he turned the laptop to face her and Bree.

"That's him," was all she could manage.

Blue eyes the same unusual hue as her own stared back at her, and the light shadow of facial hair darkened the young man's cheeks. His black hair was short but styled. Where she remembered a goofy, gap-toothed grin, the smile now showed off straight, white teeth.

Though Bill Black, Winter's father, had braces during his

early high school years, Winter and Justin's mother was born with a perfect smile. Without a doubt, Winter had inherited her mother's dental genes, but she, of course, never knew how Justin had fared.

Noah met Winter's gaze for the shortest of moments. "We went through all the shit Kilroy left behind." Any irritability or sarcasm was gone.

"And then we went through it again," Aiden put in.

Winter's intent stare was on the computer screen, but she saw Noah nod from the corner of her eye.

"And again," Aiden said before lifting his shoulders in a heavy shrug. "We caught a break when a woman who'd been out of the country for six months returned home and recognized Kilroy's picture as someone who utilized a storage unit close to her own."

Winter leaned forward, her breath barely wanting to leave her lungs. "What did you find?"

Aiden's glance flicked to her for the space of a second. "Among boxes of useless shit, he had a folder full of mostly useless shit. Newspaper clippings of other crimes like Ted Bundy and John Wayne Gacy's murders. But there was something else in there, something that just didn't look like it belonged."

Winter felt a new energy crackle in the air. It was hope. She knew the feeling well, and most often, despised it.

Aiden went on. "It was an unmarked envelope containing a letter about parent-teacher conferences at Bowling Green High School, the home of the Bowling Green Timberwolves. I thought it might've been Bowling Green, Kentucky at first, but none of their high schools have a team called the Timberwolves. But there's a town a little bit north of here, Bowling Green, *Virginia*, and their high school mascot is a wolf." Aiden he tapped a couple keys on his laptop. "We looked through the school's records."

When he pushed the computer toward her, another photo lit up the screen. The young man was almost identical to the first, right down to the creases at the corners of his eyes.

"Holy shit," Bree murmured.

Winter opened and closed her mouth, but she couldn't summon a single word to her lips. As she shifted her focus down to the name below the school picture, her stomach lurched.

"Jaime Peterson," she breathed. Even to her own ears, her voice sounded harried and weary, almost like she'd spent the previous night shouting.

No matter what the photograph said, she knew the kid who stared back at her was not Jaime Peterson.

He was her baby brother. He was Justin Black.

5

D r. Robert Ladwig hated making phone calls. He never knew what to do with himself during the conversation, and he often resorted to picking at a label or a sticker, anything that would give his fingers something to do.

The majority of the outbound calls made to his patients were handled by one of the two full-time desk clerks, but the dial tone that buzzed in his ear was not a routine phone call.

Months had passed since the so-called football player, Brady Lomond, had all but run out of his office. Robert's curiosity had been piqued, but when he went to double-check the man's intake form, he learned that Lomond had faked almost every piece of information.

Lomond wasn't the first person to falsify personal details, and Robert doubted he'd be the last, but the similarity of Lomond's alleged symptoms to Winter Black's was too striking to ignore.

For the fifth time in the past two weeks, Robert sat at his desk and listened to the monotonous buzz as he waited for the voicemail he was sure would come. He had been surprised to learn that "Brady's" phone number was active, and though he doubted the repeat calls would yield any useful information, he would be remiss if he didn't try.

Just as he was prepared to leave yet another generic message for whoever in the hell owned the number, he heard a light click. He pulled the smartphone away from his face to check if the line had been disconnected, but he froze in place.

The call had connected.

"Hello?" a voice finally asked.

"Yes, hello." Robert's voice was warm and soothing. The man was not Brady Lomond, but there was a real possibility that the Texan had scrawled out contact information for a friend or family member without realizing the mistake.

"Who is this?" The man sounded equal parts annoyed and skeptical.

"Hi, I'm sorry, this is Dr. Ladwig, and I'm looking for Brady Lomond. Do I have the right number?"

"Brady who? No, dude. Look, you've called this number like fifteen times and left me seven voicemails. I don't know who in the hell you are, and I don't know who in the hell Brady Lomond is. Please, take this number off your list. I'm not going to sign up for a credit card or buy a case of whatever in the hell you're selling."

"I'm so sorry," Robert said. He made sure to keep his tone pleasant. He still represented his practice. "Someone must've put down the wrong phone number. I'll make sure you don't get any more calls from us. Thank you for letting me know."

"All right, no worries. Thanks."

As Robert dropped the phone back to the wooden desk, he combed the fingers of one hand through his hair and heaved a sigh.

"Well, this isn't good, is it?" he asked the empty room.

Lomond's condition might have piqued Robert's curiosity, but he didn't want to locate Brady Lomond—or whoever in the hell he *actually* was—strictly for his own sake.

As if on cue, his work phone buzzed against the polished surface. He hadn't saved the caller's contact information, but he knew that number. With every damn call, he had committed the number to memory as he stared at the screen and forced himself to pick up the device.

"This is Dr. Ladwig." He made the formal greeting out of habit. The caller knew who he was.

"Hello, Robert," the woman purred.

Her calming voice was punctuated with just enough of a northern accent to give homage to the fact that she was not a native of Virginia or the surrounding area. The folksy pronunciations were disarming, and they belied little of her formidable intellect.

She sounded like an extra from the set of *Fargo*, not a neurosurgeon.

"Doctor Evans," he replied. He suspected the name was fake, but he honestly wasn't sure he wanted to know her real name.

"It's been a few days since we talked, so I thought I'd give you a call to check and see if you've made any progress on getting through to that Brady Lomond fellow."

Rubbing his eyes with one hand, Robert leaned back in his chair and suppressed a groan. "Yes and no. The only progress I've made is to officially establish a lack of progress."

"Well, that's interesting," she said with a laugh. The sound contained a hint of mirth, but whenever Dr. Evans laughed, he was sure the humor she found had a darker meaning.

"All the information Lomond provided was fake, right down to the address and the insurance information. I've looked seven ways from Sunday to see if any of it is affiliated with someone related to him in some way, but it seems like it was all random. The address he provided is a pizza place at the edge of downtown Richmond, and his parents' names are Al and Peggy, probably from *Married with Children*."

That light laugh again. It lifted the hair on his arms. "Clever."

He suppressed a sigh. "The phone number was valid, but it was another dead end. I ran it through a couple different databases, and it looks like it's been affiliated with a few different people, none of whom have any connection to a guy named Lomond. As I said, it's a dead end, Dr. Evans."

"It's curious, though, isn't it?" She didn't wait for him to answer the question before asking the next. "Why would someone come to your office with the exact same symptoms as your other patient and forge all his contact information? Do you suppose he's law enforcement?"

Robert gritted his teeth. "It crossed my mind. Everything for my practice is in order, though. The police would have no reason to be here, and I think the fact that he hasn't shown back up is testament that they weren't conducting an investigation. At least not into my staff or me."

"Right, of course. Well, Robert, I'm afraid I've got some disappointing news too. This newest patient, the man from Pennsylvania, has given me a whole lot of nothing. You know, we'd make a lot more progress on this research if I could take a look at someone who's actually manifested these phenomena, these *visions*, as you've called them."

Of course, that was what she wanted. That was what she *always* wanted. Robert thought he had caught a break when Brady walked into his office, thought he had been given a ticket to get Sandra Evans off his back for longer than a week.

But he knew what Dr. Evans did to her so-called patients, and he knew what her idea of "progress" entailed. As soon as Sandra had mentioned her interest in examining Winter

Black, Robert had purged any mention of Winter from his records, both digital and physical.

He'd checked, double-checked, and triple-checked to make sure there were no traces of Winter left behind.

Sandra Evans took every precaution to avoid detection for her gruesome experiments, but Robert didn't want to put her stealth to the test by handing her an FBI agent.

The feds took the kidnapping or harm of their own as a personal affront. As smart and well-connected as Evans was, Robert wasn't about to risk the bureau breathing down his neck.

If Winter Black had presented with brain abnormalities after she sustained severe trauma to the head, then there had to be others who experienced the same phenomenon.

And right now, Robert would much rather take his chances with someone like Brady Lomond.

"No," he said to return his attention to the conversation. "You know that Patient Zero isn't an option."

The term "patient zero" was used to refer to the person responsible for the start of a disease outbreak, but Patient Zero was his preferred method to refer to Winter Black when Dr. Evans brought up the topic.

Evans didn't know if Patient Zero was a man or a woman. All she knew was that the symptoms had begun after a traumatic brain injury at approximately age thirteen.

"Fine, Ladwig." She pronounced each word slowly, and he felt the start of a chill creep down the back of his neck. "But I hope you know this is starting to test my patience. If you won't give me Patient Zero's information, then you'd better come up with a replacement soon."

With a light chime, the call was disconnected before he could formulate a rebuttal.

If he didn't reach a viable alternative soon, he would be forced to decide whether he wanted to test the wrath of the

Federal Bureau of Investigation or the wrath of Sandra Evans.

After his dealings with Dr. Evans over the past seven years, there was no doubt about whose ire he would rather face.

6

By the time midafternoon rolled around, Noah thought he had done an admirable job avoiding Winter. Since their little group dispersed from the conference room, he hadn't even seen his friend.

His former friend? Honestly, he didn't know. He didn't pretend to understand what went through Winter's head on any given day.

At the irascible thought, his stomach dropped.

He was so sure he had the right to be upset with her for the unannounced departure and silent treatment, but when her face fell at the announcement of their theory that Douglas Kilroy had followed Justin Black's entire life, he felt like an idiot.

Even Autumn's words of wisdom, words honed by almost eight years of intense study of human behavior, couldn't drive the pang of guilt from his head.

"You're permitted your feelings," she'd told him over dinner one evening, "and you shouldn't minimize them just because you think you understand why she did what she did.

What's important is what you do with those feelings, how you express them. But it's not healthy just to pretend they don't exist."

He could almost hear Autumn's voice as he stepped into a hallway to make his way back to his home department.

For most of the day, he had spent his time talking to members of the tech department. They had scoured the internet for social media accounts that might have been affiliated with Justin Black, now also known as Jaime Peterson, but they'd come up empty-handed.

As he approached the elevator at the end of the corridor, he tapped the down button with one hand and stifled a yawn with the other. Stealth was exhausting. Maybe he would call it good and head home for the day. He might not understand how Autumn was capable of sleeping for twelve hours straight, but right now, he'd be more than happy to try.

With a cheery ding, the silver doors slid open.

As his gaze fell on the single occupant, his mouth suddenly felt like it had been stuffed with cotton balls. He clenched one hand into a fist to ward off the tremble that came with the unexpected rush of adrenaline.

When Winter's blue eyes flicked up to meet his, he felt like they were suspended in their own isolated bubble of space time.

Shit.

He wasn't ready for this. He hadn't prepared, had no idea how to broach the topic of her absence without sounding like a needy asshole.

"Afternoon, Dalton." Her voice was soft, and he expected her to brush past him without another word, but instead, she stepped back and waved a hand to the empty space at her side.

"You're not..." he started, pausing to glance over his

shoulder. To his chagrin, the hall was empty. "You're not down here for something?"

When he returned his attention to her, she narrowed her eyes.

"Okay then," he muttered under his breath.

His hope that another agent would rush over to the elevator at the last minute was dashed as the doors eased closed. Their ascent had only just started when Winter moved forward to smack one of the plastic buttons.

As the car lurched to a stop, he shot her a fervent look. "Is that a good idea? An unexpected elevator stop in an FBI building?" He tried to keep the accusatory tinge out of the question, but he wasn't sure how effective his effort had been. To his surprise, the shrill alarm of the elevator didn't go off. Just what he needed, to be stuck in a busted elevator with an enraged Winter.

"I don't give a shit," she spat, flicking her long braid over her shoulder. "It'll just take a second, anyway. Apparently, that's about all the time you can stand to be around me, isn't it?"

"What?" He gawked at her, truly stunned. "Is that really what you think?"

She was projecting. He was sure of it. He'd only ever been glad for her presence, but he couldn't say the same for how she felt about him.

"Right now, Dalton, yeah. Yeah, it is."

"Are you fucking kidding me?" he exclaimed, throwing both arms in the air.

So much for Autumn's words of wisdom. There was only so much of these dejected, run-down feelings he could take, and Winter's petulant observation had just pushed him over the limit.

She opened her mouth to speak, but he cut her off. "Do you have any idea what that did to me? What *you* did to me?"

For the second time, she tried to talk, and for the second time, he cut her off.

"No, Winter…just, no. If you want to do this, then we'll do it. But right now, here's the thing. I get what you went through. I mean, I don't entirely get it, but there's this thing I like to use called *empathy*. I know you've walked through your whole life like you're the only one who understands what you're dealing with, and you're not wrong. But this shit you're pulling now, this playing the victim bullshit, I'm fucking tired of it."

Her mouth popped open again, an angry glint sparking in her eyes.

He didn't care. He plowed on, unable to stop the words now that they had started. "You shut out all the people who want to help you because you don't think they can possibly get a grasp on what you've been through. Just because we didn't experience the exact same thing, you think we're incapable of helping you. Honestly, darlin', it's a little insulting. It's like you're telling your friends that they aren't good enough. Like you're waitin' around for someone who'll fit the bill, and it sure as shit ain't any of us! You know when the last time I saw you was?"

When he paused this time, she didn't try to respond.

"Last time I saw you was in that damn church with Douglas Kilroy's blood splattered all over one side of your face. And then after that, you just, you what? You disappeared! Did you stop to think for a fucking second what that might have felt like to me? To Bree? To *Parrish*?"

In the silence that ensued, the rush of vehemence started to subside, and he felt the first pangs of guilt cut through the righteous indignation.

With a sigh, he ran a hand through his shaggy hair. He needed a damn haircut, he thought as he tilted his head back to stare at the ceiling.

"I'm sorry," he managed. "That was shitty and mean, and I didn't want any of it to come out that way."

"Maybe," Winter's voice was quiet and strained, "but it's not inaccurate. I've been such an asshole to you, and you've only ever been nice and understanding to me. I've been such a shitty friend."

Eyes wide, he glanced back to her just as she swiped at her cheeks with the sleeve of her black blazer. Tears. The woman who didn't cry had tears gleaming in her eyes.

The sight nearly brought him to his knees. "What? No, you haven't." He fisted his hands to keep from reaching for her. "Winter, you opened up and brought me into your family because you knew I didn't have anyone around here. You're the first friend I made after I moved east, and you're part of the reason I don't feel homesick. I've got you here, so it doesn't feel like I left everything I cared about behind in Texas."

Her eyes grew shiny again. "Noah, I—"

"None of what I said came out the right way," he continued, needing to say what needed to be said. "It's just, with you leaving like you did, it didn't feel like I was important to you. And you're *so* important to me, and that difference, that disparity, it seemed like it was this fucking canyon, this giant hole in the earth, and I didn't have any way to cross it. And if I tried, I'd fall into that massive pit of nothingness, and I'd be lost trying to find something that was never there in the first place."

Amber light caught the droplets in the corners of her eyes before she had a chance to wipe them away.

Noah could feel the sting of tears, and he sniffled as he dabbed at the glassiness in his own eyes.

"They need to do something about this," Winter started, her voice scarcely above a whisper.

He gave his head a little shake, trying to figure out what she was talking about. "About what?"

She sniffed and gave a little embarrassed-looking grin. "The onions in this damn elevator. I don't know who in the hell cuts onions in an elevator, but they need to knock it off." The conviction in the quiet statement was so sincere, he thought for a split-second that the remark was genuine.

"Oh my god." He laughed, and the feel of it caused most of his muscles to relax. "I missed you, Winter."

With a wistful smile, she met his eyes. "I missed you too."

Just as he was about to ask whether or not she should press the button to resume the elevator's movement, she took a swift step forward and threw her arms around his shoulders. He knew hugs were not in Winter's normal repertoire, but he wasted no time wrapping her in a tight embrace.

The familiar scent of her hair, of strawberries and citrus, was more than enough to drive away any lingering doubts about their friendship. Even if their relationship never went beyond platonic, he knew he would just be glad to have her in his life.

"We should see if this elevator will start back up before the fire department gets here." He offered a light kiss to the top of her head before pulling away from her, stuffing his hands in his pockets.

"Right," she agreed. Nodding, she reached out to tap the glowing button. "Do you want to go get some coffee? I've been drinking the stuff from the breakroom all day, and it's, well, I'm not really sure it's fit for human consumption."

He grimaced. "You've been *drinking* that?"

As she snickered in response, some of the leaden weight appeared to have lifted from her shoulders. "It's nice outside again today too. Seems like a good day for a walk."

And just like that...they were friends again. The

awkwardness began to disappear, almost as if it had never been there.

On their way through the office, he gave her a summary of the mostly uneventful months since Kilroy's death. Aside from Sun Ming's injury and the information he and Aiden Parrish had unearthed on Justin, they had gone about business as usual.

Once the commotion from the mass shooting died down, Noah's main focus had shifted to the items and documents left behind by Douglas Kilroy. Aside from a letter that pointed them in the direction of Bowling Green High, Kilroy's belongings were all but useless.

Even after an extensive examination of Kilroy's life, the conclusion about his motives had changed little. Kilroy was a sociopath, and both he and his father had exhibited symptoms consistent with paranoid schizophrenia. Their breaks from reality came in the form of religious experiences, and according to Aiden Parrish, such a manifestation wasn't uncommon with schizophrenia.

The conversation between him and Winter didn't become personal again until they were out of the coffee shop, drinks in hand, and away from the prying ears of any bystanders. Their route to the café had been straightforward, but the path they decided to take back to work wound through a handful of residential neighborhoods and passed by a park. Winter dubbed it "the scenic route."

"So, are you officially back? At work?" he asked, glancing over as she took a sip from the paper cup.

"Not quite. I talked to Max about it earlier. I was gone for so long because, well, there are a lot of reasons, but my grandpa wasn't doing so well. He was having a lot of pain, and the doctors ran a ton of tests looking for anything they could find, but they didn't get anywhere. I was staying with him and Gramma Beth so I could help them and just recuperate, I guess."

Noah was immediately concerned. He liked the old man. "He's all right, though?"

Before he finished the question, Winter nodded. "Yeah, that's why it took me a little while to get here, actually. He was in the hospital, and that's when they found out that he has lupus. He's probably had it for a long time but didn't realize it. It sounds bad, but it's a relief to have an actual diagnosis. I hung around while he started treatment, and when I left for Richmond, he seemed like he was doing a lot better."

"Lupus," he echoed. "Yeah, my aunt has that. She's been dealing with it since she was thirty-something, though. We aren't blood related, so I guess that's good news for me."

"Wait, what? What do you mean you and your aunt aren't blood related?" There was a twinkle of amusement in her eyes when she looked up from the sidewalk.

"She's my stepdad's sister, my Aunt Hazel."

"Your parents are divorced?"

"Since I was five." He lifted a shoulder. "Dad, *Eric*, moved away and married the woman he'd been cheating on my mom with. Started a new family, you know the type. Mom didn't get married again until I was something like ten. I was too old to be the ringbearer, I remember that."

"Wow." Winter stared at him, the paper cup resting on her lower lip, but she didn't drink. "I'm sorry, Noah. I had no idea."

"Please," he laughed as he waved away the sympathetic words, "don't be. Chris, my stepdad, he's a great dude. His sister, Hazel, used to be a concert pianist. If my mom hadn't divorced my dumbass father, she'd never have met Chris and his family."

A flash of pain passed over Winter's expression, but she hid it with a smile. "They sound wonderful."

Noah nodded. "The Alvarez family is like the epitome of what a family ought to be. Nothing but love from them, which is more than I can say for any of my dad or his kin. They're a bunch of stuck up pricks like…" He trailed off and shrugged before he could say the man's name. *Like Aiden Parrish.*

"Huh, all right." Winter offered him a thoughtful glance. "Well, good for your mom, then. I'm glad it all worked out for you guys. You'll definitely have to tell me more about your family because I didn't know *any* of your history." She laughed, her cheeks turning pink. "Shit, have I really been taking up that much of our conversation space? So much that all we've done is talk about my family, but I didn't even know that your parents were divorced? Or that you had a stepdad? Or that your biological father is an asshole?"

"Knock it off, Winter." He grinned, giving his head a little shake. "That's how friendship works. When one friend is going through some rough shit like you have been, the other one's there for them. I know you'd do the same for me, right?"

"Of course." There was no hesitation, no pause, and all he wanted to do was hug her again.

"See. Now, any time you're feeling guilty, just remember that. Just because it hasn't happened yet doesn't mean it's not going to. Someday, I'll be the one apologizing to you about, what did you call it? Hogging all the conversation?"

Her laugh sounded closer to a snort as she nodded. "Yeah, basically."

For close to an entire block, they walked in silence. The din of the nearby busy street melded into the whisper of the summer breeze, and birds chirped from the branches overhead.

"I'm worried about Justin." The quiet statement snapped his attention away from the scenery and back to the woman at his side.

He reached out and squeezed her shoulder, but only for a quick moment. "We'll find him."

"I know." Even though the response was reassuring, there was a flicker of darkness on her face as her eyes fell on his. "But I think that's part of what I'm worried about. We'll find him, but *who* will we find when we do?"

7

Lips pursed, Aiden glanced over Jaime Peterson's meager school records for what felt like the fifteenth time. The kid was smart, and the only grade lower than a B was during his senior year chemistry class. Otherwise, his academic record was impeccable.

Well, at least we don't have to worry about him throwing together a bomb, Aiden thought, frustrated beyond measure.

The conclusion did little to stifle the unease that clung to the darker recesses of his mind. Aside from the records of his graduation at Bowling Green High, searches for a nineteen-year-old named Jaime Peterson turned up little and less. Aiden had checked colleges throughout the state, even bordering states, but none had records of a Jaime Peterson matching Justin Black's description.

As far as Aiden was concerned, the null search results were an ominous sign.

He knew from his research on Douglas Kilroy's formative years that the Kilroy family had been just short of nomadic. None of their stops lasted even two years, and based on the year and a half that Justin had spent at Bowling Green High, the pattern still fit.

Had Justin been *raised* by Douglas Kilroy? Or had Kilroy spared the young boy because of some deeply ingrained sense of misogyny that insisted he could brutalize women, but that he spare males whenever possible? Had he intercepted the letter about parent-teacher conferences from the people who had *actually* raised Justin?

If Kilroy had been a bystander during Justin's adolescence, then the kid might have stood a chance. But there were too many question marks, too many aspects of the discovery that didn't make sense.

Aiden was careful to keep the sentiment to himself. The pained glint behind Winter's eyes had been plain for him to see, and he hadn't wanted to add his pessimistic theory to her bereaved mind.

When the hell had he started *that*? Since when did he withhold pertinent information in an effort to spare someone's *feelings*? Facts were facts, and the way they made someone feel wasn't supposed to matter.

And maybe those feelings didn't matter most of the time, but with Winter, it was different.

When it came to her wellbeing, he felt like he tripped over himself in his effort to ensure she was okay. But of all the people he knew, she deserved a sense of peace.

He would keep the theory about Kilroy's motivation for kidnapping Justin Black to himself until he had more to backup his assessment than a hunch.

In the world of research, the absence of evidence was a poor method to prove a theory. But no matter the number of hours he'd sunk into familiarizing himself with statistical analyses and behavioral research, he already knew he was right.

Kilroy hadn't left Justin alive because of a soft spot, not

even because of his set of twisted ideals that insisted men were superior to women. The Preacher, the man responsible for a body count that rivaled any serial killer in existence had not decided to spare Justin's life because he *cared* about that life.

In fact, Aiden wasn't so sure that his goal had even been to *spare* Justin's life in the first place.

Serial killers as entrenched in their methodology as Douglas Kilroy didn't decide one day to change their routine. Those men and women adhered to a ritual, and the only deviation from the established modus operandi occurred gradually over a number of years and a number of bodies.

The brutal murder of the Black family and the disappearance of six-year-old Justin Black was far too different from Kilroy's previous crimes to be a change in the man's MO.

There had been a reason he targeted Jeanette and Bill, and that reason was Justin Black.

Aiden was sure of it. And he was beginning to think that he understood why.

Sure, Kilroy had intended to kill Jeanette and Bill, but his selection of a family with children was no accident. Kilroy had never married, and he had never procreated, that anyone knew of, at least. But the man was a fanatic, and like his father before him, he was not about to leave his work half-finished.

In the twilight of his life, Kilroy had searched for a young boy to become his protégé.

Even if Justin had spent the first six years of his life in the loving environment provided by his parents, he wouldn't have stood a chance under the guardianship of someone like Douglas Kilroy. Any semblance of morality the boy possessed would have been malleable at his tender age, and Kilroy would have exploited the early stage of development.

If Justin, or Jaime, or whatever the hell he was called now, had been raised by Douglas Kilroy for the past thirteen years, there was no doubt in Aiden's mind that the kid was just as fucked up as the man who had kidnapped him.

❄

WHEN SHE GOT the text message from her new friend, Autumn groaned. She had planned to eat a sleeve of Saltines, drink a glass of ginger ale, and then sleep for sixteen hours in hopes that when she awoke, the pain in her stomach would be gone.

Though she had only just turned twenty-eight, she was convinced that the stress from her final year as a Ph.D. student had given her an ulcer.

In the last two weeks, she had dropped a full five pounds, and aside from the impromptu chimichanga eating contest with Noah Dalton, she couldn't remember the last real meal she'd eaten. She had always prided herself on her ability to eat as much in one sitting as a linebacker, but she had tapped out well before her Texan friend.

And, to top off her decreased appetite, she had tossed and turned all night as she fought against throwing up the three chimichangas she'd eaten.

I'm meeting Bree at The Lift tonight. You should come hang out with us. My friend Winter will be there. Noah's text message ended with a smiling cat emoji and another emoji that was just a pint glass of beer.

She'd expected the muscular, broad-shouldered Texan to be a dog person, but his adamant love of cats had taken her by surprise. Apparently, his grandmother's affinity for kittens had worn off on her grandson.

Before she could rationalize an excuse to avoid going out to meet Noah's best friend, she composed a response to advise him she would be on her way within the next fifteen minutes.

The clatter of nails against the hardwood floor drew her attention, and she rolled to her side and stretched out an arm to waggle her fingers at the little dog that approached. Her cat, Peach, was asleep at the other end of the sectional couch.

"Come here, Toad," Autumn cooed.

Wagging his fluffy tail, the Pomeranian mix trotted over and hopped up to sit beside her.

Toad's namesake wasn't the Mario Brothers character of the same name, and as far as Autumn was concerned, her cat wasn't named after Princess Peach.

Peach was a ginger tabby with fur roughly the same color as a peach, and Toad was a fluffy mutt with an overbite. Some people might have thought Toad's goofy face made him ugly, but Autumn thought his less than flattering jaw made him just the right combination of ugly and cute. Thus, the name Toad had been born.

After she scratched behind his pointy ears, she pushed herself to sit, and then to stand. Maybe while she was at The Lift, she would make another attempt to eat real food. Pedialyte and plain Cheerios provided adequate nutrition, but the flavor profile left a lot to be desired.

Though Autumn walked to the nearby bar as often as she could, she didn't feel up to the trek while her stomach turned and twisted with each lance of pain. She pushed the grimace off her face as she shoved through the familiar set of double doors.

Seated at the same booth he and Bree usually selected, Noah waved as a wide grin brightened his face. Chuckling to herself, she returned the gesture as she made her way to the little group. Bree scooted to the wall to make room for Autumn as the third member of their entourage watched her approach. The woman's dark blue eyes were vivid, and her stare was intense despite the slight smile on her pretty face.

Autumn liked her already.

"You must be Winter," Autumn started before Bree or Noah could make the introduction. With a grin, she extended a hand to the woman.

As Winter leaned forward to accept the handshake, the amber light caught her glossy black hair. "I am. You're Autumn, right?"

"Right." Though Autumn's smile didn't falter, she fought against grating her teeth together as her hand met Winter's. Sometimes her "gift" for reading people was a blessing, and other times it was a curse.

Winter Black had seen some shit, and she'd been through a hell most people could only imagine. But amidst all the turmoil, there was a calm resolve. A resolve to close the dark chapter of her life, to heal the open wound and find her place in the world. It was a feeling Autumn Trent knew well.

"It's nice to meet another seasonally named person." Winter's smile seemed lighter as she spoke, and Autumn didn't have to touch her to know that the words were sincere.

"So, Noah, Bree, what in the hell is this?" Autumn arched an eyebrow at one friend and then the other. "It's my night off, from this *and* school, teaching, whatever in the hell you want to call it. And you guys decide to meet up at my work?"

The corners of Bree's eyes creased as she laughed, and Winter chuckled while the man beside her offered a wide grin.

"Hey, you said it yourself, all right?" Noah tapped the plastic menu with an index finger. "This place has the best damn chili cheese fries in town, and you know how seriously I take my chili cheese fries."

"Okay." Autumn held up a hand in surrender. "Next time we get together, I expect we'll be at the FBI building, you hear me?"

Winter's quiet chortle turned into full-blown laughter at the offhand remark. "As long as we aren't there for coffee," the dark-haired woman said. "That shit tastes like, well, like shit."

"Like it was brewed in a dirty sock," Noah put in with a noncommittal shrug.

"That's what you said about my beer!" Autumn held out her hands to feign exasperation.

"More than one thing can be brewed in a dirty sock." His tone was so matter-of-fact, she thought he might have been answering a math problem.

For what was far from the last time that night, Autumn covered her mouth to stifle an outburst of laughter.

And, god, it felt good.

8

Robert Ladwig had never received two calls from Sandra Evans in a span of less than twenty-four hours before, and as he stared at the screen, he thought about returning the ringing phone to the polished surface of his desk. Maybe she meant to dial another person. Maybe her phone was in a pocket, and his number had been selected because of their recent contact.

Right, and maybe that lotto ticket I bought yesterday is a jackpot winner, he thought.

At the last second, he swiped his thumb across the green key and raised the device to his ear. "This is Dr. Ladwig," he answered.

"Good morning, Robert," Dr. Evans replied, her voice as velvety and warm as fresh caramel.

"What can I do you for, Evans?" The effort required to keep his tone level was monumental. This conversation would have to be short, or he was liable to lose his mind.

"I'm sure you need to get to work soon, so I'll only keep you a moment. I've been thinking about Patient Zero."

He gritted his teeth. "And?"

"And I've been thinking about the lack of success I've had replicating Patient Zero's particular brain abnormality. Brain structure is a funny thing, but I'm sure you know that. You went to medical school, too, didn't you, Robert?" She laughed. "More or less."

Though her query was casual, there was a sinister undertone to each and every word. Then again, wasn't there always a sinister undertone with Sandra Evans these days?

"I did," he answered, then snapped his mouth closed.

"Basic brain structure doesn't vary dramatically from person to person, but when it does, it can cause some significant outcomes. Take schizophrenia, for instance. Schizophrenics have a different brain structure than people without symptoms of schizophrenia. Now, there are many elements that can affect someone's brain structure after they're born."

It grated Ladwig to be lectured like this, but he held his silence, unwilling to stir this woman's wrath.

"Things like stress, environmental agents, and genetics," she said, continuing her lecture. "Genetics can predispose someone's brain to behave a certain way when it encounters a specific type of stressor. Diathesis-stress is what it's called, right?"

"That's a simplified version of it, but yes." He knew where her anatomy lesson was headed, and he felt like a cold hand had clamped down on his stomach.

"In any case, life events and environments are only half of the story." She sounded even more excited now. "The other half comes from a person's genetics, and sometimes, I think our little realm of the scientific community forgets just how powerful genes can be."

"You think there's something in Patient Zero's DNA that predisposed them to the abnormalities they experienced after their head trauma?" he surmised.

"I do." Her laconic response bordered on venomous, and

even though he was alone in his office, he wanted to crawl under the desk to hide.

In the agonizing seconds that followed, he considered blurting out Winter's name. He could let Dr. Evans deal with Winter Black and the fallout that would accompany the disappearance of a federal agent.

Evans was smart, but more than that, she was ruthless. If anyone was fit to contend with the feds, it was her. But if she was caught, the damn woman would drag him down with her. Probably even use him as a scape goat. Push him off a cliff.

But his own personal safety wasn't the only thing that worried him. For some reason he couldn't understand, he didn't want to lead the little dark-haired girl he used to talk to every week to slaughter.

But would it be slaughter?

Surely, Evans wouldn't kill Winter. Would she? The sadist doctor needed her alive to monitor her brain function, to parse through the inner workings of her mind. But Robert had seen Sandra's handiwork. If Winter fell into the surgeon's custody, death would be a kindness. And if Robert didn't come up with a way to appease Dr. Evans soon, he would be on the receiving end of ire he couldn't begin to fathom.

For a split-second, Ladwig wished Douglas Kilroy, The Preacher, was still alive so he could punch the killing bastard for ever starting the series of events that led Ladwig to cross paths with Dr. Evans. If the delusional psychopath hadn't slaughtered Winter's family, she wouldn't have suffered the traumatic brain injury that gave rise to her unique abilities.

But Kilroy hadn't murdered her *entire* family, had he?

"Patient Zero has a sibling." Ladwig felt like someone else had made the statement in his voice. Self-preservation was a powerful force.

"Really?" To his relief, curiosity had replaced Sandra's anger.

"Yes. A brother. His whereabouts are unknown, but I can begin searching for him."

During her time as Ladwig's patient, Winter had recalled the last time she had seen her brother in detail, but the FBI had no leads on Justin Black's fate. Though he kept the notion to himself, Ladwig had his own theory on the younger Black sibling's disappearance.

The Preacher had wanted Justin.

Alive or dead? That was the question, but Dr. Ladwig thought it was the former.

Sure, Sandra might be able to trace back to Winter through her younger brother, but Ladwig would cross that bridge when he came to it. For now, he needed a way to appease Dr. Evans before she turned her wrath on him.

"All right," Dr. Sandra Evans finally agreed. "Find the brother."

❆

WINTER HAD JUST PULLED her car key from the ignition when she felt the faint vibration from the pocket of her black slacks. Narrowing her eyes at the unfamiliar number, she swiped the screen and raised it to her ear.

"Agent Black," she answered.

"Hello, Winter." Dr. Robert Ladwig's voice was as smooth and calm as it had ever been, but the hairs on the back of her neck stood on end at the sound.

"Do you remember what I told you the last time you called me?" Her voice was a lethal hiss. "I mean it, Ladwig. If you don't leave me the hell alone, I *will* ruin you, do you understand me?"

"There's no need for that." His response was flat, but

somehow, the hint of irritability was less unnerving than the soothing tone in which he had greeted her.

"Really?" she bit back. "Because, based on the fact that you're literally on the phone with me right now, I'd say there *is* a need for it!"

"This won't take long. Like it or not, we have a history, my dear. I'm up to date on the news, and I wanted to wish you well now that Douglas Kilroy is dead. I hope that learning more about your brother's fate will bring you some peace."

She could feel the rush of her pulse at the offhand mention of Justin. "My brother's fate?" she echoed. "What in the hell does that mean, Ladwig?"

"Well, there wasn't anything about it in the news articles I read, but I just assumed you'd found something after The Preacher was killed." He sounded puzzled, but not puzzled enough for her to dismiss the question as an innocent inquiry.

"I don't know what in the hell you're trying to accomplish here, but I've about reached the end of my tolerance for your enigmatic bullshit. If you don't have anything useful to tell me, then this conversation is over. I've got work to do, you know, in the *FBI building*. Want me to tell anyone hello for you while I'm in the office or no?" Her knuckles had turned white from her iron grip on the steering wheel, and the tips of her fingers tingled from the lack of blood flow.

"I guess well-wishing or condolences don't count as useful, do they? Fine, fair enough, then. Best of luck to you, Agent Black."

Just as she opened her mouth to tell him where he could cram his condolences, the familiar chime indicated the call had ended. Jaw clenched, she pulled the phone away and glared at the glass screen like it was responsible for the conversation.

Was Ladwig just a creep, or was there more to his call than just an unhealthy obsession with a client he hadn't seen in almost thirteen years?

With an irritable groan, Winter pocketed her phone and pushed open the driver's side door of her tried-and-true Civic.

As she glanced at the car, she remembered Autumn's bout of laughter when Winter and Noah had discussed the little Honda the night before. Noah had asked when Winter finally intended to purchase a "grown-up" vehicle, and Autumn had been quick to side with Winter to defend the Civic's honor.

At the recollection, she felt the tenseness melt away from her shoulders. Winter had been skeptical when Noah told her that his new friend was a doctoral student in psychology, but as soon as she met Autumn, her unease had been put to rest. Though the woman was a self-proclaimed nerd, she didn't exhibit the same studious, untouchable demeanor as Aiden Parrish.

If Winter had met Autumn Trent on the street, she wouldn't have guessed she would be referred to as Dr. Trent before the end of the year. Maybe the title would change Autumn into a mysterious figure like the SSA of the BAU, but somehow, Winter doubted it.

When she rounded a corner to the cluster of cubicles that belonged to Violent Crimes, she thought for a fraction of a second that her musings had summoned the tall, well-dressed man who blocked her path. His pale blue eyes flicked up from his phone to her, and that fleeting look was enough to bring on the sudden uptick in her heart rate.

And just like that, the minutes-old conversation with Dr. Ladwig was the farthest thing from her mind.

If Noah had been frustrated enough for a vehement outburst, she could only imagine what might have been running through Aiden's head as she came to a stop in front of him.

Not only had she ignored his attempts at communication for the past three and a half months, but ADD Ramirez had approved her transfer back to Violent Crimes. After Aiden's carefully planned effort to move her to the BAU, she was right back where she started.

Right back where she *wanted* to be.

"Agent Black," he greeted. His crisp, professional tone bordered on irritable.

"SSA Parrish," was her robotic response.

"I don't suppose I could get a few minutes of your time?" With an expectant glance, he pointed to an open doorway at her side.

Winter offered him a stiff nod. "Sure."

His countenance was unreadable as he followed her into the shadowy conference room. The glass and metal door latched closed with a metallic click, and the golden lights overhead came to life in short order.

Arms crossed over his chest, Aiden shifted his calm, scrutinizing gaze to her as silence descended over the small space.

"Are we just going to stand here and have a staring contest or something?" Winter blurted. "Loser owes the other one a soda, or what? The air in here dries out my eyes pretty fast, so maybe we ought to just skip the contest, and I'll head to the vending machine to get you a Mountain Dew. Or whatever in the hell you drink, I don't even know. Is it Mountain Dew?"

"Code Red," he answered with a slight smirk. "And if you tell anyone, I'll deny it. It's a guilty pleasure leftover from when I was in college."

Winter wrinkled her nose. "That stuff tastes like cough syrup."

"No, it's delicious," Aiden countered, his mouth still a flat line. "But that's not why I wanted to talk to you."

"Really, you *didn't* want to talk about how you drank straight from a two-liter of Mountain Dew Code Red while you and your college buddies played *Call of Duty* for sixteen hours straight?" Brows raised, she feigned a look of skepticism. Though his air of professionalism rarely faltered to hint at his sense of humor, Winter had known the man for long enough to understand his distinct brand of sarcasm.

"First of all, it was *Halo. Call of Duty* didn't even exist back then. And second of all, we drank beer. It *was* college."

He didn't miss a beat, and Winter felt the smile tug at the corner of her mouth. Just when she thought she had a handle on Aiden Parrish's persona, he added another layer.

The man was a damned mystery.

As he flashed her a smirk, she could have fooled herself into thinking only three days had passed since she had a conversation with him, not three months. The weight in the air between them vanished like it had never even been there, and all it had taken was a sarcastic conversation about soda.

"But no." His voice snapped her from the reverie, and she wondered how long she'd been silent. "None of those things are what I wanted to talk to you about."

"All right, what's up?"

She tried to make her voice sound casual, but she almost cringed at the sound. To her ears, the query sounded fit for a sorority sister, not an FBI agent who had never even been *close* to a frat house.

Either Aiden didn't notice the over-the-top tone, or he didn't care.

"You and Dalton plan to talk to the Bowling Green principal today, don't you?"

She nodded. Fortunately, Noah'd had the foresight to call

the school in advance so they could have anything else they'd dug up on Justin in order.

"Look, I know what a big deal this is to you." His expression had turned solemn, but the look in his pale eyes was sincere. "And I want to be clear that I'm not discouraging you when I say this, all right?"

For the second time, she nodded.

"I'm not discouraging you, but I want your expectations to be realistic. The Justin you remember might not be the Justin we find. I don't doubt that the thought's crossed your mind already, so don't take any of this the wrong way."

From his look of concern, her throat tightened, leaving her to feel like a ball of lead had dropped in her stomach. Glancing down to her shiny flats, she bit down on her tongue to keep the sadness from her face.

"Just be careful, Winter." The words were hushed, his tone grave.

Clearing her throat, she returned her gaze to his as she nodded for the third time.

"I will," she managed.

9

As Noah and Winter walked past the series of rectangular tables lining the high school's cafeteria, he caught the faint whiff of cooking food. Try as he might, he couldn't discern the *type* of food. He had never been able to tell the scent of one school lunch apart from the next. Flavorless steamed vegetables, questionable ground-up meats pressed into one of six different shapes, and a blob of gelatinous gunk for dessert. He shivered at the memory.

High school had been an agonizing four years for Noah, and even now, thirteen years later and easily a thousand miles away from the town where he had graduated, the taste in his mouth still soured as he walked through the halls of Bowling Green High.

He made an effort to displace some of the disdain as they passed a lanky girl and her shorter friend. Wide-eyed, the taller of the duo stuffed her phone into the side pocket of her backpack before she feigned nonchalance.

Like we're the damn phone police.

He had been lucky. Social media hadn't existed in its present form until shortly after he had graduated and joined the military. By then, he had been too busy getting shot at on the other side of the world to care much about Myspace or Facebook. Some of the men and women with whom he'd served had been thrilled to keep in touch with their loved ones via the online platforms, but the method of communication hadn't stuck for much longer than a month for him.

All he ever got from perusing his friends and family's status updates was a healthy dose of homesickness.

If he wanted to connect with someone from back home, he would call, text, or video chat with them. The passivity of scrolling through a Facebook timeline was not conducive to his mental health.

"What was it like?" he wondered as they approached the closed door of the school office.

"Huh?" Winter furrowed her brows as she shot him a quizzical look.

"Being in high school with social media," he answered. "What was that even like?"

With a shrug, Winter rapped her knuckles against the wooden door. "Hard to say. I don't have anything to compare it to, really. But I guess social media was just never really my thing. I had an account, but I might have updated it, like, ten times during the entire time I was in high school. People would tag me in stuff sometimes, I guess, but I never paid attention to it. I closed my Facebook account a few years ago."

"I guess that explains why we aren't Facebook friends." For the first time since they had pulled into the battered parking lot, he grinned.

"Have you added my grandpa yet?" Her eyes lit up as she returned the wide smile, almost like she had stumbled across the answer to an age-old mystery.

"Your grandpa?" he echoed. "Jack's on Facebook?"

"He is." She laughed at the look on Noah's face, which

probably closely resembled her own. "Gramma said he used to play those farm games, and he'd bombard her with requests for crops and stuff."

Just as he was about to join in her mirth, a shadow passed behind the closed blinds, and the door swung inward.

"I'm so sorry about that," the woman in the doorway started, brushing off her short-sleeved blouse as she offered them a strained smile. "Sometimes running this place during summer classes can be even more work than it is during the regular school year. Please, come on in. I'm Principal Amanda Williamson. You must be the agent I spoke to yesterday."

"That's me. Agent Dalton." With a smile, Noah stepped into the sunny office to extend a hand.

As Principal Williamson brushed a piece of dark hair from her eyes, some of the trepidation left her face as she accepted the handshake. When she turned to clasp Winter's outstretched hand, the rest of the worry dissipated.

"Agent Black," Winter offered.

"Pleasure to meet you both." Beckoning for them to follow, the shorter woman made her way past the receptionist and into a modest office. She paused at the edge of her wooden desk, and as she moved to sit in a black office chair, the scent of hand sanitizer wafted past him.

"Sorry. No offense," the principal offered, rubbing her hands together. "When you work in a high school, you get used to sanitizing your hands after just about everything you touch. I never realized before I had my own kids how gross teenagers could be. Or maybe it's just my teenagers, I'm not sure."

"Oh, I don't think it's just you." Noah chuckled as he eased the door closed behind himself. "I've got a couple cousins who graduated high school not too long ago, and my aunt used to say the same thing."

"Well, thank you. That makes me feel a little bit better," she replied as she sat. "Please, have a seat."

With an appreciative smile, he dropped down to one of two squat, armless chairs.

"I think my partner here has given you a pretty good idea of why we're here," Winter started. Though her expression was laser-focused, her voice was calm and non-accusatory.

His partner was learning, he mused.

"Yes." Principal Williamson slid a manila envelope across the polished surface of the desk. "This is everything we've got on Jaime Peterson. I made photocopies of all the documents we had so you can take them with you."

"Thank you," Noah replied with a pleasant smile.

Winter's blue eyes shifted over to him, and he merely nodded at her unasked question. A less astute observer might have missed the tremor in her hand as she reached out to pick up the folder.

"What questions can I answer for you today? Bowling Green isn't an awfully big town, so visits from any kind of law enforcement are rare, much less from FBI agents. Is Jaime all right?" A flicker of concern passed behind her dark eyes as she glanced from him to Winter and back.

"We aren't sure."

He broke his gaze away from the principal's just long enough to catch a glimpse of what he assumed was Justin Black's senior picture. He had stared at photos of the young man for long enough that he didn't need to see a color picture to know the youth's eyes were the same vivid shade of blue as his sister's.

"Jaime was a great student," Principal Williamson began and fiddled with one of the many ink pens on her desk.

"I saw that. Impressive grades. Did he talk about where he wanted to go to school? He could have gotten into some pretty good colleges." Noah finally pried his eyes away from the black and white copies and back to the principal's worried gaze.

"Not to me," she answered. "I might have heard something about Notre Dame, but I can't honestly remember if that was Jaime or one of his friends."

"Are any of his friends still enrolled that we could talk to?" Noah asked.

Before he finished the question, Principal Williamson shook her head. "No, they've all graduated. We don't have very big classes, usually only around fifteen to twenty kids. I included the names of the boys I saw him around the most often. His schedule is in there, too, so you'll have the names of his teachers. Small school or not, I've got a lot of hormonal teenagers I've got to keep an eye on, so I don't usually get to know the students as well as some of my faculty. But, well, you know how teenagers are, right? It's not like they usually share a lot with their teachers, at least not in high school."

"A fair point." He flashed her another grin as he reached into the pocket of his suit jacket. The formal wear wasn't ideal for a summer day in the state of Virginia, but it beat military dress blues.

"Could you tell us a little bit about what he was like?" Winter asked before he had unlocked the screen of his phone.

Some of the anxiety dissipated from Principal Williamson's face, and she nodded. "Of course. Well, you already know he was a great student. He was a smart young man, and not just book smart, either. I've never been a big fan of the term, but a couple of the faculty here referred to him as an old soul. He was never much for social media, and I'm not even sure that he had a smartphone."

"Is that unusual?" Noah asked.

The principal nodded. "Very. But he was outgoing, and I

don't know that there was anyone in his class who didn't like him. He might not have been into all the same music and online stuff that his classmates were, but that didn't keep him from making friends."

Winter's smile was wistful as she turned her attention to the transcripts in her lap.

"What about his parents?" Noah wanted to offer Winter words of reassurance, but he would have to wait until after they had returned to the parking lot.

"I can't say I ever remember meeting them," Principal Williamson replied. "And I can only really recall him mentioning them in passing. But that's not all that unusual. Unless they're complaining, I don't think there are a lot of high school kids who talk to their classmates about their parents."

"I know I never did." Despite the pinpricks of adrenaline on the back of his neck, Noah kept his expression pleasant as he set his phone on the desk. Pushing it toward the principal with an index finger, he kept his attention on the woman and away from the DMV photo of Douglas Kilroy.

"How about this fellow? He familiar at all?" He had to make a concerted effort to refer to Kilroy as a "fellow" rather than a "sick sack of shit" or an "evil bastard."

Lips pursed, Amanda tapped her chin as she considered the picture. "You know, yeah, he is familiar. I can't remember his name, but he did some odd jobs around the building a couple summers ago. Southern accent, sort of soft-spoken, seemed nice enough."

Noah fought against a reflexive recoil at the reference to Douglas Kilroy, the fucking Preacher, as "nice enough."

If you only knew, lady. You're lucky to be sitting here right now. Lucky he didn't decide to paint the walls of your room with your blood after he raped you and carved your body up beyond recognition.

The flash of anger surprised him.

She didn't know any better. It wasn't Amanda Williamson's fault that Douglas Kilroy had wreaked havoc on the American South for the better part of three decades.

He swallowed the rage before he dared to speak again. "Do you ever remember seeing him around Ju…" He cleared his throat. "Around Jaime?"

"No, I can't say I do." With a hapless shrug, she pushed the smartphone back to him.

Noah turned to Winter, and she nodded her agreement to the unspoken question.

"Okay, Mrs. Williamson," Winter started, producing a card from the inside of her blazer. "That's my card. If you remember anything else about Jaime or about that man, please let us know as soon as you get a chance. Otherwise, if we've got any other questions, we'll be in touch."

Pushing herself to stand, the woman nodded. "Of course, agents. I hope I was at least a little helpful."

"Absolutely," Noah replied.

"Yes, thank you for everything," Winter put in. "And please, any little bit of information helps. Even if you think it's something insignificant, just shoot me an email."

"Of course." A trace of the pleasant smile returned to Amanda's face as she reached out for a parting handshake.

Noah didn't need Winter's sixth sense to know they had gotten all the information they could get from Amanda Williamson and Bowling Green High.

He could only hope some of the names she'd provided would have a better idea of Justin Black's extracurricular activities.

10

S o many thoughts and feelings had whipped through Winter's head since she arrived at work that morning, she had almost forgotten about the odd phone call from Dr. Robert Ladwig. The conversation didn't even cross her mind until Noah pulled the giant pickup into the parking garage. Winter didn't believe in coincidences, and the man's bizarre inquiry hung in the back of her head like a leftover Christmas decoration.

"Hey…" She worried her bottom lip, wanting to bring this up the right way.

"What's up?" His green eyes flicked to her as he shifted the truck into park.

That's how I wanted *to sound earlier,* she thought to herself. Brushing aside the awkward memory, she straightened and unfastened her seatbelt.

"I think I got a weird call from Dr. Ladwig earlier. And no, I'm not trying to dredge anything up. That's all done and over with." For emphasis, she waved a dismissive hand.

"Okay?" He turned to face her. "But what do you mean you *think* you got a call from him?"

"Is that what I said? That's not how I meant it. I meant that I think it's weird. The fact that he'd call me at all is pretty weird, but he was saying shit about my brother and trying to tell me he hoped I'd found peace or something now that Kilroy's dead."

"That's a little weird, yeah. But I don't know. He was your shrink for a few years, wasn't he?"

"Yeah, but it's not like we were close."

"Maybe not, but darlin', you tend to leave an impression on people."

Almost half a year had passed since she had seen the mischievous twinkle in this man's eyes, and she'd forgotten how much she loved it. In the ensuing moment of quiet, she almost forgot what in the hell they were talking about. She tried to mask her low-key infatuation with feigned ire, but she could tell by the look on his face that she was unsuccessful.

As a last resort, she threw a playful jab at his upper arm.

"Damn it, Dalton," she muttered. "I was starting to think there was this big conspiracy going on, but you had to go and ruin it all by making sense."

"I'm sorry." He laughed. "I'll take your feedback into consideration and try to be more of a dumbass next time."

"You'd better." Despite the stressful events of the day so far, she snickered at the sarcastic comment.

Noah had a knack for lightening her darker moods, and she suddenly realized she had only ever given him grief for it. Before the wave of guilt could wash over her, she reminded herself that she didn't have to succumb to the sensation.

She could do better. She *would* do better. She would be a better friend because, of all the people she'd crossed paths with throughout her life, Noah Dalton deserved a better friend.

"Thank you," she finally said. "For being such an awesome friend, and for always being here to crack a joke and make me laugh when I'm about to cry or just lose my mind or something. I don't think I tell you that enough, so thank you."

The corners of his eyes creased as a warm smile overtook his handsome face. "Don't say it too much, though. We don't need it to go to my head." For emphasis, he tapped his temple.

"Of course not." She snickered as she reached for the door handle. "You coming in?" Brows raised, she glanced over to him.

"Nope. I've got an optometrist appointment in about a half-hour."

"An eye doctor?" She couldn't keep the surprise from her voice.

"Have you seriously not noticed that? After all the stare-downs we've had, you haven't noticed that I wear contacts?" By the time he finished the question, he had lapsed back into a fit of laughter. "My god, Winter. You might be the least observant FBI agent I've ever met."

She narrowed her eyes at him. "Okay, now you're just being mean. I don't have to put up with this shit." She raised her middle finger as she pushed open the passenger side door.

"Oh, now who's being mean, huh?"

"Shut up and go get your eyes fixed, Dalton," she shot back. Despite the hostile words, the tinge of amusement was unmistakable.

❄

BY THE TIME four o'clock rolled around, Winter was tired of phone calls. On any given day, she was indifferent about outbound calls, but when she reached the end of Principal

Williamson's list of names, she wanted to throw her phone against a wall.

Since Noah was out for the day, Winter and Bree had divided up the names—Bree contacted the teachers while Winter contacted the friends. Winter had scribbled out notes during her discussion with each person, and even though she could now say who had taken math or history with Justin, or who sat at the table with him during lunch, or who had always been on his team during gym class, she was no closer to pinning down his location. Or his current state of mind.

With a groan, she squeezed her eyes closed as she massaged her temples. She hadn't caught so much as a glimpse of a vision since Douglas Kilroy's death.

Her senses had not dulled, though, and a few weeks ago, she'd seen a glimmer of red between the cushions of her grandparents' couch after she misplaced her car keys.

Despite her frustration, she had almost laughed aloud at the unmistakable red glow. Maybe stress was the key, or if not stress, a sense of urgency. How else would her brain know which items to direct her toward?

Before she could nod off, she snapped open her eyes and stretched both arms above her head. Suppressing another groan, she glanced to the clock in the bottom corner of her computer monitor. Quarter after four.

She and Bree planned to meet up to compare notes at four-thirty, but Winter suspected that Bree's search had been as unhelpful as hers. Chances were, if Bree had come across a piece of helpful information, she would have already come to Winter.

As she turned her focus to the list of crossed out names, she frowned.

Eleven kids, and not a single one had so much as an inkling of where Jaime Peterson had gone. According to each of them, they had simply lost contact with Jaime after he graduated. No one thought the loss of communication was abnormal, especially considering Jaime's penchant for avoiding social media.

Pushing aside the piece of legal paper, a tinge of red caught her eye.

"Speak of the devil," she muttered to herself, the words barely audible.

The only pen she'd used to keep track of her progress—or lack thereof—was black, and she knew she hadn't outlined any of the text in red.

Peterson.

Why was "Peterson" important? They'd already looked through public records, criminal records, even financial records in an effort to find a hint of a nineteen-year-old named Jaime Peterson, but their search had turned up nothing.

So why was the surname so familiar? Had she merely stared at the name for so long that it now *seemed* familiar?

No, the nagging sensation in the back of her mind was more significant. Peterson was familiar for a reason, but the only case in which she had been involved over the last six months was Douglas Kilroy's. Was Peterson associated with Kilroy?

Scooting her office chair forward, Winter brushed aside the documents and notes as she pulled up the FBI database of closed cases.

She gritted her teeth as Kilroy's DMV photo appeared on the screen, but pushed past the knee-jerk anger as she scrolled down to view the details. Douglas Kilroy, born November twenty-second, 1949. His postal address had been listed in McCook, though the house to which it belonged had been condemned five years earlier. He had a P.O. box, but that too had been empty.

The man had as many aliases as Winter's grandmother had shoes.

Douglas Kilroy, also known as Barney Fife in Harrisonburg, Jared Kingston in North Carolina, George Brooks in Lynchburg, Alan Jefferson in Lynchburg and Norfolk, Harold Lee in Richmond, Robert Young in Richmond, and...

Her breath caught in her throat as she reached the seventh in the list. Thomas Peterson, referred to by friends and neighbors as Tommy.

According to the case file, he had used the alias in and around Savannah, Georgia, back during the 1990s. Tommy had worked as a locksmith, and there were a handful of his personal details available from his year and a half of employment.

Winter scribbled down the name and the social security number, her heart pounding in her chest. She typed the information into a new search bar, and though she half-expected a blank page of results, the screen was soon populated by a list of addresses and phone numbers.

A Thomas Peterson now lived in the same house in Quinton, Virginia and had done so for the past decade. The man was ten years younger than Douglas Kilroy, and he had been married for thirty-five years.

With all the questions flashing through her mind, Winter was surprised she managed to coherently write down the man's current address and phone number.

Was it possible?

Had Thomas Peterson, the *real* Thomas Peterson raised Justin? Did Thomas know Kilroy? Had Kilroy pawned Justin off on them after he murdered her parents, or had they come across Justin in another way?

The link was slim, but she needed answers, and the desperation to know Thomas Peterson's involvement in her brother's life was so strong that her breathing had become labored.

The township of Quinton wasn't far outside Richmond, but before she went to get Bree to leave for a face-to-face meeting with Thomas Peterson, she needed to pull herself together. Right now, she would be surprised if she could form a sentence that didn't make her sound like a caveman.

As she took a deep breath in through her nose, she counted to four, held still for a few seconds, and then slowly exhaled through her mouth.

What was important was that Justin was alive and healthy. All the people who had known him said he was personable, friendly, and kind. It was possible that the boy could have survived The Preacher's machinations, growing into a reasonably stable adult. Right?

Had he gone to study at a college overseas? Or had he simply moved to a more rural area to avoid the everyday hassles of the cities?

Either was a viable scenario, and in either case, he would turn up.

Once she was satisfied that the moment of blind panic had abated, she folded up the slip of paper with Thomas's address, pushed herself to stand, and started off toward Bree's cubicle at the other end of the room.

And with each step she took, she knew she was kidding herself.

But she had to try.

11

By quarter 'til four, Dr. Robert Ladwig had finally gotten a call back from a former patient, who also happened to work for the FBI. Though taken aback by his request for information on the Kilroy case, his informant had actually seemed touched that the good doctor wanted to help.

After the call with Sandra Evans, he had rescheduled all but one of his appointments for the day. Holed away in his office, Ladwig had been holding his breath until the phone rang. If this little former emotional cutter turned FBI secretary didn't come through, he would be at a loss as to how he would ever fulfill Dr. Evan's request.

He was sweating bullets.

Over the course of the afternoon, he'd been gathering his passport and important papers. He'd even been preparing to transfer money from his numerous accounts into multiple accounts overseas. He'd been ready to run when his phone rang, and his little secretary came through.

Two words were all that had been said. Two words had been all it took.

Jaime Peterson.

While he'd been waiting for that call, Ladwig had been sifting through all Douglas Kilroy's known aliases, at least the ones the media had splashed over every headline the past few months. The name the secretary gave him sounded familiar. Flipping back through his notes, he found what he was looking for...Thomas Peterson.

He ran the surname through any medical database he could find. He filtered the searches by age, gender, ethnicity, and even eye color. Less than an hour later, he had stumbled across Jaime Peterson of Bowling Green, Virginia.

Was this the one?

How did Justin Black connect to Jaime Peterson?

Was it one of many aliases The Preacher had given the boy over the years?

Puzzling through the mystery, Ladwig came to the conclusion that it was possible and continued to search for anything he could find on Jaime.

It wasn't much.

Toward the end of the boy's senior year, Jaime had broken his arm while playing football. Aside from the details of the emergency room visit, his findings were minimal.

The age progression software in which Ladwig had access might not have been as advanced as the program used by federal law enforcement, but he had recognized the young man almost immediately.

It had to be Justin Black. It just had to be.

Energy stoked, Ladwig continued to search, going meticulously through page after page of search engine results. Though Jaime had no known address listed, Thomas Peterson was labeled as a possible relative.

Not a Preacher alias. A real, living Thomas Peterson.

Ladwig researched the address, looked at the house on Google Maps. He needed to go there.

He still wasn't sure how a discussion with Thomas would

bring him closer to Justin Black, but right now, Thomas was the only lead he had. If nothing else, the man might have an idea who Jaime Peterson *actually* was.

"It damn well better," he muttered to himself as he flicked off the light switch.

He offered a departing wave to his receptionist, and the older woman smiled and nodded in response.

Any time he considered his affiliation with Sandra Evans while he was in Sue's presence, he was overcome with a wave of guilt. Sue reminded him of his mom, and Serena Ladwig was the reason he had chosen psychiatry as a career path in the first place.

His mother had only studied psychology during her undergraduate, and she had dropped out in her junior year when she got pregnant with him. She married his father, Dale Ladwig, and then she swapped her love of academia and research for the mantra of a homemaker.

When Ladwig was three, his sister had been born. Little Felicia was happy, healthy, and strong, and when his parents brought her home, it felt like she was exactly who they had waited for, like she was the perfect addition to their family.

For a month and a half, their lives were picturesque. A husband and father with a good job and an even better education, a stay-at-home mother who had enrolled in school to finish her degree, and two happy children. To top off the idyllic image, they even had a couple cats and a dog.

But in the span of two weeks, the entire world changed for young Robert Ladwig's family.

Their dog, a fourteen-year-old blue heeler mix named Rosie, had been with Dale and his family since he was in high school. Rosie was a fighter, but one of Ladwig's first memories was of his father crying into the dog's fur as they said their goodbyes.

The loss was hard enough, but Rosie had been an omen of darker times to come.

Dale had been distraught at first, but Rosie had lived a long life full of love and affection. Both Dale and Serena agreed that they would soon adopt a dog to provide the same companionship for their young children.

The three of them visited a shelter once, but they never went back.

Less than two weeks after they lost Rosie, he had awoken in the wee hours of the morning to his mother's shrieks of terror. He could still remember the way the red and blue lights from the ambulance had glinted off the plastic surface of the poster beside his bedroom window.

Felicia had died in her sleep, and even after an autopsy, the medical examiner was no closer to unearthing the reason for her untimely death. The official cause of death had been listed as sudden infant death syndrome. At four years old, Young Robert had known they wouldn't recover from Felicia's death like they had Rosie's.

And they hadn't.

A year later, his parents divorced, and a year after the divorce was finalized, Dale won full custody of their son.

Serena had succumbed to addiction, and three years after the custody hearing, almost to the damn day, she had overdosed.

She'd needed help, and instead, everyone who was supposed to care for her had turned their backs.

Ladwig never forgave his father for his role in his mother's death, but he doubted the man even noticed. Dale had remarried well before Serena died, and he had shifted his energy to his new family.

Since the seventh grade, Robert's determination had steered him to the mental health field so he could help people, people like Serena Ladwig.

As he dropped down to sit behind the wheel of his Mercedes coupe, he marveled at how far he had fallen.

Ladwig knew he should have felt a sense of shame or regret, but after seven years of Sandra Evans, he couldn't drum up so much as a pang of repentance.

To be sure, he wasn't proud of his actions. Instead, where the feelings should have been, there was nothing.

That part of him was dead, and he was sure nothing could bring it back to life.

❄

ASIDE FROM THE fact that Thomas Peterson hated to be called Tommy, Winter learned nothing from the half-hour she and Bree spent in the living room of the house Tom shared with his wife of thirty-five years.

When Winter provided Tom a picture of Douglas Kilroy, the man shook his head and advised he had never met him. Then, she produced Justin's senior picture, and Tom shook his head again.

After Winter double-checked to make sure they had run into every conceivable dead end, she and Bree bade the Petersons farewell and made their way back to Bree's gunmetal sedan.

"One brick wall after another." Leaning against the head-rest, Winter blew a couple stray strands of hair from her face. "Looks like it's back to the damn drawing board."

"I guess so. None of the teachers I talked to had any insight on where Justin might have gone. He never talked much about college, aside from Notre Dame a couple times. One of the guys I talked to thought that might have just been because he liked basketball, though. Notre Dame was his favorite college team."

"Basketball," Winter echoed. "Can't say I was ever really a

fan of it. Or any sport, honestly. I ran track for a little bit in high school, but there's no way I'd ever go to a track meet just to watch it for entertainment."

"You and me both." Bree chuckled. "I played softball. Freshman through senior year, all four summers. Softball or baseball are things I throw on if I want to take a nap or something, though. Going to the games is fun, but that's as much about the environment as anything."

"I like the Olympics," Winter put in. "The gymnastics always blew my mind. Still do, I suppose."

"Just about everything at the Olympics blows my mind. Oh, shit, that reminds me. You know Autumn's aunt, right? Or at least you've heard us mention her? She owns The Lift."

"I think I saw her when we were there the other night, yeah." The mention of the auburn-haired graduate student came with an unfamiliar twinge of worry. Irrational, stupid worry that Noah had developed an affinity for the redhead that went beyond platonic.

"She was in the Winter Olympics a while back, in snow-boarding. She didn't win a medal or anything, but she was still *in* the Olympics. Which is pretty badass, if you ask me."

"Yeah, that's pretty cool," Winter managed.

As they sped away from the quiet, small-town neighbor-hood, the only sounds were the quiet voices from the radio and the drone of the road.

How long had Noah known Autumn? How had he befriended her?

The pang of jealousy was stupid and immature, but try as she might, she couldn't push the sentiment from her mind. If she knew more, maybe then she could put her sudden concern to rest.

"Can I ask you something?" She enunciated each word with the same precision she would use in a surgical procedure.

Bree's dark eyes flicked over to Winter as she nodded. "Of course."

"Is there something going on with Noah and Autumn? Going on as in, like, well, you know."

Smooth, Winter. Real smooth. As she repeated the question in her head, she winced.

A glint of amusement flitted over Bree's face. "No, there isn't. And you don't have to ask twice, because I'm one-hundred-percent sure about that. Autumn told Shelby about the night they met, or at least the first time they talked to one another about something that wasn't a missing person."

In spite of the wave of awkward anxiety, Winter let out a quiet snort of laughter. Bree's ability to laugh at herself was uncanny, and in truth, Winter admired the quirk. Someday, she hoped she could be as light-hearted as the seasoned agent in the driver's seat.

"Anyway, Shelby told me about it," Bree went on, her lips curled into a slight smile. "I almost felt bad for Dalton. I mean, almost."

"What do you mean?" Winter asked, wrinkling her nose as she flashed Bree a puzzled look.

"Well, he stayed at The Lift one night after Shelby and I left, and he went up to hang out at the bar. They shot the shit for a little while, and when Autumn's shift was over, she got her stuff and went to head out. She told Dalton to let her aunt know if he needed anything, and that's when he offered her a ride home."

"Really?" Winter scoffed. "For the love of god. I mean, trying to pick up the bartender at a place you guys go on a regular basis doesn't seem real smart, does it?"

"No, not a bit." Bree laughed. "He's lucky Autumn's a bartender, and that she's nice. I tended bar for a little bit back when I was in college, and you get really good at turning dudes down. It was easy for me, though. I'd just tell them I was into chicks, and then they'd usually back off. Or..." she paused to hold up an index finger, "and this happened more than you'd think, but they'd just double down and get extra creepy."

"I don't know how you guys do it." With a sigh, Winter propped her elbow along the doorframe to rest her cheek in one hand. "What happened then? Did she tell him to go fuck himself?"

Bree raised a hand to her mouth to stifle a sudden fit of laughter. "Kind of, yeah. She shut him down with rugged quickness, just laid down the law like it was her damn job."

"Sounds like it kind of *is* her job."

"Kind of." Bree snickered. "You're not wrong. She told him he was being a creep, and I don't know how she did it, but she got him to agree that he was being a creep. Then, they went to this Mexican place down the street, and she almost ate as many chimichangas as he did."

"Damn, really?" The words felt perfunctory. Her mind had already begun to wander away from the conversation.

"Yeah," Bree confirmed with a nod. To Winter's relief, she didn't add to the response.

By just about anyone's standards, Noah was an attractive guy. But as much as Winter puzzled over Autumn's reason for shooting down the advance without so much as a lingering doubt, she was glad for the woman's rebuff.

She didn't feel she was entitled to envy. Even if Autumn had accepted the offer, even if the attraction had spanned more than one night, Winter didn't think she was allowed to be jealous.

Sure, the lines between her and Noah's friendship had started to blur, but as long as she was uncertain, she couldn't hold him accountable to an unrealistic set of expectations. She couldn't expect him to wait around while she made up her mind, while she decided what she wanted from her life.

Autumn had shot him down, but how many other women had said yes?

At the realization, the cold clasp of adrenaline settled in beside her heart, and her mouth felt like it might have been a desert.

Was that what he had been doing for the entire time she was gone? Had he been picking up women to take home for the last three and a half months? And if he had been, why did she care?

Noah was an adult, and he could be a barfly if he wanted. He didn't owe her anything. Didn't owe her his loyalty. Didn't owe her some bizarre vow of chastity.

So why in the hell did it sting so much to think of someone else in his warm embrace, smelling the familiar scent of fabric softener and peppermint that so often clung to him?

She could try to reason with herself and dismiss the ugly twinge of jealousy, but the effort was for naught.

The sentiment was there, and it was there to stay.

※

ROBERT LADWIG HEAVED a sigh as he watched the gunmetal Audi back out of the driveway. Even from the distance, the dejected expression on Winter Black's face was obvious. Thomas and Jaime Peterson had been a dead end.

The sedan had long since vanished from sight by the time Robert managed to turn the key over in the ignition.

Tomorrow, he would be forced to tell Sandra Evans that he had been unable to find Patient Zero's brother, and he would have to come up with a damn good reason to withhold Winter's name.

Or maybe he just needed to transfer those funds and brush off that passport after all.

12

Autumn's morning class had been canceled the night before, and she thought the happiest moments of her adult life occurred when she tapped the "dismiss" button on her first alarm. If there was one feeling she could bottle up for an emergency, she would choose going back to sleep after shutting off an alarm.

She drifted back to sleep in short order, and the next time she awoke, she did so of her own volition. With a contented sigh, she stretched both arms above her head before she went about her morning routine.

If she hadn't scheduled an appointment to look into the pain in her stomach, she would have lounged around on the couch while plugging away at her dissertation.

Maybe that was why she felt sick all the time, she thought. Maybe the stress of graduate school had started to eat its way through her stomach. She needed a vacation or at least a week off where she didn't feel obligated to work on an extensive research project.

The topic was fascinating, and clinical psychology was a lifelong goal, but she needed time to herself. She wanted to lounge on the couch and watch television, to watch a competitive cooking show, not write about the differences in offending patterns between male and female serial killers.

Snatching her car keys from their hook next to the front door, she glanced over to where Peach had curled up into a ball on the center of the sectional. On the cushion beside the ginger tabby, Toad watched Autumn as she bade them farewell and slipped out into the hall.

More often than not, the hallways in her apartment complex smelled like dirty socks, but today, the only scent she caught on her way out was a hint of citrus. Someone had finally cleaned, and she hoped the scent was a good sign for the remainder of her day.

Given her choice in career, her distaste for doctors' offices might have seemed counterintuitive to a casual observer.

After all, hadn't she devoted her life—not to mention a substantial sum of money—to working in a healthcare field? And which type of doctor did people dislike more, a regular physician or a shrink?

Most of the time, she was pretty sure the average person trusted a witch doctor more than a psychologist. It was a thankless job, but she figured it was one that someone ought to do. Never mind that her specific line of study would lead her to a career wherein her clientele were hardened criminals bound to the justice system.

After she had received her Juris Doctorate as part of the Ph.D. program for forensic psychology, she had debated dropping the clinical program to become a lawyer. But then, she realized that if there was an occupation the average person hated more and trusted less than a psychiatrist, it was a lawyer.

She might not have been the only person who was leery

of the doctor's office, but Autumn's reservations were atypical.

Her insurance was good, and she was fortunate enough not to have to worry about the expense. But each time she visited a new physician, she had to go through her entire family and medical history all over again. And each time, she had to put on a face to pretend that the topic didn't bother her.

The drive to the sleek office was uneventful, and for much of the trip, she let her mind wander. Only when a nurse stepped into the waiting area to call her name did she return her focus to the present.

"Autumn?" the woman called.

With a practiced smile and a nod, Autumn pushed herself to stand and made her way to follow the blue-clad nurse down a quiet hallway and into an exam room.

"So, what brings you in today, Ms. Trent?" Clipboard in hand, the corners of the woman's green-flecked eyes creased as she offered a warm smile.

"My stomach," Autumn answered as she rested a hand over her belly. "I've been experiencing a lot of stomach pain and nausea."

"Are you on any medications?"

Autumn shook her head. "Just the occasional allergy pill. For pollen, though. I'm not allergic to anything else that I know of."

"When's the last time you had sex?"

Even though she had expected the question, she still couldn't help a snort of laughter. "I'm a grad student, so I don't know exactly, but my ex and I broke up before Thanksgiving, if that's any indication. Nothing since."

"So, seven months?" the nurse surmised.

"Sure." Autumn shrugged. She didn't mind the topic of discussion when she was around one of her girlfriends, but with a perfect stranger, she always felt like she was being judged.

"Any history of surgical procedures or any chronic illnesses?"

HIPAA or not, she was always reluctant to answer the question.

"Yeah," she started. "No chronic illness, but I had a traumatic brain injury when I was eleven. I had to have surgery to relieve the pressure. I was in a medically induced coma for a couple weeks."

She left out that she had to repeat the sixth grade because she spent so long in the hospital, and she left out that during those months, her only visitor was her math teacher.

She also left out that, when she awoke, her senses had been overloaded to the point she thought she was losing her mind, or that she had woken from her coma in a different dimension. It took years for her to get a handle on the newfound keenness.

Even before the injury and the subsequent surgery, Autumn hadn't been fond of physical contact, especially with people she didn't know. But after she woke from the medically induced coma, she avoided touches even as innocuous as a handshake.

She hadn't known what was happening when she touched another person, but the onslaught of foreign emotions—feelings that were most definitely *not* hers—made her even more uneasy.

In the seventeen years since the head injury, she hadn't told a soul about the inexplicable sixth sense.

But Autumn was nothing if not determined, and she had learned to use the ability to her advantage by the time she was a sophomore in high school.

"Any family history of serious illnesses? Stroke or heart attack, cancer, anything like that?" The nurse's question snapped her out of the reverie and back to the little exam room.

Biting back a knee-jerk *hell if I know*, she shrugged. "I'm not sure. I think there might have been a stroke or something on my mom's side, her great-grandfather, but it wasn't until he was getting close to a hundred. Both my parents are dead, but not because of a medical issue."

Not unless you count a syringe or a bullet to the chest.

Autumn glanced down to where she had folded her hands in her lap.

If the pain from the last few months hadn't been so pervasive, she would have stayed at home. And if the nurse asked her how she had sustained the head injury, she would be inclined to hop down from the exam chair to walk out the doors altogether.

To her relief, no such inquiry was forthcoming. The nurse took her blood pressure, her pulse, and asked for a more in-depth description of the stomach pain. After a quick smile and a promise that the doctor would be with her shortly, the shorter woman departed.

There, she thought. *The worst part is over.*

None of her experiences with doctors had been bad, and she wondered how realistic the fear that her ability would be discovered was.

She'd been through so many MRI and CT scans of her head that she'd lost count, and none of the tests or images had revealed an abnormality that might have pointed to her enhanced senses or her ability to size someone up with a touch.

Whatever in the hell had happened to her was not easily captured in an image, even with the aid of modern medical technology.

Regardless of what her rational mind knew, Autumn's fear of being discovered and subjected to a series of experimental procedures was still persistent. And every time she stepped foot into a hospital or a doctor's office, that trepidation reared up to smack her logic and reasoning away like it had never been there in the first place.

If anyone had the know-how to discover the abnormality, it would have been the woman who had performed Autumn's surgery in the first place.

Despite the impression conveyed by her folksy, northern accent, Dr. Catherine Schmidt was one of the best pediatric neurosurgeons in the entire state of Minnesota.

Dr. Schmidt took a personal interest in many of her patients, especially those who didn't have much in the way of a support system. Once Autumn awoke from the medically induced coma, Dr. Schmidt had been the second person to visit her.

The bedside table in Autumn's room had been sparse—the only items were a couple cards and flowers from the hospital staff, and then a potted African violet from her math teacher. Autumn still had the flower, and she had even topped the soil with rocks so her animals wouldn't dig at it.

A couple hours after Dr. Schmidt had gone through a handful of medical questions with Autumn, she had returned with a box of cookies and a bouquet comprised of candy. Autumn hadn't been able to conceal her excitement, and despite her tendency to avoid any form of physical affection, she threw her arms around the surgeon's shoulders.

Though Dr. Schmidt's warm smile remained, Autumn could still remember the sensation that had overtaken her at the close contact. At the time, she was still unfamiliar with her new sixth sense, but she knew enough about what she felt to keep the sentiment to herself.

Before the embrace with Dr. Schmidt, a couple different nurses had taken Autumn's pulse and listened to her breathing with a stethoscope. Their slight touches had conveyed a deeply ingrained sense of kindness and sympathy that had helped to put her at ease.

When her math teacher, Mr. Sellers, had hugged her, she had been struck by a fatherly affection she doubted she would have received from her biological father.

But with Dr. Catherine Schmidt, Autumn's mind had plummeted into a shifting abyss, a place of eerie nothingness tinged with little more than ambition and anger.

Autumn might not have known much about her ability at the time, but she knew that Dr. Schmidt was not what she seemed.

13

As Aiden replaced the stout glass atop the coffee table, the last swig of the pricey scotch burned its way down his throat before it settled in to warm his stomach. Though he had started to compile the information while he was still in his office, he realized soon that this was the type of sensitive work he would be wise to keep out of the building.

The ability to throw back a stiff drink as he sifted through the files was an added bonus.

The day's search for Justin Black had turned up little and less, aside from confirmation that Jaime Peterson was a stolen identity.

No matter Aiden's personal distaste for the man, he knew Noah Dalton was a keen observer, and he knew that regardless of her personal stake in the outcome of the investigation, Winter was just as sharp as her Texan friend.

And then, of course, there was Bree.

From organized crime in Baltimore to violent crimes in Richmond, the woman had seen it all. She'd put away murderers whose notoriety rivaled, even *surpassed*, that of

Douglas Kilroy, and she'd landed the arrests before most of them had even thought to pursue an FBI career.

Bree Stafford had put away *mob bosses*. Over a career that spanned more than twenty years, she'd been face to face with the worst of the worst, the lowest of the low.

All three of them—Noah, Winter, and Bree—were better than good. They were some of the best.

But when it came to Justin Black, he couldn't help but wonder if they were blinded by the potential to find the kid intact, both physically and mentally. Aiden did not doubt that Justin was physically healthy. After all, Douglas Kilroy wouldn't have harmed his protégé.

Or had all Aiden's years analyzing the motivations of mass murderers and psychopaths jaded his perception? Was *he* the one who was biased? As he scrolled through Bree and Winter's handwritten notes, he doubted it.

By all accounts, Justin—or Jaime, as he had been referred —was outgoing and personable. None of the friends who Winter contacted had a bad word to say about Jaime, and only one teacher had vocalized even a hint of concern. However, the older man's worry had more to do with the fact that he had never met Jaime's parents than anything.

High school hadn't been a joyous experience for Aiden. He had been tall, thin, and awkward. He had no interest in sports, and he was too shy to approach his classmates to make new friends. Until he graduated, his only friends were the same group of geeky outcasts he had associated with since the fifth grade.

His high grade point average gave him a way out, and he took the opportunity as soon as it arose.

In a new city, surrounded by unfamiliar faces, by people who did not know about his social standing in high school, he reinvented himself.

The loss of his older sister, Emily, came with a new,

cynical outlook, and with that outlook, the awkward Aiden Parrish from South Chicago vanished.

More outspoken and assertive, he found himself with a new circle of friends almost overnight. He changed his major from engineering to a double major in criminal justice and psychology. At first, he had been determined to maintain a spotless academic record to earn a spot in a competitive graduate program for clinical forensic psychology.

However, after a handful of discussions with the graduate students who oversaw behavioral research at the university, he formulated a backup plan.

Clinical psychology programs were among the most competitive Ph.D. tracks, and often, students who "knew somebody" were selected for the coveted spots. No one in Aiden's family had even gone to college, so he decided not to hedge his bets on a path that was so full of uncertainty.

All in all, the realization had been for the best.

Forensic psychologists were not profilers, they did not carry a badge and wear a Glock on their hip. Though the profession was responsible for much of the understanding of criminals' motives, he hadn't wanted a career in a clinical setting.

After Emily's murder, he wanted the badge, and he wanted the Glock.

Sure, he still wanted to understand the motivation that drove murderers like Emily's husband, Dave Lemke, but he did not want to try to treat them.

He wanted to put them away. And if Justin was one of them, then Aiden would put him away too.

Swallowing against the sour taste in his mouth, he forced his attention back to the laptop.

From what Aiden had dug up via social media websites, Justin's friends at Bowling Green High had belonged to a few distinctly different sets of social cliques. By itself, the knowledge was not damning, but when he sifted through the differing accounts of Justin's personality, a clearer picture formed.

Around one set of friends, Justin was soft-spoken and humble. He went to Wednesday night youth groups and even joined their families for dinner.

Then, with another group of friends, he had been brash and daring, cocky, and rebellious. He'd tell those friends stories about his antics in previous school districts, about how he had gotten into fights and openly disobeyed his teachers.

With yet another cluster of friends, Justin had been creative and thoughtful.

Justin Black, also known as Jaime Peterson, was a chameleon.

All his friends loved him because they all thought that he was just like them, and they didn't know that he was pretending to be someone else when he was in the company of a different group. As luck would have it, Justin hadn't stuck around Bowling Green long enough for all his classmates to compare notes.

But as luck would also have it, Aiden could compare those notes to form a more complete picture of the true nature of Justin Black.

So far, the picture was bleak.

❄

ROBERT LADWIG DIDN'T HAVE a client scheduled that morning, and when Sue called back to his office to tell him he had a visitor, his stomach dropped.

The night before, he had ripped off the band-aid and called Sandra Evans as soon as he returned home from the trip to Quinton. Each statement he made had been greeted with a laconic response that bordered on curt. By the time the call ended, his hands shook.

He spent more of the night tossing and turning than he had sleeping, and as he strode out to admit the visitor, his only goal was to get the meeting over with.

As he suspected, the only occupant of the waiting area was a familiar woman.

Her amber, gold-flecked eyes were fixed on the saltwater fish tank that his other receptionist, Kiera, had convinced him to install. Even as she watched a little octopus scuttle along the colorful rocks, he could tell that she had noticed his arrival.

"Dr. Evans," he declared. "It's been a while."

With the slightest smirk, she nodded as she turned to face him. "It sure has. Looks like you're doing pretty well for yourself here, eh, Robert?"

He fought against bristling at the cool indifference in her voice. Nodding, he swept his arm toward the hall. "Come on back, Sandra. I just brewed some coffee if you'd like some."

"Of course, that sounds great." Sandra flashed the woman behind the reception desk a quick smile." Thanks again, Sue. It's so nice to meet you."

"You, too, Dr. Evans." Sue returned the pleasant expression as if nothing was amiss.

Then again, as far as Sue was concerned, nothing *was* amiss. As far as Sue knew, Sandra was just another colleague from the medical community. As far as Sue knew, the blonde, middle-aged surgeon was just another visitor.

"What are you doing here, Evans?" Though he had closed and latched the heavy wooden door, Ladwig kept his voice hushed as he spun around to face her.

"Wow, that's not much of a greeting." With feigned exasperation, she crossed both arms over her white button-down blouse.

Every emotion Sandra Evans had was feigned, Ladwig knew. The woman was a fucking sociopath.

"Cut the bullshit, Evans. You know how risky this is, don't you?" He made sure to keep his tone cool and dismissive. The pediatric neurosurgeon might have terrified him, but he wouldn't reveal the abject fear in her presence.

"I'm aware." Her response was flat, and he didn't miss the dangerous glint behind her gold-flecked eyes. "But we need to talk, and it's about time we had a face-to-face discussion about Patient Zero."

"Fine. Sit down." Grating his teeth together, he made his way around the desk and dropped to sit.

The ghost of a smug smile was on her lips as she took a seat in one of the two chairs that faced him.

"You want Patient Zero's name, don't you, Evans." The vocalization wasn't a question. Not at all.

"The people I do this work for are starting to get impatient, Robert. And believe me when I say that when they get impatient, bad things happen."

If it hadn't been for the grave look that replaced her self-assuredness, he might have been inclined to think she was lying.

He knew there were others involved, and though he tried not to give the idea too much consideration, the discovery of how Winter came into her enhanced senses would be a lucrative breakthrough for Sandra's associates.

"What do you want me to do about it?" he finally asked.

"I think you know the answer to that."

"And you know my answer to *that*. Patient Zero is off-limits, and for a good fucking reason. Listen, Sandra. If you and your employers want me to take your word about this 'research,' then you'll have to do the same for me. You have to trust that I'm keeping Patient Zero's identity a secret because involving this individual would be a bad idea. A *very* bad idea."

Eyes narrowed, she leaned forward. "And why might that be?"

"He's in federal law enforcement," Rob answered through clenched teeth.

Despite the changing demographics of the last decade, the vast majority of law enforcement agents were men. Referring to Patient Zero as a man would throw Sandra far enough off the correct trail that the likelihood of discovering Winter would be minimal.

At the same time, the lie held enough truth to come across as believable.

"*Federal* law enforcement?" Sandra echoed. To his relief, her tone was free of doubt or suspicion.

"Yes."

"Which agency?"

"Does it matter? Do the people we work for have a preference? Would they be all right with starting a fight with, say, the ATF as opposed to Homeland Security? Or vice versa?"

"No." She tapped her lower lip with a carefully manicured finger. "You were right, Robert. I'm enough of an adult to admit that. Well-connected or not, none of us want to pique the interest of a federal law enforcement agency. Homeland, ATF, FBI, it doesn't matter which. We don't want to be caught, and poking the bear seems like a sure-fire way to get caught."

"I appreciate your understanding, Evans." Even as he forced the agreeable look to his face, he wanted to shout at her to get the hell out of his building.

"Do you suppose you could give me an overview of how you came across this man? Of what events led up to these unique abilities of his?"

With a sigh, Robert leaned back in his chair and brushed

a hand through his hair. Fortunately, he had become a good liar.

"He was about thirteen when it happened," Robert started. "It was an accident on a merry-go-round. You're familiar with how much teenage boys like to do stupid shit, aren't you?"

The corner of her mouth turned up in what would be known as amusement for most human beings, but Ladwig knew this woman wasn't amused. She nodded, and he rushed to go on.

"Based on how he told it, he tried to jump onto the merry-go-round after one of his friends pushed it to get it to spin as fast as he could. He said he must have tripped, because he hit the back of his head on one of the metal handles. His friend thought he was dead, but after a three-month long coma, he woke up with the abnormalities you already know about."

"Do you think you could send me a synopsis of his treatment?" she asked, tapping a slender finger against her cheek.

"Sure. But that's all I'm sending you."

He wanted her to leave, and once she was gone, he intended to update the go-bag he had thrown together a year earlier. More money. Not just the financial transfers, but more cash. And a fucking shotgun.

"Of course," she replied with a smile.

And that look was all he needed to confirm his suspicion.

If she suspected he was lying, she would have simply picked up her phone and ordered his death. If he was lucky, his death would be mercifully quick. If he wasn't lucky—and Robert was rarely lucky—she would knock him out, have one of her goons load him into a van, and drive him out to wherever in the hell she kept her victims.

He wondered how many men and women had seen that same smile in the final seconds before they died.

14

Once the dinner rush died down, The Lift's flow of business returned to its usual weekday tedium. Autumn had come in at the last minute to help the servers and the bartender after one of the women scheduled had to take her nephew to the doctor.

According to Autumn's Aunt Leah, the poor woman worked two jobs, attended college classes at VCU, and babysat her nephew while her sister worked the night shift.

"The struggle is real," Leah had told her.

And if anyone would know, Autumn figured it would be Leah. From Olympic athlete to small business owner, Leah had worked her ass off for everything she had. And in an economy that was stagnant, Leah's everything wasn't much.

With a sip from her glass of soda, Autumn forced herself to focus on the short essay she had started to grade. During the summer months, she earned her graduate stipend by teaching two different sections of Abnormal Psychology.

This week's assignment had been straightforward enough, but she was still taken aback by the lack of effort put forth by some students.

To those who weren't psychology majors or minors, Abnormal Psych was like a novelty. They could "ooh" and "ahh" at all the mental health maladies listed in their manual, and they could use the fleeting knowledge to diagnose their crazy uncle. And when the time came to grade papers—even short article summaries—she could tell who those students were.

"Damn it," she muttered to herself.

She had spaced off again, had retreated to her private headspace to avoid the half-assed attempt to summarize an academic journal article about schizophrenia. If she was at home, she suspected she would have passed out with her face on the keyboard by now.

A flicker of movement caught her eye as the double doors swung open to admit a new patron. Pushing the slim laptop closed, she rose to her feet to greet the woman. The closing bartender was lounging in a booth for his lunch break, and as soon as he returned, Autumn would be clear to go home to suffer through the remainder of the papers.

As her gaze settled on the familiar set of vivid blue eyes, she expected to see either Bree or Noah on the newcomer's heels. Autumn slid the computer into her messenger bag, but when she looked back up, the dark-haired woman was still alone. She made no effort to conceal the puzzlement from her face.

"Hey, Winter. Is it just you?" she asked.

"Yeah." Winter nodded and hopped up to sit on a stool at the edge of the horseshoe-shaped bar.

"Are Bree and Noah busy chasing down UFOs tonight or something?" Eyebrow arched, Autumn took another drink of her soda.

"Some kind of lake monster, I think," Winter replied without missing a beat. "I'm not sure. They didn't tell me much about it."

"That explains it." Autumn nodded as she leaned against the counter. She didn't have to reach out to shake Winter's hand to know that something weighed on her mind. "You want a shot? On the house."

"It's been a long week." Winter's eyes skimmed the choices behind Autumn's shoulder. "Yeah, a shot sounds just about perfect right now."

"I hear that. Whiskey all right?" As she produced a couple shot glasses, she offered Winter a questioning glance.

"You read my mind."

The overhead lights glinted off the polished glass as she and Winter tapped the shots together with a merry clink. Quality booze or not, Autumn still grimaced at the potent flavor. Her stomach had been calm for the past twenty-four hours, and she hoped she wasn't pressing her luck by drinking straight whiskey.

To her chagrin, the doctor she'd seen the day before had referred her to a specialist. He agreed that stress was the most likely cause, but based on the persistence and the sheer level of pain, he wanted to err on the side of caution. Autumn couldn't find it within herself to argue, but she'd scheduled the appointment two months out in hopes that the pain would disappear and she would be spared from another office visit.

"So," she started, pulling herself back to the present. "Do you want anything to drink?" Still no nausea or stabbing pain. Well, that was good, wasn't it?

"If I say I want a beer, it looks like there are about six hundred possibilities." Winter's blue eyes were fixed on the line of taps as she scooted forward in her seat. Her gaze flicked back over to Autumn, and she offered a hapless shrug. "Any recommendations?"

"I hate when people ask me that," she muttered. "I always recommend my personal favorite, but I'm starting to think I ought to just respond to everyone with 'Bud Lite' or something standard like that."

"Boring." Wrinkling her nose, Winter shook her head.

"I know, right? But really, I can tell you what the majority of normal human beings order, or I can tell you what I usually drink. I'll let you decide."

"Red pill or blue pill." A faint smile crept onto Winter's face. "Sorry. I watched all those movies with my grandpa when I was a sophomore in high school. He doesn't seem like a sci-fi kind of guy, but he loves some *Star Trek* and *Matrix*. He was Captain Picard for Halloween one year, but I don't think any of the kids who showed up at our door knew who the hell he was."

"Well, if he was here, or if I was there, he'd be in good company." Autumn chuckled, poking herself in the chest for emphasis. "I've been in college for eight years, so I guess it's not a huge surprise that I'm a giant nerd."

"You know, I was so damn focused on a career while I was in school that I never really ventured into too much of that stuff. It always seemed like it was cool, but I guess I never really sat down to consider it."

"So, you focused on school during school? That's arguably even nerdier." Shrugging, Autumn retrieved a pint glass.

With a half-laugh, half-snort, Winter nodded. "Apparently, if I wanted to be cool, I needed to be playing *Halo* and drinking beer."

"I did that in high school. It was *Halo 3* by then, though."

"I don't suppose you happen to be a fan of Code Red Mountain Dew?" The grin that crept to Winter's face insisted there was more to the question than Autumn knew, but she returned the expression.

"I feel like I'm playing into an inside joke here, but yeah, that stuff is great."

"No, you're not." Winter snickered. "It's just a fun fact I

found out about an old friend today. And believe me, if you knew the guy, you would *not* have guessed."

"Fair enough. All right, Neo. Red pill or blue pill?"

"Red. Definitely red. Let's see what this beer everyone hates is all about."

"According to Noah, it tastes like it was brewed in a dirty sock. At least that's what he said when he tried it for the first time. But if you were wondering, it's called Black Star IPA. They sell it in cans at some liquor stores." Dropping a coaster atop the polished wooden bar, Autumn set down the glass and pushed it to Winter.

Brushing a piece of jet-black hair from her eyes, she gingerly picked up the beer and took a tentative drink. Rather than fix Autumn with a sour look, Winter flashed a thumbs-up.

"Really?" Autumn's response was more reflexive than doubtful.

Winter took another, longer drink. "Yeah, I like it. It's like a punch in the mouth, but in a good way. I mean, if I was sleepy and I was at the bar with my friends, I could get one of these, and I feel like it'd wake me up *and* give me a buzz."

"It's nine-percent alcohol," Autumn advised.

"Even better." For emphasis, Winter took a deep drink. By the time she set the glass down, almost half the dark beer was gone.

"Damn, girl." Autumn laughed. "You looking to get blitzed tonight or something?"

"I wouldn't be opposed to it," Winter muttered. The edginess Autumn had spotted upon her arrival was back, and she couldn't help but wonder what had motivated her to venture out to a bar by herself.

She bit back the curiosity and gestured over to the other bartender as he stepped out of his shadowy booth and stretched. "If you can hold that thought for a couple minutes, that'll give Eli over there plenty of time to go have a smoke before he comes back in here to take over for me. Then we can grab a couple drinks and decide how plastered we want to get."

With a quiet chuckle, the dark-haired woman nodded. "Sounds like a plan."

Autumn offered her a wide grin and stuck out her hand.

Some of Winter's wariness had worn away, but the brief physical contact came with an onslaught of different emotions. Of contentment, frustration, regret, and trepidation. Winter's solo trip out to The Lift had not been made because she wanted to drink away her problems.

To Autumn's surprise, the driving force was to speak to her. There was no malice to be found, but the lack of anger only made Autumn more curious.

They made casual conversation while she waited for Eli. She learned where Winter was from as well as the names of her grandparents, and in exchange, she offered up the names of her adopted parents. Before their conversation could venture too near their respective families, Autumn switched the topic.

There was a flicker of relief in Winter's eyes at the abrupt change.

Though Autumn could admit to a polite curiosity about Winter's reluctance to discuss her family, she was the last person who would dig into such a sensitive subject. Outside the psychiatric couch, at least. And as far as Autumn was concerned, the further away they stayed from talking about their families, the better.

Once Eli made his way back behind the bar, Autumn filled a pitcher with the dark IPA and retrieved a pair of chilled pint glasses. Shouldering her messenger bag, she nodded in the direction of the corner booth where Bree and Noah usually sat.

"I'll take those glasses," Winter offered.

"And I won't argue with you."

As Winter reached out to accept the cold glasses, her index finger brushed against the back of Autumn's hand. The frustration had abated, and as best as she could tell, the anxiety had been replaced with a twinge of optimism.

Autumn couldn't help the smile that crept to her lips at the simple act of friendship.

By the time the conversation shifted to their college careers, Autumn's head felt lighter, and she noted that Winter had become more talkative.

"I went to SUNY," Winter started as she poured some more beer into her glass. "In Albany. It was pretty good, at least aside from the dude who robbed a bunch of students at gunpoint."

"Wait, what?" Autumn chortled. "Holy shit, really? I applied to grad school there, and they turned me down."

"Yeah, it was a big deal. Some rich jackass, probably just doing it for kicks or to support his coke habit. Who the hell knows. I was the one who found his last victim. I thought she was dead for a second, but she pulled through. The news made it sound like I was some kind of superhero, but really, it was just a lucky hunch."

"Well, you are a federal agent, so my guess is there was some skill involved there too." Grinning, Autumn held up her glass.

"Thanks." Winter tapped their glasses together. "What about you? What exactly are you going to do when you're a forensic psychologist?"

"It's not quite what they make it look like in *Criminal Minds*." She lifted both shoulders. "No private planes, no badge and gun, no field work."

"Will you be doing any profiling? Or, I guess, is that what you want to do? Because if it is, you know, you've got a few

FBI friends now." With an exaggerated wink, Winter sipped her drink.

"I'll admit, it's pretty cool to have friends like that. I had no idea that The Lift would be the place to meet Feds, but here we are. To answer your question, though, no. That's not the plan. It'll probably sound weird, especially since you're in law enforcement, but the reason I went into this field is that I think there are a lot of people who've been branded 'criminals' who could just use some help."

She waited for a scoff or a snort, but Winter just looked at her solemnly. "At times, I'm sure you're right."

"It's a little more scientific and a lot more treatment oriented than profiling. I mean, it's one thing to pin a list of attributes to an offender in the interest of understanding their motive, but it's another thing entirely to understand that motive and find a way to prevent it from happening in the future, you know? It's being proactive versus being reactive."

Tapping an index finger against her glass, Winter paused, her blue eyes thoughtful. "That's admirable. And for what it's worth, I think you'll be really good at it. You're down to earth, and I don't think that's a quality that a lot of shrinks have."

"I think you've been associating with the wrong shrinks if that's been your impression." Autumn laughed into her glass as she polished off the remaining beer.

When Winter joined in her mirth, Autumn felt her smile widen. In her entire life, she had never been able to call more than two people a friend at any given time. Now, with the addition of Winter Black, she had four friends.

15

As Beth dropped down to sit across from her granddaughter, she stretched her legs and sighed. Winter had been back at the house for almost a week, and Beth could tell she had already grown restless.

At the disturbance, Winter's vivid blue eyes snapped up from her smartphone.

"What's on your mind, honey? And don't even say nothing. I know that look." Beth made sure her knowing glance was over the top, and Winter's slight smile told her she had been successful.

The past six days had been markedly different from the three and a half months Winter had spent with them after Douglas Kilroy was shot. Winter and Jack had competed with one another for the higher score in a silly mobile game about slicing fruit, and every night, they all ate popcorn and sat together in the living room to watch *Star Trek: The Next Generation*.

Though Winter had only spent a few days in Richmond, she soon revealed that she had made a new friend, and that the new friend was not another federal agent. Beth had been thrilled at the news, but she knew better than to show Winter the full extent of her joy.

"Do you think it's weird that I want to go back to work?" Winter's gaze had returned to the cup of coffee beside her phone.

"It's not weird," Beth started. "It's not like you work in a call center or something. Then, I think it'd be weird. But you know how important the work you do is. It's more than just work."

The smile remained as Winter nodded her understanding. "And no offense, but I think I'm getting stir-crazy. Max, my boss, told me that I could come back whenever I was ready, but that I didn't have to rush into it. It's hard to explain, but while we were working on that investigation when I was there, it just felt like everything made sense. Like I was doing something right by being there. It's been a couple weeks since we ran out of leads, but I think maybe I ought to go back anyway. Even if we aren't looking for Justin."

"It makes sense to me." Beth returned Winter's faint smile with a grin. "Go ahead, sweetie. Your grandfather is doing much better. The only reason he isn't awake and out here with us is because he stayed up too late last night watching Jean-Luc Picard and the Enterprise."

"Okay," Winter chuckled. "Well, maybe this *will* sound weird then. Watching that show has been like a weird source of inspiration. They're just a bunch of good people out helping others around the galaxy, and no matter what, they always do the right thing."

Six months ago, Beth might have bit back the words she was about to speak. She might have kept them to herself for fear of the despondency they would bring to her grand-daughter.

Now, however, she knew how silly such a line of thought was.

"You know, Winter," Beth started, raising an index finger. "Your mother used to do the same thing. She'd stay up with Jack until twelve on a school night watching *Star Trek*. They'd always sneak out to the living room after I went to bed, like I didn't know what they were doing. And then the next day, they'd both be a couple zombies."

"Really?" Though there was a wistful tinge in Winter's eyes, her smile widened, and Beth knew she had made the right decision.

"Really," she answered. "Your grandpa and your mom were a couple of nerds. When Jean was old enough, Jack bought her all the *Lord of the Rings* books. I don't know how many months it was, it might've even been a year, but they'd walk around talking to one another in Elvish. It was the most ridiculous, adorable thing I've ever seen."

"I had no idea." The sound of Winter's laugh filled Beth's heart with joy. "She must have hidden it pretty well."

"I'm not so sure about that, honey." Beth waved a dismissive hand. "She married a college professor."

Winter covered her mouth to stifle a burst of laughter.

Beth wasn't sure how long they sat at the circular table while they recalled stories of Jeanette and Bill, of Jeanette and Jack, or of all three. But by the time she made her way around the living room and kitchen to shut off the lights for the night, she felt like an impossible burden had been lightened.

❄

I NEVER WANTED any of my patients to die. To watch them close their eyes that one last time was a testament to my failure, and in some ways, I mourned their loss.

Human beings were fragile creatures, their lives fleeting and ultimately insignificant. But every time I watched one of them die under my care, I thought of what they could have been. Of the greatness they could have achieved, and the lasting effect they could have had.

Jensen Leary had shown promise, but promise didn't always equal progress. And in Jensen's case, I suspected he had simply not been equipped with the right genetic profile.

A person's genetic makeup was responsible for so many of their physical attributes. I was sure there had to be a marker that determined whether or not they had the capacity to develop the same abnormalities as Robert Ladwig's Patient Zero.

Unfortunately, Jensen had not been in possession of the ever-elusive marker.

With a sigh, I pulled down the plastic face shield I used during autopsies.

There were a number of television shows that depicted surgeons as a studious lot who listened to classical melodies while they tended to both the living and the dead. And sure, there were some of my colleagues who played Beethoven or some other dead man's compositions while they prepared for surgery.

But, to be honest, I'd always thought it made them look pretentious.

Just because I had the letters "MD" behind my name didn't make me a classical music aficionado, and just because I could remove a brain tumor from a six-year-old kid's head didn't mean I could tell Beethoven apart from any other famous composer. As far as I was concerned, Sebastian Bach was the front man for an '80s hair band, not a classical composer.

I used different playlists for different occasions. For surgeries performed on the living, specifically in a hospital, I preferred upbeat tunes.

Though I was sure it drove the other doctors and nurses

insane, my latest preference was Korean pop. Anything more down-tempo than K-Pop was not conducive to the right train of thought for surgery, in my opinion.

Autopsies, on the other hand. Those were different. Sure, cutting into a dead man's brain to discern what had led to his untimely death took precision, but precision was second nature to me. I was about to turn fifty-three, and I'd been performing surgeries since I was in medical school.

When I conducted an autopsy, I liked to take a stroll down memory lane. The follow-up song was different each time, but I always started the procedure with one of my favorite songs to come out of the '90s, "Kiss from a Rose."

The process was long and messy, and if it had not been for the mix of tunes from the '90s and the present, I didn't think I could stand to finish it all in one sitting.

In addition to examining the brain and a handful of other vital organs to check for damage and abnormalities, I had to remove any pieces or parts that could be used to easily identify the poor son of a bitch.

In the past, that had only meant teeth and surgical implants. Now, pacemakers and other devices were all outfitted with serial numbers that could make identifying the deceased as easy as if they had been buried with their driver's license. Killers had been identified with less, I reminded myself.

I wasn't a killer, but I knew better than to think the police would agree. They were incapable of stepping back to view the bigger picture. They couldn't tell the forest from the trees.

The strongest acids were monitored heavily due to their use in explosive devices, but lye was still just as easy to buy as plant fertilizer. Though potent, lye by itself or with water was not quite enough to eliminate human bone. Methods existed to speed up the process of dissolution, but they required much more water along with large, expensive pieces of equipment that would raise more than a few eyebrows.

For the time being, I'd have to make do with a fifty-five-gallon drum, a few pounds of lye, and a healthy dash of water. It was still risky. For a human skeleton to completely decompose in such circumstances, it would take at least four years for no DNA or RNA to remain. Which was the end goal, needless to say.

So, I had to be clever and bury the barrels in places they wouldn't be discovered. As luck would have it, I was very clever.

Even the men and women in charge of the larger operation would never know where I buried the bodies.

There was one person I trusted with that knowledge.

Myself.

16

Brad Rathbun thought he would head to the construction site at the edge of town like he did every day. He thought he'd ride around in a Bobcat to dig space for future basements like he always did. He'd been in the construction business for more than twenty years, and he had seen almost every little oddity and quirk that came with the occupation.

Once, about six years back, he and his crew had even come across a body.

It had been a skeleton, and the old-timey dress and shoes were stained and frayed. According to the medical examiner, the lady had been dead for over a hundred years.

A single gunshot to the back of the head left little doubt that she'd been murdered. Brad looked up the old case on occasion, but they still hadn't identified the poor woman, much less discovered her killer.

After that, he was sure he had seen everything, but on this ordinary Tuesday morning, he was about to be proven wrong.

A flicker of movement snapped his attention away from

the panel of gear shifts and controls and up to the windshield. Pete's neon yellow vest glimmered in the sunlight as he waved his arms. He looked like he was making an attempt to fly away, but Brad curbed his amused chuckle as soon as he saw the man's expression.

"What is it?" Leaning his head out the window, he glanced from Pete and then over to the new guy, Will.

"I don't know," Will answered with a shrug. "Pete, what the hell's going on?"

"There's something here. You hit it, Rathbun! I think you dented it, but I can't tell if it's broke open or not." Pete hopped up from the wide, shallow dirt pit and made his way to stand beside Will. "Back that thing up, will you?"

"Yeah, yeah," Brad muttered.

He and Pete had been friends for years, and his feigned exasperation was all in good fun. Turning the key over to kill the engine, Brad climbed down to the grass.

"It's a barrel," Will announced as Brad returned. "Fifty-five gallon, by the looks of it."

Brad raised his hardhat to scratch at his sweaty head. "You think it's full of oil?"

"Shut up, guys." Pete reached into the pocket of his well-worn jeans to produce his phone. "Nothing good ever comes in a fifty-five-gallon drum buried out on the edge of town. I'm calling the cops."

Pete was normally a jovial guy, and his grave tone was more than enough to set Brad and Will on edge.

As it turned out, this Tuesday morning was anything but ordinary.

❊

THREE WEEKS EARLIER, Aiden had come to the conclusion that Justin Black was a sociopath. And three weeks earlier, Bree and Winter had hit a brick wall in their pursuit of Justin's whereabouts. For three weeks, the only reason Aiden went home was to sleep.

His time hadn't been spent chasing after Jaime Peterson or Justin Black. He'd bounced from case to case in his own department as he provided much-needed insight to the members of the BAU.

For three weeks, he'd done his damn job, and that was *all* he'd done.

Even after all the work they'd put in to find just a trace of evidence to lead them to Justin, Aiden had only crossed paths with Noah Dalton on a handful of occasions. And on none of them had he felt it necessary to strike up a conversation.

Unlike Winter's disappearance after Kilroy's death, she had left them all with a brief email to announce her absence. The explanation was half-assed, but he figured it was better than nothing.

Before the login screen on his computer had even finished loading, a shadow of movement behind the closed blinds of the door was followed by a sharp clatter as the visitor knocked.

"It's unlocked," he called.

As the door creaked open, he reached for his usual cup of coffee. When he swiped at air, he was abruptly reminded that he had not bothered to stop at a café on his way to the office. In the interest of saving a few minutes, he had convinced himself that he could subsist on the breakroom muck until he had a chance to walk to the coffeehouse down the street.

At the thought of the bitter brew provided for free in the office, he wondered what the hell he had been thinking.

He felt the corner of his mouth turn down in a scowl, and when the morning visitor stepped into the dim room, the expression of distaste deepened.

"To what do I owe the pleasure, SAC Osbourne?" His tone was laden with sarcasm.

He might not have had a personal issue with Max Osbourne at the beginning of summer, but a month had passed since their pointed conversation about Winter's absence.

Though he would never admit it to Max—or anyone, for that matter—the seasoned SAC's words about Aiden's behavior toward Winter had hit a nerve. And unflattering observations only hit a nerve with Aiden when they were accurate.

A twitch of amusement passed over the man's lined face as he took a seat in front of the polished, wooden desk.

"Good morning to you, too, Parrish."

Leaning back in his chair, Aiden crossed his arms over his black suit jacket as he fixed Max with a flat look. "Good morning, SAC Osbourne. *Now*, to what do I owe the pleasure?"

"Right down to brass tacks. That's one thing I've always liked about you." For emphasis, Max held up a manila folder before setting it down in front of Aiden.

"What's this? A case file?" He flashed Max a questioning look before he flipped to the first page.

An autopsy report with more blank spaces than filled. Beneath the diagram were a handful of glossy, eight-by-ten photographs of a human skeleton. Well, the majority of a human skeleton. The bones were brittle and worn, almost like they had been retrieved from an archaeological dig site. Flashes of memory poured through Aiden's mind as he shifted through the folder's contents.

"This is the new one." Max's voice snapped Aiden's attention away from the picture as the man produced a folder nearly identical to the first.

This folder, however, held even less information than the

other. Rather than a skeleton, the solo photograph showed a fifty-five-gallon drum amidst a heap of fresh earth.

Tapping a finger on the newer folder, he shifted his gaze back up to Max. "How old is this?"

"Found on Tuesday morning. So, about twenty-four hours since discovery. That's why there aren't any autopsy charts or pictures of the body. We don't have them yet."

"All right. Now, aside from the fifty-five-gallon drums, what else do these two cases have in common? Disposing of a body in a barrel isn't exactly unique. The cartels and the mafia all like to dump bodies in barrels like this, so what's to say this isn't some cartel shit?"

"That first one, I guess you didn't get to the back of it. You're right, Parrish. You usually are." Max didn't pause long enough for Aiden to soak up the compliment. "Cartels and Italian crime families do like their barrels, but they also like to leave calling cards. Warnings for other gangs not to fuck with them. There was nothing like that at either of these sites, and considering who worked on the first one, I'd say it's a safe bet that organized crime doesn't have anything to do with it."

"Who worked it?" Even as he asked the question, he already knew. Even so, he turned to the agents' notes at the back of the file.

"You and Agent Stafford," Max answered.

"Thirteen years ago." Aiden glanced up at the SAC and then back down to the chicken scratches he recognized as Bree's handwriting. "Stafford was the case agent. Shit, we never even figured out who the victim *was*. Based on the fact that her name's still listed as Jane Doe, it doesn't look like much has changed."

"It hasn't," Max admitted. "But it might now. I just got word from the ME's office that your John Doe there has the same precise marks on his bones as Jane Doe. Some of them are even in the same spots. And, just like Jane Doe, someone cut open his damn head."

Aiden nodded, remembering the marks vividly.

"I'm bringing it to you first because I figured you'd want to take it," Max went on. "Stafford's already on board, and I'm going to assign a couple more of my people to it too. Because whoever the hell is doing this has a lot of experience doing it, and I sincerely doubt that these are the only two bodies like this out there. Sheriff already handed it over to us. They don't have the resources to identify bodies in this state of decomp."

The golden light from Aiden's desk lamp glinted off the silver band of Max's watch as he raised his arm to check the time. "Fifteen minutes, Parrish. Downstairs, in the briefing room. Provided you want in on this, that is."

With a self-deprecating chortle, Aiden stacked the folders to hand them back to Max. "You know the answer to that, Osbourne. I'll see you down there."

"Oh, real quick," Max started, glancing back to Aiden as he pulled open the glass and metal door. "Agent Black is back for good starting today. Stafford ran out to get a cake, even though I told her not to. Hope you like German chocolate, because apparently, that's Agent Black's favorite."

He ignored the cold creep of adrenaline as he nodded. "German chocolate is good."

"Great. See you in a few."

In the minutes he had to spare before the trip down to VC, he drank a cup of breakroom coffee as fast as he dared. The brew tasted just as foul as he remembered, and he mentally vowed never to make the same mistake again. After fishing a piece of gum from a desk drawer, he made his way to the VC briefing room.

Like they were guided by a laser, Winter's eyes snapped over to him as soon as he stepped through the doorway. He offered her a practiced smile and nod before he took a seat beside Bree.

When Noah Dalton walked into the room, Aiden didn't miss the taller man's eyes go wide as he spotted Winter.

Apparently, Winter's return was a surprise to everyone. Everyone other than Max, at least.

Brian Camp and Miguel Vasquez filtered in not long after Noah, but as soon as Aiden caught a glimpse of the next attendee, he purposefully averted his gaze. There was a light clatter as Sun Ming eased the door closed behind herself, but he didn't look back to make note of her arrival.

Dropping a little paper plate into the trash can at the front of the room, Max dusted off his hands and glanced around.

"Looks like that's everyone," he said. "This case is going to be anything but, so I'll try to keep this briefing short. Yesterday morning, a construction crew building new houses at the edge of the city was digging up a lot to start laying foundation." Max paused to press a button on the remote in his hand.

From where it was projected onto the whiteboard at the man's back, the dark earth and the navy-blue drum seemed washed out and faded.

"A fifty-five-gallon barrel buried underground," Miguel remarked. "Never a precursor to anything good."

"It sure isn't, Agent Vasquez," Max replied. "In all my years with the bureau, I've never gotten a call from the local PD to tell me about a barrel they dug up and cracked open that was full of candy. I'm still holding out hope, but it's looking less and less likely as the years go by."

Vasquez's tanned skin darkened even more. "No doubt, sir," he said with a little salute thrown in.

"Anyway, I'm sure no one's surprised that there was a decomposed body in that drum. The Haz-Mat people geared up and went in to check it out after one of the guys at the construction site mentioned a nasty smell. And it's a good thing they did because John Doe's body had been doused in lye."

No one said a word, but Aiden felt more than saw the grimaces.

"To say it was a mess is a serious understatement. I don't know how they did it, but they got what was left in that barrel to the ME's office. They're still processing the scene, trying to find something that whoever put John Doe there might've left behind, but so far it doesn't look promising."

"Shit," Vasquez muttered.

"You're not all working on this." Max pressed the remote, and a picture of a different barrel in a different mound of dirt lit up the whiteboard. "But I wanted you all in here so you know what we're dealing with. Because John Doe isn't the first body we've found like this."

"It's not uncommon for the mob to get rid of bodies like this." To her credit, Sun always managed to keep the tinge of condescension out of her voice when she spoke to someone she liked or respected.

"It's not the mob." Bree's tone left no room for debate, and Aiden fought against a smirk.

"How can you be sure?" Sun pressed. Aiden had expected a respectful tone when she addressed Max, but he was surprised by the lack of condescension in her question to Bree.

"Because the mob leaves calling cards." It might have been his imagination, but he swore he saw a self-assured smirk flit across Bree's face as she answered. "The mob, the cartels, the Russians, they all leave calling cards. When someone comes across a body, they want them to know who put it there."

"How do we know there isn't one here?"

"Because I worked the Jane Doe case." Bree finally paused to glance back to Sun.

"You did," Max proclaimed. "You and Parrish both did. Which is why you're working it now too. And you two." He waved a hand toward Noah and Winter. "Agent Black, Agent Dalton. You're going to help them. They'll be expecting you out at the dump site soon. Don't worry, you've got plenty of time to get some of the cake that Agent Stafford brought in."

The man shifted his gaze over to Sun, his countenance flat. Max expected Sun to put up a fight to be assigned to the John and Jane Doe case, but Aiden knew better. Sun wanted to improve her record, and a decomposed body in a vat of lye with little to no physical evidence was not an effective method to get another case closure under her belt.

"That's all I've got for now. Make sure you pay attention to what's going on with this one because there's a good possibility you'll be helping in some way or another. Otherwise, you're dismissed."

As the others rose to stand, Bree turned her head to offer Aiden a smile. "You want some cake?"

"Sure," he replied. "I might as well have something in my stomach to throw up when we go to check out John Doe at the ME's office."

Bree wrinkled her nose. "Dry heaving is the worst."

❋

THE STRING of four-letter words Bree spat out as the stench of decay greeted them was almost enough to make Aiden do a double-take. Instead, he threw in a few colorful phrases of his own and tightened the flimsy paper mask over his nose. The basement of the medical examiner's office wasn't usually a place for welcoming aromas, but the odor of human flesh rotting away beneath a layer of lye was overbearing even for a veritable morgue.

"Damn, agents," the medical examiner started. His voice was muffled from beneath his own mask, but the corners of his dark eyes creased in amusement. "I was in the Navy for six years, and I think you'd make a lot of those guys blush. Don't get me wrong, that's a compliment. Impressive wording."

"Thanks, Dr. Nguyen," Bree muttered.

"Aiden, it's been a while. Congrats on the promotion. I had a feeling it wouldn't take you long to get there."

"Thanks, Dan," he managed through the abundance of saliva in his mouth. "Congratulations on yours too."

"I fully expect that Agent Stafford over here will just leapfrog over both of us one of these days. We'll wake up, and suddenly she'll be the director of the whole damn FBI." Chuckling, Dan beckoned them toward a stainless-steel table with one gloved hand.

"I don't know about that, but I appreciate the vote of confidence," Bree replied, swallowing hard as the stench increased by degrees.

"Fuck me." Aiden couldn't help the exclamation as he spotted the remains of their John Doe.

The body, or what was left of it, had been laid out atop the metal surface much as an intact corpse might have been. However, the shape of the skeleton was where any resemblance to a human being ended. Rather than sallow, decayed skin, John Doe's soft tissue—again, what was left of it—resembled gelatin.

"Shit," Bree murmured, pressing the paper mask closer to her nostrils. "How long do you think he was in that barrel, Doc?"

"It's hard to say exactly." Dan shrugged. "It'd depend on the temperature of the environment around the drum, the amount and quality of the water they poured in with the lye. But if I had to make an educated guess based on what I've seen so far, I'd say he's been in the ground for somewhere in the neighborhood of six months to a year. Lye will definitely eat through skin, but unless it's got water and heat to speed it up, it takes a little while. You guys ever heard of alkaline hydrolysis?"

Aiden and Bree both shook their heads.

"Well, it looks to me like that's what the person who dumped him in here was going for. A less sophisticated version of it. Basically, alkaline hydrolysis is the process of cremating a body using water, lye, and a fair amount of heat. For it to work most effectively, the solution has to get to about three-hundred-degrees. The vats they use for that look like giant pressure cookers. You've got to have permits, registrations, all kinds of shit to get one. And if our killer had one, I doubt we'd be here talking about John Doe right now."

"What types of injuries have you found so far?" Aiden asked, careful to keep his gaze on Dan Nguyen and away from the putrid sight of John Doe's corpse.

"Yeah, honestly." The trace of mirth vanished from Dan's face. "That's what I think is the most troubling about this whole thing. I've been doing and assisting with autopsies now for almost twenty years, and believe me, I've seen my fair share of people dissolved in lye in a fifty-five-gallon drum. But this guy's wounds, the marks on his bones, these aren't injuries I forget. I know why you guys are here instead of someone else, and honestly, that's the reason I'm down here instead of someone else."

Aiden looked grim. "These types of cases are hard to forget."

"Whoever our John Doe was, he went through some serious surgery. *Brain* surgery. It was harder to tell on the

Jane Doe case I worked with you guys a while back, but I think the same thing happened to her."

"And that is?" Aiden pressed.

Heaving a sigh, Dan glanced down to the silver table and shook his head. "Someone autopsied this guy after they killed him. I'll know more once I can get a better look at the bones, but the marks I've seen so far, they were made from something capable of precision. Not something your average Joe keeps sitting around in their garage at home. And, here's the really weird part."

"The rest of that *wasn't* weird?" This time, the remark came from Bree.

Aiden expected at least a quiet chuckle or a smile from Dan, but instead, there was just more wariness.

"Agents," he said, "John Doe's brain is missing."

17

"You don't *see* anything?" Noah asked as he turned his quizzical glance to Winter.

Her blue eyes flicked over to his, and she shook her head. She knew what he meant by the emphasis. "No. I've *seen* nothing. I even walked around the perimeter over by where they're starting to build the house next to this one. Nothing."

"Shit," he spat. "All right. Well, we already talked to the guys who found that barrel. Looks like this trip was a bust."

"Looks like it," Winter sighed. "You ready to head back?"

Noah nodded his response. They handed business cards out to the three men who had made the initial discovery, bade them farewell, and started back toward the gravel parking lot.

For the duration of the trek, neither he nor Winter spoke.

He'd made his best effort to respect her boundaries, but the past few months had been, for lack of a better term, a fucking roller-coaster.

First, there had been the awkward kiss in the kitchen of her apartment, a kiss that he did not initiate. Sure, he had hoped that she would respond to his professed feelings with some enthusiasm, but he hadn't wanted *that*.

Then, for three months, she might as well have moved to the moon.

Complete and total radio silence for three damn months. Once she returned, they'd had a heated dialogue that ended with Winter tearing up and wrapping him in a bear hug.

And two days after their stop in the elevator, she had vanished again. This time, at least, she'd responded to his attempts to reach out to her.

Every time he and Winter's friendship took a step forward, it was followed abruptly by two steps back. Noah tried to be understanding, tried to give her time and patience, but it had become exhausting.

As he took his place in the driver's side of the nondescript sedan, he stopped short of turning the key over in the ignition. Maybe he needed to be just a *little* more persistent, he thought. Persistent enough to show he cared, but not so persistent that he was overbearing.

"Hey," he started as he glanced over to her. "You want to grab a drink tonight after work? Catch up?"

"I can't tonight, I'm sorry." There was no deception on her face, nor was there uncertainty in her voice.

"Got a hot date?" He asked the question before he stopped to think it through. He really needed to work on that.

With a trademark half-snort, half-laugh, she shrugged.

In the seconds before she elaborated, he thought he felt his heart stop. Every muscle in his body tensed as if in preparation for a physical confrontation. Pulse hammering in his ears, he tightened his grip on the steering wheel until the tips of his fingers tingled.

"I don't want to say no because I think it'd almost be insulting to Autumn," Winter finally answered.

All at once, the strain vanished, and the first waves of relief rolled over his tired muscles. Even though he had been sure that Winter and Autumn would get along, there had still been a pang of worry when the two women were introduced. Worry that Winter would feel like he was forcing a friendship on her when she just wanted to be left alone. Just because he'd learned how helpful the support of a friend could be didn't mean that Winter would be inclined to the same feel-good sentiments.

But to his surprise, the women's steadfast friendship defied any of his lingering doubts. Apparently, they had become such good friends that they planned outings about which he did not even know. The sting of disappointment was accompanied by a hint of jealousy, and he almost scoffed aloud at himself. Winter and Autumn didn't have to involve him in everything they did just because he had introduced them.

To think he held a monopoly over their friendship was chauvinistic at best and outright mean at worst. No, the twinge of envy wasn't due to some need for control or a possessive streak. He simply missed his friends.

As he pulled himself out of the reverie, he glanced over to her. The glint of petulance in her eyes was unmistakable, and the first chill of adrenaline rushed up to greet him.

"I'm sure you agree that Autumn's a hot date, right?" She spat the question as much as spoke it.

Even as he nodded, he narrowed his eyes. "This seems like a trap, but alright. I'll spring it. Yeah, Autumn's a good-looking lady. So are you. So is Bree, and so is Shelby. What're you getting at here, darlin'?"

Winter paused as her expression turned thoughtful. The venom was still there, he noted, but unlike him, she carefully contemplated her next words.

"You've got a point." She blew out a long breath. "That's the wrong way to go about this, isn't it? She's just doing what we all do, trying to look and feel good about herself. It's not her fault that she gets creeped on by guys while she's working. Bree used to be a bartender too. I guess there are a lot of guys who don't really give a shit when a woman says she's not into them."

"You're still being pretty vague here. Are you pissed that Autumn has to deal with creeps at work? I mean, on some level, we should all be pissed about that, shouldn't we? What was it Autumn said? Something like 'creeps are just representative of our society's tolerance for their creepy bullshit.' Something like that. I think she had a better technical term than 'creepy bullshit,' though."

"Damn it, Noah!" Winter exclaimed. "You're the creep here! You! You're the one who creeped on her!"

"Oh." As he scratched his unshaven cheek, he hoped the shadow of stubble would be enough to hide the flush. *Maybe I should grow a beard*, he thought.

"Oh?" Winter echoed. Enough venom dripped from that single syllable to kill ten full-grown men.

"Did she tell you that?" The weak question was all he could manage.

"For the love of...does it matter?" she snapped. "But no, she didn't rat you out. No one ratted you out! I asked Bree if there was something going on between you and Autumn, and she told me about how Autumn shut you down when you tried to creep on her."

Fuck.

He didn't think he had uttered the word aloud, but when Winter glowered at him, he realized he had.

"And just in case it's crossed your mind, don't try to blame any of this on Bree or Autumn. If you didn't want anyone to know about you being a sleazy jackass, you shouldn't have *been* a sleazy jackass. Is that your thing now, Dalton? Just picking up women when you go to the bar? Or, I guess in this case, *trying* to pick up women."

"That's not," he started. But the words sounded so stupid, he hesitated before he went on. "That's not what that was. It's not what it sounds like."

"For shit's sake," she spat, rolling her eyes. "Is that it? That's all you've got to explain this? You come to me and tell me that you have these feelings for me, and then, what? I don't know what in the hell you thought that was, or how in the hell you thought I took it, but I took what you said to me pretty damn seriously!"

If he'd had enough oxygen in his lungs, he would have snorted.

"Believe it or not, I really, *really* thought about it," she railed on. "I thought about it because I thought you meant it, but then a few weeks later, and I guess it slipped your mind. Or was that just how long it took for you to lose interest? Is that just the norm for you? It's fine if you're out picking up women and getting laid, but if I do it, you'd lose your fucking mind, wouldn't you?"

He managed to open his mouth. "I—"

"You'd take it as some kind of personal slight." She poked him in the arm with an index finger that felt like a knife. "Well? Tell me I'm wrong, Dalton! Tell me that isn't what your pissing match with Aiden is all about!"

He was damn sure going to get a word in now. "No," he practically shouted. "It's...no, the guy's just an asshole. He's not an asshole to you because you've got history with him, but he *is* an asshole. No, Winter, that's not what any of this is about. I didn't even, I had no idea you...took it seriously." He paused to grit his teeth to will away the stammering. "The next day, you were just gone, and no. I didn't think you took it seriously or honestly gave a hot damn."

She crossed her arms over her chest and managed a snort that was loud and long.

"It's always been easy for me to talk to people," he went on before the snort could turn into words. "I like talking to people, getting to know them, all that shit. But just because I can do that doesn't mean I've got a menagerie of best friends in my back pocket that I can turn to when life gets hard. I'm a thousand miles from home, Winter. I've *been* a thousand miles from home for years, and with you just disappearing like that, it felt, I don't know. Lonely doesn't really cover it, but I guess that's it."

"Noah, I—"

"And yeah, maybe it sounds pathetic to you, but that's why I tried to get Autumn to go home with me. But she didn't, and it's a good thing because she's been a damn good friend. And it turns out *that's* what I needed. I needed a damn friend, and I lucked out and got one even though I acted like a dumbass."

As Winter leaned back in her seat and turned her gaze to the windshield, he watched the bluster drain from her face. In the wake of the anger, the shadows beneath her eyes seemed more pronounced.

The silence that descended on them felt like a noxious haze, and once he was sure she didn't intend to break it, he turned the key over in the ignition.

He was done with this day.

The digital clock read 12:17, but unless they returned to a major development in the John Doe case, he was finished. Maybe he would go make good on Winter's less than flattering observation about his penchant for picking up chicks.

Never mind that he could count on both hands the number of times he had even made an attempt at a casual hookup, or a one-night stand, or whatever in the hell people called it.

But if that was the impression he gave to one of the most important people in his life, he figured he might as well live up to it.

18

Winter was still reeling from the unexpected, emotional conversation with Noah a few hours earlier. Their drive back to the FBI office had been made in complete and utter silence, and Winter was sure that in all her twenty-six years of life, those twenty minutes were among the most strained she had ever experienced.

After Noah had explained the driving force behind his decision to try to go home with Autumn, the unmistakable burn of shame had overtaken the ire that had motivated her to bring up the topic in the first place.

When Winter showed up at Autumn's door later that afternoon, she was greeted with a warm embrace. Her eyes widened at the unexpected gesture. Over the past few weeks, she and Autumn had at least one conversation about how neither of them was keen on hugs.

In fact, as best as Winter could tell, Autumn was not a fan of most physical contact. Half the time, she was even leery of a handshake.

"What was that for?" Winter asked as she handed Autumn

her contribution to their meal that night: popcorn kernels and a jug of Hawaiian Punch.

Autumn flashed her a quick smile before she turned to make her way across the open floor plan to the kitchen. "I'm basically a shrink, remember? I've gotten pretty good at reading people. You seemed like you could use a hug."

With a sigh, Winter nodded and brushed the ebony hair from her eyes. "Yeah, it's been a day, all right."

"Disagreement with someone?" Autumn asked. Her expression was curious but understanding.

"Something like that," Winter muttered.

"Well, you know I'm here if you want to talk about it, but you also know that you don't have to talk about it if you don't want to." As she stepped out from behind the breakfast bar, Autumn offered her a reassuring smile and held out a glass of bright red punch.

Winter's smile was weak as she nodded her understanding. She thought to ask Autumn for her perspective on Noah's self-proclaimed jackass behavior, but she realized suddenly that the mention would only make the woman feel guilty. And even though Winter may not have known the full breadth of Autumn's history, she could tell there was enough on her plate.

"We're starting season three today, right?" Winter asked as they dropped down to sit at their usual spots on the long sectional.

The clatter of nails on the hardwood was followed in short order by a quiet huff and the jingle of Toad's collar. The little ball of fluff always had to greet Winter before he returned to his human mother's side.

"Hi, Toad," Winter cooed, scratching behind one pointed ear.

"Yeah, season three," Autumn confirmed. "The final one is season eight, so we've got a ways to go."

"We going to try to guess how many people die again?" As Toad scuttled across the couch, Winter reached for her drink. Three weeks earlier, Autumn had proposed that they watch the entire *Game of Thrones* series together. Winter had heard Bree mention her and Shelby's obsession with the show, and aside from providing her with another topic to discuss with Bree, binging six hours of television at a time was a good way for her and Autumn to unwind.

Laughing, Autumn shook her head. "I don't even want to try."

Just as the screen flickered to life, a loud knock at the front door snapped both their attention over to the short hallway. Though Toad's ears perked up, the pup did not make a sound at the disturbance. Unless Autumn purposefully incited it, Toad rarely barked. Between his size and his pointy ears, Winter thought Toad behaved more like a cat than a dog.

"Were you expecting someone?" she asked.

Autumn's gaze flicked back to Winter as she shook her head. "Probably someone trying to sell me something or convert me. Just a sec, I'll take care of it."

After a couple metallic clicks, Winter heard the door creak open. Scooting to the center cushion, she leaned over until she could see around the edge of the hallway. As she caught sight of the visitor, the icy clutch of adrenaline edged its way in beside her rapidly beating heart. When Noah's green eyes settled on hers, all she could manage was a half-assed wave.

Why in the hell was he here? Was this some ploy of Autumn's to get Winter and Noah back on good terms with one another? No, that didn't make any sense. Autumn didn't even know about the heated conversation outside the dig site. Unless, of course, Noah told her about it.

Even if he had, Autumn wouldn't have staged a surprise

visit for them to hash out their differences. She would have encouraged them to be honest with themselves and to communicate their feelings, as she often did, but she wouldn't have tried to trick anyone into divulging information they didn't wish to share.

"Hey," Autumn greeted. Her voice snapped Winter away from her fixation on Noah, though the man's gaze had already returned to Autumn.

"Hey," he replied, his voice hushed. "Uh, is this a bad time?"

"What?" Autumn looked confused, wrinkling her nose as she waved the taller man into the hall. "Why would you say…" She trailed off as she and Noah stepped into the living room. "Oh."

"It's all right, I can go." Noah held up his hands and took a step backward.

"Tell you what," Autumn started, gesturing from Winter to Noah. "Clearly something's going on right here, and something tells me it doesn't involve me. Not directly, at least. Right?"

"Um." Now it was Noah's turn to look confused. "No, I guess not. Are you trying to read our minds or something?"

Autumn's cheeks grew pink. "No, but I'm observant. Not that it takes an observant person to see that the tension in here is so thick I could spread it on a piece of toast. You know what, Toad probably wants to go for a walk. You two stay here, figure out whatever the hell is going on. As much as I like toast, I'm not a big fan of the air in here right now."

Brushing off the front of her loose-fitting t-shirt, Autumn stepped into a pair of moccasins and retrieved a retractable leash. With an excited snort, Toad leapt off the couch and ran over to her.

Once the door latched closed, the room lapsed into silence.

Noah made no move to advance from where he stood beside a small end table, and Winter kept her gaze fixed on her hands.

"I didn't know you'd be here. I thought you meant you two were going out..." His voice was strained and quiet, and she felt a stab of guilt at the dejected tone.

"I'm sorry." Winter finally managed, the volume of the words scarcely above a whisper.

"Yeah." As she glanced up at him, shadows shifted along his face as he clenched and unclenched his jaw.

"I'm sorry, Noah. I rushed to judgment, and I shouldn't have done that."

"It's all right," he replied with a slight shrug. The words sounded perfunctory.

"No, it's not," Winter said, shaking her head. "It's just like, for all those years, ever since I was thirteen, my life's had this singular purpose. All I'd been determined to do was either put Kilroy in a prison cell or put a bullet between his eyes. But then after that was done, it felt like I had all this unresolved shit to deal with, shit I'd just been pushing to the side, and I didn't even know where to start."

Compassion etched itself across Noah's handsome features.

"Grampa wasn't doing well..." Damn, the burn of emotion had her blinking hard. "And we didn't know what was going on with him. At the time, it really felt like I might lose him, and that, that just broke something in my head, I think. I didn't want to burden you with it, but more than that, I think I was ashamed of myself for it. For not knowing how to deal with it. I mean, that was the point I'd wanted to get to for my entire life, but once I was there, then what?"

With a tired sigh, he nodded his understanding as he moved to sit beside her on the arm of the couch. His expression was still strained, but the suspicion had vanished. "I get it. Look, I know I'll never understand how it felt to lose your family like that, but that feeling you just described. Not knowing how you fit into anything anywhere after you're finished with your task, I know how that feels."

"You do?" Before he could respond, she held up a hand and shook her head. "I'm sorry. I didn't mean to sound like I doubted you. It's just hard to picture you *not* fitting in, you know?"

His gaze fell to the cat, who'd chosen that moment to go batshit crazy and shoot across the room. "I guess. But yeah, I do. It wasn't as bad for me as it was for some of the other guys I was overseas with. That's one of the big problems a lot of combat vets have when they get back to the States. They're used to being on high alert all the time. Their brains are tuned into that frequency, and some people have a harder time tuning out of it than others."

She looked at him. Really looked at him. This was the first time he'd really talked about his experience in the military.

"We came back from a warzone, from a place where we had to kill to survive, and everyone just expected us to fit right back in like we'd never left. Believe it or not, the skills you learn as an infantryman aren't compatible with a lot of civilian jobs. Not with jobs that aren't some entry level nonsense, anyway."

He turned to face her, then reached for her hand. When he was only inches from touching her, he pulled away, rubbing his palms on his pants.

"You just got back from a combat zone, darlin', and you don't need to be ashamed of not knowing what to do next. It's normal, and you're not alone. I'm sorry I acted like a jackass. I knew you were going through some shit, and I just threw myself a pity party like some kind of butthurt teenager."

Winter felt the corner of her mouth turn up in a smile.

"Apology accepted. And I'm sorry I just took off without telling you anything about, well, about anything. That was a jerk move, and I don't think you were the only one who threw yourself a pity party like a butthurt teenager."

"I guess not." He chuckled. As his eyes met hers, his wistful smile was more noticeable. "It's all right to not be all right. I'm your friend, and I'll never think any less of you because you're not all right."

She felt the telltale pinpricks in the corners of her eyes as she leaned over to wrap her arms around his shoulders.

"Thank you," she murmured as she tightened her grasp.

"You know," he said, breaking a spell of quiet. "If you keep doing this, keep hugging me, you're going to have to change your mantra about not being a hugger."

She chuckled softly as she glanced up at him. "Only for you, Noah."

Had it not been for the metallic click of the door latch, Winter wasn't sure what might have happened next. Part of her was glad for the interruption, and part of her was disappointed.

The creak of the front door was followed by the clatter of paws on the hardwood as Toad rushed over to greet them.

"Toad is happy to see you," Autumn said.

Noah crouched down and straightened the pineapple print bandana around Toad's neck before he scratched behind one fluffy ear.

"You know," Autumn said, her green eyes flicking from Winter to Noah and then back. "It's the first time you've both been over to hang out with me at the same time. Maybe that's not exciting to you guys, but for me, it's kind of a big deal. This is the most people that've been in my apartment at one time since I moved here two years ago. And if there was one more person here, that'd be an all-time high for me since I moved to Virginia."

"Come to think of it," Winter chuckled, "I think three other people in my apartment would be an all-time high for me too."

"Same here," Noah put in.

Autumn arched an eyebrow. "Really?"

"Why does everyone think that I've got like a hundred friends?" He threw his arms up and sighed in feigned exasperation.

Flashing him a smug look, Winter crossed her arms over her chest. "See, I'm not the only one."

"I've only got ninety," he huffed. "Get it straight, ladies. Autumn, where's your cat?"

With a sarcastic grin, she raised the popcorn kernels to gesture to the short hallway to the side of the front door. "Pretty sure she's on my bed."

The open invitation to wander unaccompanied into their host's bedroom might have struck Winter as odd if their host was anyone other than Autumn Trent. The woman's level of tidiness surpassed even Aiden's, and it rivaled Bree's.

For the first visit, Winter had felt like the place was so orderly that she should refrain from touching anything. When she returned home that day, she had cleaned her apartment from top to bottom.

"Are you a cat person, Noah?" Winter asked.

"I feel like there's a lot of stereotyping going on here right now," he replied as he made his way to the hall. "And I don't appreciate it. Yes, Winter, I like cats. My Grandma Eileen has been fostering kittens since I was in grade school. Little dogs like Toad are cool, too, but big dogs, not so much. There were some dogs that hung around Grandma and Grandpa's ranch, and those things were *mean*."

Winter laughed. "Hard to believe you're afraid of anything."

He rolled his eyes. "Might be a little unconventional, but

that's when I learned to shoot a gun. Once we got rid of the mean-ass dogs, we started seeing feral cats around more often. Feral cats are a whole different story. They just run away from you and hiss if you get too close. Plus, they'd keep all the critters under control, mice and ground squirrels and shit. In a roundabout kind of way, the cats were great for Grandma and Grandpa's garden. Grandma and I used to catch some of the cats and take them in to get them fixed and vaccinated."

"A whole family of cat people," Winter remarked with a grin.

He returned the pleasant expression and nodded. "A whole family of cat people."

At the look, at that perfect, disarming smile, she felt the start of an unfamiliar flutter in her stomach. But no matter her lack of experience with the sensation, she knew what it meant. Something between them had shifted, and the change was irreversible.

Whether the shift was good or bad, she wasn't sure.

❄

THE MAIN REASON Ladwig turned on the news during dinner that night was to learn more about the thunderstorms that were slated for later in the week. Richmond wasn't usually tornado territory, but Sue and Kiera had discussed tornadoes for the better part of the morning. He had been skeptical at first, but the weather app on his phone had supported the weather women's observations.

White and blue light from the flickering screen glinted off the end of his metal chopsticks as he stuffed another pot sticker in his mouth.

Ladwig liked to cook, but as the years dragged on, he found the motivation to make a meal for no one but himself had all but vanished. So much time had passed, he assumed he would have to season his cast iron cookware all over again before he used any of it to prepare a meal.

"In what is still a developing story, authorities yesterday unearthed the remains of a man whose body had been sealed in a fifty-five-gallon drum." The young man on the screen looked like he was merely reciting a recipe for marinara sauce. "Police have said that lye was used to speed up the decomposition process. We go now to our field reporter, Jenny Harris. Jenny?"

The screen flipped over to a dark-eyed woman who held a microphone in one hand as she nodded.

"Thanks, Clark. I'm just outside the city limits where workers are preparing to start the construction of some new homes. Yesterday, while they were digging out the basement for one of these houses, Brad Rathbun and Pete Timson came across a metal drum. According to the two men, the lid was still sealed, though the equipment used in the dig had dented the side of the barrel.

"Now, the county sheriff's office has handed the investigation over to the Federal Bureau of Investigation. At this point, the victim's identity remains unknown, but I did have a chance to talk to one of the deputies earlier today. According to the medical examiner, there are marks on the skull of the deceased that indicate they went through a series of surgeries not long before their death."

Though the woman still spoke, all her words turned to dust before they had a chance to drift into Ladwig's ears.

Lye. A sealed drum. Surgical marks on the skull.

And now the FBI was involved?

If the Feds had taken over the investigation, that meant they likely had another body. Surgical tools left distinctive marks on bone. They left *precise* marks.

Ladwig didn't know the full extent of the weight behind

Sandra Evans' work, but he knew enough to understand that the men and women who called the shots held positions of considerable power. Maybe they could have dealt with a county or a city investigation, but he doubted any of them could contend with the resources of the Federal Bureau of Investigation.

His mouth had gone dry, and he knew the arid sensation wasn't the result of the salty takeout he had picked up for dinner. With a desperate drink from his glass of water, he tried to sort through the litany of thoughts that flew through his mind.

Now that he was thinking more clearly, he knew he couldn't just leave.

He'd dealt with Sandra Evans for seven years, but he'd opened his practice more than a decade ago. That practice, coupled with the years he'd spent as a physician and a psychiatrist in the military, had paid off not only his extensive student loans but the cost of the building out of which he worked.

That practice paid for him to live comfortably. That practice was his whole damn life, it was all he had left, and even though he'd been ready to flee a couple days ago...

Not now. He wanted to stay.

Sandra and her people had to have safeguards in place for an eventuality such as this. They'd be stupid not to, and if there was one thing Sandra Evans was not, it was stupid. He would let her and whoever in the hell employed her deal with the unidentified body in the barrel. This wasn't Ladwig's fight.

It had never *been* his fight.

As the television cut to an earlier interview of a sheriff's deputy, Ladwig swore he felt his heart stop.

Before the scene could switch away, he snatched the television remote from the coffee table and pressed pause. Even though they were not in focus, the man and woman standing at the edge of the dig site were clearly visible thanks to the high resolution of Ladwig's new television.

The afternoon sunlight glinted off the woman's sunglasses as she pushed them to rest atop her head, and the man's aviators had been clipped to the breast pocket of his black jacket. The sight of Winter wasn't a surprise, but the man was a different story.

The man at Winter's side was Brady fucking Lomond.

19

Max Osbourne was in a meeting about a different matter, and he had tasked Aiden with updating their little group about the John and Jane Doe cases. Behind the same podium from which he had announced Douglas Kilroy's identity, from which he had effectively solved the case that had stumped them all for decades, he prepared to advise that same group of people of the scant evidence they had uncovered for their newest case.

All three agents—Bree, Noah, and Winter—were seated, but a flicker of movement at the doorway drew their attention as Dan Nguyen strode into the room. He wore his usual agreeable expression, and the casual smile was a far cry from the gravity of their most recent encounter.

"I think you all know Dr. Nguyen already," Aiden started as the newcomer moved to stand at his side. Though Dan was an inch or two shorter than Aiden, he always forgot how tall the man was. During a typical interaction, Dan was either seated beside a body, behind a desk, or hunched over an exam table.

"Agents." Dan offered Winter and Noah a quick smile. "Nice to see you again, even though I wish it was under better circumstances. I was in the area, so I figured I'd come by and make sense of what I've included in my report so far."

Aiden nodded and stepped aside. "You're the one with the medical degree. Go ahead."

"Warm welcome as always, Mr. Parrish." Dan chuckled, but his expression remained grim. "To start with, I'm sorry to say that we still don't have any idea who John Doe is. All his teeth were pulled, and none of his skin was intact enough to pull any kind of print. We'll be lucky if we can get DNA from any of the tissue that was left. Lye degrades DNA, and John Doe was doused with a hell of a lot of lye. We'll test bone, of course, but even so, DNA only helps us if he's in the database. And, I'll be honest, the odds aren't in our favor there."

"Any update on the cause of death?" Aiden asked.

"None. With the tissue as decayed as it is, we aren't likely to get much from a tox screen, but we're going to try to run one anyway. I've got a theory, but at this point, that's all it is."

"That's about all we can ask for right now," Aiden put in. "Let's hear it."

"There were some interesting marks on John Doe's bones. Specifically, the bones here." He paused to draw the shape of a Y over his black suit jacket. With his vintage hairstyle and pricey watch, Dan almost looked like he was in the employ of a marketing firm, not the medical examiner's office.

"Like an autopsy." Bree's words were not a question.

"Exactly like an autopsy. And the tools that were used to make those marks weren't just some set of knives in a psychopath's garage. Those marks were made by precise surgical tools. They're the same marks left behind after an autopsy. An autopsy performed by a *professional*, by someone with a medical degree and years of experience. And that's not even the weirdest or worst part of it."

"It's not?" Noah furrowed his brows.

"Nope." Bree sighed and leaned back in her chair.

"No, it's not. John Doe's head was split open like a coconut, and his brain was gone." Dan's dark eyes shifted from agent to agent as the shocking realization registered on their faces. "That's *still* not it, though. There was a lot going on with John Doe's head, as it turns out. He'd recently undergone a surgery that involved cutting open the back of his skull."

"You're saying someone performed *brain surgery* on him before he was killed?" Winter surmised. Her laser focus didn't drift from Dr. Nguyen.

Even under the intense stare, Dan didn't so much as miss a beat. "I can't say with complete accuracy when it happened, but yes, more or less. The surgery is recent, within the last few months before he died, at least. Now, that was on the *back* of his skull, the parietal bone, but at the front, right in above the temporal bone on his left side, there was an old, healed injury. There were some marks to indicate that he'd undergone surgery for that injury too."

"As a child?" Winter asked, the hair raising on her arms.

Nguyen nodded. "My theory is that whoever killed him and took his brain would have wanted it intact. Rather than a bullet or another type of physical injury, I think they euthanized him in the same way a veterinarian would euthanize a sick animal. John Doe was anywhere from thirty to fifty years old, probably Caucasian."

"Sick bastards," Noah muttered.

"Jane Doe, the case from thirteen years ago, she's got the same autopsy marks as John Doe. A forensic anthropologist estimated at the time that she was between twenty and thirty. Also consistent with John Doe, Jane's head was split open. The body was too decomposed to tell, but I'd be willing to bet that her brain had been taken too.

"They didn't make a lot from it at the time, but she had an old head wound as well. Hers was on the back of her head, near the occipital bone. I think it stands to reason that you've got two murders with a really distinct pattern, but I'm just here to relay the physical evidence. Making a behavioral sketch is SSA Parrish's job."

"Thanks for stopping in, Dr. Nguyen." Aiden reached out to clasp the man's hand in a parting shake.

With a grin, Dan nodded. "Always a pleasure working with you guys. I'll keep you in the loop as to what we find. The autopsy, if that's what you want to call it, has been a mess, but we're not leaving any stone unturned. Hopefully, I'll have more for you guys soon."

Dan waved to them as he pulled the glass and metal door closed behind himself.

"Well, shit," Noah muttered.

Aiden suppressed a sigh. "Yeah. 'Well, shit,' about sums it up."

"What do you have so far?" Winter asked.

"Not much." Aiden stepped behind the wooden podium and flipped open the manila folder. "As we just learned, both victims had similar surgical procedures conducted on their heads. The wounds had started to heal in both cases, so those surgeries were conducted while they were still alive. An autopsy was performed on both victims, but it centered around their head.

"We don't have a lot here in terms of physical evidence, but these deaths were both really, really specific. The killer has a specific set of skills, and based on how recent John Doe's body is, they're still in the city somewhere. They've been using lye to dissolve their victims' bodies for at least thirteen years, and they added water to John Doe's to speed up the process.

"This is someone who knows what they're doing, both in terms of the procedures performed during and after the victims' lives. They know how to destroy identifying evidence, and they know how to keep a person alive after they cut open their head and poke around in their brain."

"You think we're looking for a surgeon?" Bree surmised.

"Yes," he answered. "Most likely a neurosurgeon. This isn't another Jeffrey Dahmer chopping people up in his bathtub. This is someone with a medical degree, at the very least. Probably someone with specific experience performing surgery on the brain. The surgical tools used to make these cuts and to saw open the skulls were medical grade, but that doesn't necessarily mean that our surgeon is practicing. They could have been fired for malpractice."

"Or happily cutting into patients at a hospital right now," Noah muttered.

Aiden nodded. "It is likely they are still practicing, still seen as a competent physician. Considering the previous head trauma experienced by both victims, there are a couple different ways the killer could have found them. They could've looked through medical records and decided they wanted these specific people, or these people could be previous patients of theirs. There's no doubt here that we're dealing with a serial killer, and I don't think there's any doubt that Jane and John Doe are just two of many."

Drumming her fingers atop the polished table, Bree glanced over to Noah and Winter and then back to him. "We pull missing persons reports from the past year with a focus on those submitted in the past seven months. Check through those people to see if any of them have any history of traumatic brain injuries. Meanwhile, we look through hospital personnel records to see what kinds of brain surgeons around here have been slapped with malpractice suits."

"Sounds like we're sleeping here tonight, then." Noah leaned back in his chair, his jawline grim. "I hope someone has their own coffee maker because, if we're all relying on the shit in the breakroom, we'll be dead before we can find out who John Doe is."

20

In the past forty-eight hours, Winter estimated that she had managed approximately three hours of sleep. As soon as her head hit the plush pillow of her bed—as opposed to the scratchy couch cushions in the breakroom—she was out. Despite the soft mattress and the warm blankets, her fretful slumber was marked by bizarre, vivid dreams.

Though the digital clock at her bedside indicated she had slept for almost a full seven hours, she felt like she had rested for only two out of the seven. Pushing herself to sit, Winter rubbed her eyes and yawned. She could feel a dull ache at the base of her head, but she wasn't all that surprised to wake up with the start of a headache after a night of such fitful rest.

Before she could scoot over to swing her legs off the edge of the bed, the room blurred as the pain sharpened to a stab. Months had passed since her last vision, but the sensation was so unlike any other that it was easy to differentiate.

As darkness ate away the edge of her vision, she reached one clumsy hand over to the tissue box on the nightstand. She had only just pressed the balled-up tissue to her nose when the world went black.

❄

THROUGH THE DUSTY glass of an old window, Winter watched a flurry of fat, white snowflakes whip by on a mournful gust of wind. The beige windowsill was specked with dirt, and chips of paint had begun to peel away from the cheap wood.

She snapped her gaze away from the snowy scene as she heard the faint whisper of music. The sound grew clearer as her senses tuned her into the little bedroom, and she soon recognized the song as a popular rock anthem during the late 1990s.

Atop an overturned milk crate was the clunky, old-school boombox that blasted the well-known tune, and beside the makeshift nightstand, a girl sat cross-legged on a twin-sized bed. The bright greens and blues of the comforter were faded, and the edges were frayed in spots.

As Winter stepped away from the window, the girl's attention didn't break away from where it was fixed on the book in her lap. Though she was no older than ten, she wasn't reading a children's book or even a comic book.

This ten-year-old kid was reading a full-length novel.

The clatter of a door snapped the little girl's gaze up to the shadowy hall at the other end of the room. Even in the muddy gray daylight, her green eyes shone like a pair of emeralds. As soon as Winter saw those eyes, she knew who the girl was.

"Autumn," a woman called, her voice muffled. There was an unmistakable slur to her voice. Whoever she was, she was three sheets to the wind.

Shoving the paperback closed, Autumn scrambled to the end of the mattress to press the power button on the radio with a shaking hand. She scooted back to the corner where the bed met the wall, grabbed a stuffed kitten from the pillow, and clutched the cat to her chest.

As Winter glanced back and forth between the doorway and the young girl, she could feel her heart rate pick up, each beat pushing the chill of adrenaline throughout her body. Autumn was terrified, and now *Winter* was terrified too.

She wanted to tell herself that she was standing in the middle of an event that had never transpired in the real world, that the fear she felt was a nightmare Autumn had experienced when she was young. But Winter couldn't so much as entertain the idea.

Whatever in the hell she was watching had happened. Whatever caused the sickly sense of fright to hang low and heavy in the air was real.

A flicker of movement drew Winter's gaze away from Autumn and over to the doorway, and she took in a sharp breath as the woman shambled into the room.

The resemblance between her and the Autumn that Winter knew was uncanny, but what surprised Winter the most was how young she looked. She was hardly halfway through her twenties.

"Autumn," the woman repeated, "why are you looking at me like that?" The query was as weary as it was accusatory.

The dull afternoon light glinted off the tears as they streaked down Autumn's pale cheeks. With a sniffle, she brushed the droplets away and shook her head.

"You're drunk." Autumn's words were little more than a whisper, and Winter could feel the pinpricks at the corners of her eyes.

There was more melancholy in the little girl's voice than there ever should have been in someone her age. At ten, Autumn had already seen more pain and suffering than most adults would witness in their entire lives.

"I'm not drunk." The slur with which she spoke was almost ironic.

Heaving a tired sigh, the woman brushed off the front of

her denim miniskirt as she dropped down to sit at the end of the bed. With one hand, she combed the pieces of bleached blonde hair away from her hazel eyes.

"Okay," she giggled, "maybe I'm a little tipsy."

In response to the lessened distance between them, Autumn's grasp on her orange stuffed kitten tightened.

"I'm not going to hurt you, sweetie." As she reached a hand toward her daughter, Autumn jammed herself farther into the corner.

"That's what you always say," Autumn whispered.

If Winter hadn't been in the midst of a memory, she would have pushed the woman off the bed, punched her in the jaw, or both.

"I know." Shadows along the woman's throat shifted as she swallowed.

"Why do you hate me, Mom?"

As the woman shook her head, Winter caught the glassiness in her green-flecked eyes. "I don't hate you. I'm just, I'm going through a hard time right now. But it's about to get better. I promise it's about to get better. We're going to get better. I'm going to stop using, I'm going to stop drinking. I just had to go out one last time before I got well, okay?"

Autumn's only response was another quiet sniffle.

"Honey, your dad is going to move back in with us."

"W-w-what?" Autumn stammered. "When? Why? He can't, we can't." Shaking her head vehemently, Autumn tucked her knees up to her chest. She looked like a cornered animal. If she was frightened of her mother, then she was outright terrified of her father.

"He's going to help me." The woman made another tentative move toward her daughter, but when Autumn bristled, she stopped in place. "We aren't going to drink anymore. We're going to go back to school, and we're going to get good jobs. Everything's going to be okay. I promise."

Winter half-expected the young Autumn to nod and accept her mother's reassurance, but the look of abject terror didn't even lessen.

"You never keep your promises, and neither does he."

There was a glint of ire behind the woman's hazel eyes, but before Winter could watch the rest of the interaction play out, the scene shimmered out of existence. When she blinked, she was suddenly outdoors. The stairs to the splintered porch were worn, and a handful of persistent weeds pierced through the cracks in the concrete.

She could tell right away that the girl who walked down the pockmarked sidewalk to the rundown house was the same girl she had just seen. And like the scene in Autumn's room, Winter knew she was in the midst of another memory.

Tightening her grip on the straps of her purple backpack, Autumn paused before she climbed up the first step. The afternoon sunlight gave her caramel-colored hair a golden tinge, and Winter was reminded that she was not a natural redhead.

Ever since she was a freshman in high school, Autumn had dyed her hair. She had even shown Winter a picture of the vivid purple and blue hues she used before she moved to Virginia to start her postgraduate work.

By the time Winter pulled herself from the short reverie, Autumn had opened the tarnished front door. In spite of the shouts she heard from inside the house, or perhaps because of them, Winter didn't hesitate to follow the girl.

A blond, muscular man with a handful of tattoos printed on each arm stood beside a plush couch, and in front of him was Autumn's mother.

Her hair was now a deep, chocolate brown, and the dark circles beneath her eyes were more pronounced. Maybe she had made good on her promise to quit drinking, but whatever her new substance of choice, Winter suspected its effects were far worse.

Try as she might, Winter couldn't focus on the words the two hollered back and forth at one another, but without warning, the man snapped one arm up to crack the back of his hand across the woman's face. Reflexively, Winter covered her mouth to stifle the sound of her sharp gasp.

Autumn's words were just as indistinguishable as her parents' as she set her books atop the coffee table to rush over to her mother.

"Go to your room, Autumn!" the man ordered, jabbing an index finger at a set of stairs beside the entrance to the kitchen.

"Leave Mom alone!" Autumn returned as she positioned herself between the two adults.

"Get the hell out of here!" His voice was just below an outright shout.

"Fuck you, Jeff!" the young girl shot back. "Why don't you just leave? I know that's what you want to do anyway, so why don't you just get it over with?"

"I'm your *father*, Autumn," he grated in response. "You'd best watch your damn mouth, you hear me?" His green eyes had narrowed, and his dangerous expression made the hair on the back of Winter's neck stand on end.

"Whatever you're going to do," Autumn ground out, her tone strained, "just get it over with, you piece of shit!"

Curling his right hand into a fist, Jeff took a swift step forward, arced his arm backward, and swung.

At the precise moment the blow landed on Autumn's cheek, Winter felt a searing pain just above her forehead. Autumn's lids fluttered closed, and with a sickening crack, her head struck the corner of the sturdy, wooden coffee table.

If Winter didn't know better, she would have thought she had just witnessed Autumn Trent's death.

But before the pool of blood could grow, before the mother's shrieks could echo through Winter's ears, the scene changed again.

The environment was calm and tranquil, a far cry from the chaos of the cramped living room she had just left. Autumn held the same stuffed kitten to her chest as she pulled up the blankets on her hospital bed. White gauze wrapped around her head, and to her side, the light of the television glinted off a metal IV stand.

Winter's breath caught in her throat as the heavy door cracked open.

Vision or not, if either of Autumn's parents walked through the doorway, she would find a way to push them back out.

To her relief, the visitor was a middle-aged woman clad in navy blue scrubs and a white lab coat. The corners of her amber, gold-flecked eyes creased as her gaze met Autumn's. Brushing away a piece of blonde hair that had fallen over the girl's forehead, she made her way to the cushioned chair beside the bed.

"Dr. Schmidt," Autumn greeted, a portion of the doctor's warm smile reflected in her face. "I didn't think you were going to be here. The nurse told me I'd be doing all the rest of my checkups with her or a different doctor."

"Maybe some of them," Dr. Schmidt replied, her smile unfaltering. "But I always like to check in to make sure my patients are okay after surgery."

Autumn nodded. "Yeah, that makes sense."

As the doctor asked the young girl a series of questions, the rest of the room faded to a listless gray.

By the time the darkness crept back into the edge of

Winter's vision, everything other than Dr. Schmidt was black and white.

※

WINTER SAT bolt upright and sucked in a deep breath. The headache was gone, and not even a twinge of the sharp, stabbing pain had been left behind. Only a smudge of red dotted the tissue, but when she looked to the digital clock, she groaned.

She might have only been out for fifteen minutes, but she and Noah had agreed to carpool to work in an effort to save a little cash. They made decent money, but scholarships or not, Winter still had her fair share of student loans to repay.

If she had been unconscious for fifteen minutes, that meant Noah was fifteen minutes ahead of her.

As she hastened through her morning routine, Winter mulled over the events she had just watched. There was still no doubt in her mind that the visions were memories, and that those memories indeed belonged to Autumn Trent.

But why?

So far, all her visions had been relevant to a case. Even without the profile put together by Aiden and Bree, Winter knew Autumn wasn't responsible for the body they'd found earlier that week.

The Jane Doe case was more than thirteen years old, and as smart and capable as Autumn was, Winter doubted the woman would have been able to pull off a brain surgery turned murder when she'd just been fifteen.

So, why had Winter just watched three distinct snippets of Autumn's past? If Autumn wasn't the perpetrator, then it meant she was...

"Shit," Winter spat as she unlocked the screen of her phone.

If Autumn wasn't the perpetrator, then she was a potential victim. Like Kayla Bennett, like the armored car personnel in the Presley case, or like Bree in the Kilroy investigation.

I'm in the parking lot, Noah had written.

Her fingers flew across the screen. *Be right there. I need to talk to you.*

She was so wrapped up in the possibility of a cold-blooded murderer gunning for her friend that she hadn't considered how the sentence "I need to talk to you" might have been construed.

About the case, she added quickly.

Dropping the phone into her handbag, she went through a mental checklist of essential items—her phone, wallet, badge, weapon—and then scooped up her keys and made her way out into the summer morning.

The sun was blanketed by a layer of clouds, and to the west, the sky darkened with the first hints of the forecasted storms. Gray daylight glinted off the lenses of Noah's aviator sunglasses as he turned them over in his hand. His gaze was fixed on the horizon, but as soon as she stepped onto the lot, his green eyes flicked to her.

"Mornin'," he greeted, stifling a yawn with one hand.

"Did you sleep like shit too?" she asked as she pulled open the passenger side door of the red pickup.

He only managed a nod in response as he yawned again.

"It's stress, probably." With a sigh, Winter squeezed her eyes closed and rubbed her temples.

"Maybe we should ask Autumn if she's got any recommendations. She's a double expert when it comes to stress, you know? She's a grad student, which is stressful, and then she's a clinical psych major." He glanced to her and offered a noncommittal shrug.

"That's not a bad idea," Winter muttered as she fastened

her seatbelt. "But that's part of what I wanted to talk to you about. I think she's involved in this John Doe case we're working."

Eyes going wide, he shot her a questioning look as he turned the key over in the ignition. "Involved? How?"

She wanted to know what was going on, but the vision hadn't been forthcoming. Winter took in a deep breath to push past the sudden bout of impatience. "I had a headache. You know, one of *those* headaches."

He opened his mouth, but before he could speak, she held up a hand.

"I'm fine. Honestly, compared to some of the other ones, this wasn't even really that bad. Plus, I was sitting on my bed when I lost consciousness, so I fell onto a pillow instead of the floor." She emphasized her point with a sarcastic smile.

She wasn't worried about herself. She'd dealt with these visions for years, and right now, she was concerned for her friend.

It was a strange feeling, she thought suddenly.

For the first chunk of the Douglas Kilroy investigation, her actions had been driven as much by a lust for revenge as worry for the wellbeing of others.

Winter wasn't proud of her motivation in those months, nor did she like how she had behaved toward her friends and colleagues. Maybe the whole Machiavellian attitude worked for Aiden Parrish or Sun Ming, but manipulating people to get what she wanted was not Winter's scene.

How in the hell those two had ever sustained a romantic relationship for anything longer than a week was beyond her comprehension. At the thought, she felt a twinge of irritability. The feeling bordered dangerously on envy, and she pried herself from the introspection and glanced to Noah.

"A vision?" he surmised.

"Yeah." Winter nodded. "It was weird. Not that any of

them are normal, so to speak, but this one was like I was skipping through time to watch different events."

As they pulled out of the parking lot, she walked through each scene she had viewed, and she spared no detail. For all she knew, what seemed trivial to her might have struck someone else as important.

And she was right.

By the time she finished the recollection, they had pulled into the drive-thru of a Starbucks. Noah was clean-shaven, and Winter could swear she watched most of the color drain from his cheeks as she went through the memories.

As he rolled down the window to give the barista their orders, he looked like he had just come face to face with a ghost.

"Jesus Christ," he muttered, raking the fingers of one hand through his dark hair.

"Yeah." Winter sighed and leaned against the headrest. "You remember the vision I had with Kilroy's victim, Officer Delosreyes? During that one, it was like I *was* her, like I lived through that trauma just like she had. This one was almost the same way. I mean, I didn't see it through Autumn's eyes, but I was right there, and I felt every single thing she did. When she was scared, so was I, and when she hit her head on the edge of that coffee table, it *hurt*."

"Yeah, I remember that. And I think what we should do right now is try to set aside a lot of that. Set aside the knowledge that her parents are a couple serious, high-grade pieces of shit, and just try to figure out what the stuff you saw has to do with the John Doe case. Because if she's a target here, we need to take care of that before we can even really think about all the rest of it. Not trying to sound like a dick, either. Because, believe me, I'm not about to just forget about the rest of it."

"Me neither," Winter all but spat. "But you're right. I agree completely. We need to figure out what she's got to do with this case first so we can make sure she's safe."

"She hit her head, right?"

"Right. And if I hadn't known she was still alive, I would've thought that it had killed her."

Noah inched closer to the pick-up window. "Traumatic brain injury, right?"

"Right." She saw the connection already, but she didn't interrupt him.

"John Doe and Jane Doe both had traumatic brain injuries too. From what the ME said, the injuries were older. And he said that they'd undergone surgery for those, plus the surgery that the killer, or at least we assume the killer did before they overdosed them on morphine or whatever in the hell it was they used to kill them. So, since they were able to keep these people alive after a damn brain surgery, we're looking for a brain surgeon, right?"

Winter stared at him. "Do you think...?" It was like the rest of the words were stuck in her throat.

"That doctor you saw," he finished for her. "Yeah. Dr. Schmidt, right? Schmidt is a common name, and we don't know where the hospital was."

"Yeah, Autumn grew up in Minnesota, but for procedures like that, sometimes people get life flighted pretty far away from where they were when they got hurt."

"We don't have enough for a subpoena." Thoughtful gaze fixed on the windshield, he tapped the steering wheel with an index finger. "Could we just ask her?"

"How?" Winter held out her hands as she shook her head.

There were only a few people alive who knew about her sixth sense and her visions, and one of them was bound by a Hippocratic Oath. As much as Winter liked Autumn, and as much potential as she saw for the future of their friendship, she could not take the risk.

Not only would revealing her so-called ability put her career in jeopardy, but there was a real chance that Autumn would think she was insane.

To her relief, Noah needed no elaboration. "Good point."

"I feel bad about it, but I can't think of another way. We need to find out who Dr. Schmidt is. And you're right, we don't have enough for a subpoena, especially not for medical records. But we can look through what we do have, and then we can *get* enough for a subpoena."

"If we look hard enough, we might not even *need* a subpoena."

21

The search for background information about Autumn Trent started out slow and tedious. For a student with a massive amount of loan debt, Autumn's credit score was good. In fact, Winter thought it might have been higher than hers.

Her academic record was spotless—she had been on the Dean's List for every semester of her undergrad. Autumn had graduated with "highest distinction" after she wrote an honor's thesis about bystander intervention. A couple years ago, she'd been awarded her Juris Doctorate, and once again, she had been at the top of her class.

None of the school records were news to Winter. She and Autumn had engaged in plenty of discussions about their respective college careers.

A list of addresses and potential relatives gleaned from public records indicated that Autumn's adopted father had passed away, and that her adopted mother, Kimberly Trent, still lived in Minnesota.

Again, Winter already knew about Autumn's adopted parents.

Before they were even twenty-four hours into their search, Winter and Noah had hit a dead end. They didn't know the surname in which Autumn had been born, and despite sifting through at least seven different databases, they hadn't even found a clue to point them in the right direction. Her adoption records were sealed, and all they could discern was that she had been thirteen at the time.

There were Child Protective Services records, but they were closed up even tighter than the adoption documents. Other than the fact that Autumn was labeled "victim" in each case, they weren't even given a date or a year when the events had taken place.

When they left the office on the first day, Winter had been sure they would come back in the morning with a refreshed perspective. She was sure they would find *something*.

But when they departed on the second day, her conviction had begun to waver.

Concocting a series of lies so she could ask Autumn about her past was an absolute last resort. But as Winter dropped down to sit on her couch, she figured her time would be better utilized by coming up with a believable cover story.

The idea left a sour taste in her mouth, but she would rather lie to her friend than watch her get hurt, especially if she knew she could have prevented it.

A clatter sounded from the wooden coffee table as the screen of her smartphone lit up the shadowy living room. She spotted Noah's contact picture as she leaned forward, and she swiped the answer key before the device had a chance to buzz again.

"Hey," she greeted. "What's up?"

"I've got something." His breathing was labored, and she wondered what he had been doing.

"About the case?"

"Yeah. Is it cool if I stop over?"

"Of course." She pushed herself out of her seat and started toward the kitchen.

"Good, because I'm already here."

When he rapped his knuckles against the nearby door, she couldn't help but laugh.

Flicking the deadbolt, she pulled open the door and stepped aside to give him room to enter. He had abandoned the black suit and blue tie he wore to work that day in favor of gym shorts and a worn band t-shirt.

"Nirvana?" she asked, furrowing her brows to flash him a puzzled glance. "You don't strike me as a Nirvana type of guy."

"There you go stereotyping me again," he huffed with feigned exasperation. "I listen to everything, thank you very much."

"Kurt Cobain did lead us out of the darkness of the hair band era." Winter grinned at him. She couldn't stand '80s hair bands, and Noah had been subjected to a couple of her tirades when they accidentally came across Poison or Def Leppard on the radio.

"They're not all terrible, I'm telling you. You've got to have an open mind sometimes, Winter." With one of the matter-of-fact looks he had perfected over the last year, he produced a silver laptop from beneath an arm. "Don't worry, I'm not going to use this to pull up a ten-hour loop of 'Unskinny Bop.' I found something about our case." When he paused, she didn't miss the flicker of guilt behind his green eyes.

"About Autumn." She kept her tone gentle, but she was relieved to know that she wasn't the only one who felt like an asshole for snooping around in their friend's past.

"Yeah."

"You want something to drink?" Winter jerked a thumb

over her shoulder as he dropped down to sit in the center of the couch.

"Sure."

"Okay, what do you want?" she prodded.

Shrugging, he glanced up from the computer. "Surprise me."

As she made her way to the refrigerator at the end of the galley kitchen, she entertained the idea of pouring him a mug of Southern Comfort.

She went so far as to open the cupboard where she kept the coffee cups before remembering why he was here in the first place. He was here so they could rip open their friend's dark past in hopes they would be able to connect her to a serial killer who happened to be a brain surgeon.

Her stomach dropped, and she wondered if she should pour *herself* a mug of Southern Comfort.

With a sigh, she pried open the stainless-steel fridge and retrieved two bottles of beer. Autumn had recommended the seasonal brew, and now Winter and Noah were obsessed.

"Thanks." Noah accepted the bottle from her outstretched hand and took a quick swig.

"What did you find?" she asked as she dropped down to sit at his side.

"Her name."

Winter tightened her grasp on the cool glass. "Her last name?"

"Yeah. She and her adopted parents changed it at the same time they officially adopted her. Her last name before then was Nichol, and her parents were Regina Petzke and Jeffrey Nichol. And their records." Shaking his head, he left the observation unfinished as he opened a new window. "I didn't spend very long on them before I came over here, but from what I saw, neither of them were good people."

"Her mom looked really young," Winter put in.

"Sixteen." Noah tapped a few keys. "And her dad was nineteen when she was born. So, based on the age you thought Autumn was when you saw her, I looked through his criminal record. The dude dropped off the face of the planet after the state pressed charges. And I mean, he *really* dropped off the face of the planet. Didn't leave so much as a bread-crumb behind when he did."

"Fuck him," Winter muttered.

Noah nodded. "Hopefully, he got eaten by a shark or sucked up by a tornado or something. I found the date that it happened, April twenty-third, 2002. Little less than a month before Autumn's eleventh birthday. And that's when I called you to tell you I found something."

Winter reached for her notepad. "Now, we look for news articles and other reports from that day. There ought to be something out there that'll mention which hospital they took her to."

"And then we look up their personnel records and find the woman you saw."

"And then we've got a suspect, right?"

He paused to offer her a noncommittal shrug. "I don't know about that. I mean, obviously *we'll* know she's a suspect, but I'm not sure how we explain that to anyone else. Especially Autumn."

Winter hesitated before she made the next suggestion. She knew he wouldn't like the idea, but at this point, she figured they were desperate enough that he would still agree.

"We can take it to Aiden," Winter finally said, then held up a finger. "I know, but before you say anything."

Propping both elbows on his knees, Noah shifted his green eyes to hers. "You're right," he started. "No offense because I know he's your friend, or mentor. Whatever. But the guy's manipulative as shit. If anyone'll be able to come up with something to use for us to talk to Autumn, it'll be him."

Though Winter's first inclination was to protest, she stopped herself before the words had formed on her lips.

Well, he wasn't wrong, was he?

"All right," she replied. "Yeah, something like that. I'm going to go get my laptop so I can help."

❄

THOUGH THEY SPENT over an hour sifting through the records of the hospital, the time was minimal compared to the two days that had yielded no useful information.

Winter was the first to locate records for the surgical staff during the month of April in 2002, and as soon as her eyes had settled on the familiar blonde woman, she took in a sharp breath.

Noah's attention snapped over to her laptop screen before she even announced her finding.

"That's her." Winter gently tapped the woman's picture with an index finger. "Dr. Catherine Schmidt. Pediatric Neurosurgeon. It says she only worked there for a couple more years after 2002."

"I'll see what I can find in the FBI databases."

Her fingers were already moving. "Okay, I'll see what I can find online."

A silence enveloped them, but it was broken within a matter of minutes as Noah heaved a sigh.

"What?" Winter asked, pulling her focus away from the screen and over to her friend. "Did you find something?"

"Yes and no," he muttered. "You said she only worked there for a couple more years, right? So, she would have left there about fifteen years ago. As luck would have it, all her records left right along with her. No utilities registered in her name, no cell phone, no car, nothing. She just disappeared like she was never even there to begin with."

"Did she have any family? Anyone else we could follow to maybe get to her?"

"No. She's divorced, but her ex-husband died last year of natural causes. Her parents are both gone too. Cancer in both cases." Running a hand through his hair, he flopped back in his seat and groaned. "It's one dead end right after another."

"Do you think she could have died too?" Winter suspected she knew the answer, but they were grasping at straws.

"If she did, it happened off the grid. No records of anything. It's just, one day she was there, and then the next." He paused to snap his fingers. "She was gone."

"Our luck, huh?"

With a dry chuckle, he nodded. "Pretty much."

"You should take a break." Winter waved her hand toward the kitchen. "Get yourself another beer and kick back for a little bit. I'll keep looking."

Eyebrow arched in feigned suspicion, he returned his laptop to the coffee table. "Do you want a beer? Is that why you think I should take a break?"

Despite the strain from a frustrating, morally questionable search into Autumn's past, Winter laughed at his dripping sarcasm.

"It's not," she managed, "but yes. I'd appreciate it."

Flashing her a grin, he pushed himself to stand. As he made his way to the kitchen, Winter returned her focus to the search.

When she first caught the glimmer of red, she thought the screen of her laptop might have been acting up. The computer wasn't even a year old, and if she had to jump through a series of hoops to get a replacement due to a manufacturer's defect, wouldn't that just be the icing on the damn cake?

But as she scrolled, the out of place glow moved with the text.

"A study," she muttered to herself. The link led to the abstract of an academic journal article. As a bright, crimson glow crept along one of the authors' names, she felt her jaw go slack.

"What?" From the corner of her eye, she saw Noah approach, a beer in each hand.

She wished he had retrieved the Southern Comfort from the top of the fridge instead.

Wordlessly, she turned the screen to face him and pointed to the second to last author.

"Holy shit," he managed.

As she met his wide-eyed stare, she nodded. "Dr. Robert Ladwig."

22

Glancing from the two people at the circular table and then back to the hallway, Noah eased the glass and metal door closed. As he approached Winter and Aiden, he felt like he should have walked on his tiptoes.

He didn't make a hobby of sneaking around the FBI office, but as of late, it had become unnervingly common. Noah took his seat, and Aiden's pale eyes flicked from him to Winter and back before he spoke.

"What did you find?" His tone was just as cool and casual as if he was asking for directions to the breakroom.

"Robert Ladwig," Winter told him. "He's the shrink I saw after I started getting these weird headaches and *visions,* or whatever in the hell you want to call them."

Wordlessly, Aiden nodded for her to continue.

"Maybe we should start at the beginning," Noah suggested.

"Probably," Winter muttered. "Speaking of those visions... I had one a few days ago."

"Why didn't you say anything?" Aiden rested both elbows atop the polished wooden surface as he narrowed his eyes.

The flash of indignation on Winter's face was unmistakable, and Noah had to fight to keep himself from smirking.

Before she could reprimand the patronizing query, Aiden shook his head. "Don't answer that. That was a stupid question. Go on."

Noah was almost impressed. Maybe Parrish had finally learned that Winter was capable of making adult decisions. He bit down on his tongue to stifle an amused chortle.

"It was about our friend." Winter folded her hands in front of herself.

Noah's mirth was short-lived as she went over every detail of the recollection, just like she had when she told him.

When Winter finished, Parrish clenched and unclenched his jaw, a spark of ire simmering beneath his composed exterior. It was the most human behavior Noah thought he had ever seen from the man.

Maybe he wasn't an automaton, after all.

With a reassuring smile and a nod, Noah took over for Winter and regaled their painstaking search for the doctor's identity. By the time he explained the significance of discovering Robert Ladwig's name on a scholarly journal article co-authored by Catherine Schmidt, Aiden's cool visage had returned.

"She could be using a fake identity," the man proposed. "We've been seeing a fair amount of those lately."

"Or, she could be dead," Winter put in. "We did some more digging in Dr. Ladwig's history this morning, and he was in the military for close to ten years. He got his medical degree while he was working as a medic in the Army."

"He's got the skillset." Parrish said the words more to himself than Noah or Winter.

"He might," Winter replied. "And he called me out of the blue a few weeks ago. I didn't think too much of it at the time, but it was a little…off."

"Maybe he's the killer." Even as he said it, Noah didn't think it was the right answer. But what else did they have? "And maybe that's why Catherine Schmidt dropped off the face of the planet. What if he killed her because she found him out? Or what if she was one of his victims?"

To his surprise, Aiden nodded his agreement. "It's always seemed like there was something off about that guy. What about your friend?"

Noah frowned as he leaned back in his chair. "Do we really even need to bring her in for an interview at this point?"

"Yeah, I don't really know what we'd get from it," Winter agreed.

Parrish was shaking his head before she even finished. "Just because we like Ladwig for this doesn't mean that's the only route we pursue. Your visions have all been right so far, and Ladwig *wasn't* in that vision. Your friend and her surgeon were." Winter opened her mouth again, but Parrish raised a finger, and she snapped it shut. "Look, you two are her friends, so you bring her here and I'll talk to her."

Noah couldn't help a derisive snort. "You're going to interrogate her?"

"She's a witness." Aiden's response was so flat that it bordered on outright irritable.

"Right," he replied with a roll of his eyes. "Tell you what, Parrish. Since you're such a delightful guy, I'll ask her to be nice to you."

"You're sweet, Dalton." Unsurprisingly, the man's response was laden with condescension.

They both turned their attention to Winter as she covered her mouth to stifle a sudden bout of laughter. "You know," she started, pausing for another chortle. "Usually, you guys are just annoying when you do this shit, but this was actually pretty funny. So, thanks, I guess."

23

When Aiden made his way to meet Winter's friend on the first floor, he wasn't sure what to expect. But when he stepped into the tiled hallway just past the main entrance, he realized he hadn't expected *this*.

Both women sat on a wooden bench against the wall, but before he spotted them, he heard their laughter. There was a brightness on Winter's face that he didn't think he'd seen since before she started her FBI career. Or maybe ever.

And then there was her laugh. Not dry, not sarcastic, not mocking. This laugh was genuine. After Douglas Kilroy, he was sure he'd never hear that sound again.

The other woman held a smartphone, and both her and Winter's attention was fixed on the device. The corners of Winter's eyes creased as she and her friend both lapsed back into their fit of laughter.

"Where do you *find* this shit?" Winter managed, holding her hand low on her belly.

"One of my students told me about it," the friend snickered.

She opened her mouth to add to the explanation, but then

her gaze flicked away from the screen as he approached. As the lighthearted expression started to dissipate, he almost considered backing away to let her and Winter return their focus to whatever had given them so much amusement.

Winter turned her head to regard the source of her friend's sudden distraction. "Afternoon, SSA Parrish. That was fast."

"It's important." He forced an agreeable expression to his face as he inclined his chin toward the other woman. "I didn't want to waste your friend's time."

"Right."

Winter was clearly unconvinced, but he brushed away the skepticism.

Autumn Trent, formerly Nichol, stood just a touch taller than Winter's five-seven, and he realized in short order that her DMV photo didn't do her justice.

As her emerald eyes flicked over to Winter, he let his gaze linger. Her auburn hair contrasted with her fair skin in a way that was almost ethereal. A teal shirt beneath her black and white striped cardigan clung to the hourglass shape of her body like it had been made specifically for her, and her slim-fitting jeans gave the same impression.

When Winter cleared her throat, he snapped his attention back to her.

Based on the malevolent glint in her blue eyes, she hadn't missed his less than polite observation of her friend. Autumn, on the other hand, seemed oblivious to the exchange. He didn't personally know the redhead, but he thought he would have rather had her notice the drawn-out look than Winter.

"You must be Miss Trent," he said to pull himself out of the sudden haze. With a slight smile, he extended a hand.

"I am, but please call me Autumn." She nodded as she accepted the handshake. The smile that crept to her lips was sugary sweet, but there was a cunning behind her bright eyes that made him second-guess his assertion from moments earlier.

"Since you're such a delightful guy, I'll ask her to be nice to you," Noah Dalton had said the day before.

"I'm Aiden Parrish, Supervisory Special Agent of the Behavioral Analysis Unit here at the Richmond office of the FBI."

"That's a hell of a title," Autumn chuckled. "I hope it's got an abbreviation."

"SSA," Winter offered, "and BAU."

"Alphabet soup." Glancing over to Winter, Autumn shrugged. "All right, well, I suppose I'll see you back here in a few. Thanks again for the ride. I don't know what the hell is wrong with my car, but I'm really hoping it isn't something to do with the transmission. I definitely do *not* have transmission money."

"I wish I knew enough about cars to be helpful," Winter replied. "I'm going to go get a coffee from down the street. Do you want anything?"

"Actually." Autumn tapped a finger against her cheek. "Yes. Salted caramel mocha. The biggest one they have. If they've got one of those giant gas station cups, fill that."

Winter grinned, and once again, Aiden was surprised at how relaxed she looked around the other woman. "I wish."

"I'll pay you when I'm done with this." For emphasis, she gestured to him.

"Don't worry about it." Winter waved a dismissive hand. "Consider it a payment for having to deal with the FBI."

If he hadn't known better, Aiden would have thought the two women had been friends for their entire lives.

Before she turned around to make her way to the exit, Winter flashed him a dangerous look.

Ignoring the implied threat, he led Autumn back into the

heart of the building, and he paused in front of the silver elevator doors.

"I've got an office upstairs," he said as he met her curious glance. "Or there are a few interview rooms down the hall. Wherever you're more comfortable."

"You know," she offered him a sarcastic grin, "I think I'll take the interrogation room. I've been in a few of those, but I've never been in a Fed's office."

"What is life if not the opportunity for new experiences?" With an exaggerated shrug, he waved toward the corridor.

"Thanks, Socrates, but it just seems like it'd feel too much like a job interview," she replied, unfazed. "After you. I don't know where the hell I'm going."

Chuckling lightly, he nodded. "Fair enough."

Despite the moment of amusement, he started to wonder about Dalton's sarcastic comment the day before. Federal agent friends or not, he had expected Autumn to be intimidated by a stroll through the FBI office. Even as he held the door for her to enter a windowless interrogation room, her calm didn't waver.

"I overheard you say something about one of your students earlier." He pulled out a rickety metal chair to sit. "What do you teach?"

"Teach?" she echoed. "Oh, right, that. I'm not a teacher. I'm a graduate student, and I teach so the school will give me my stipend."

"What are you studying?"

"I half-expected you to know all this stuff already," she laughed. "Or do you know it, and you're just screwing with me?"

"I am not," he replied as he rested his arms atop the stainless-steel table. "And no, I don't know anything about your academic record. Winter and Agent Dalton didn't tell me any of that."

The corner of her mouth turned up in the start of a knowing smirk. "Clinical forensic psychology. I defend my dissertation at the end of August, but I've already gotten my JD."

"A law degree?" No wonder she wasn't nervous. In a couple months, she would have more letters behind her name than he had in front of his.

"Oh, don't worry. I haven't passed the bar or anything. It's just part of the forensic psych track at VCU."

Try as he might, he couldn't tell whether she was mocking him or merely being informative. "I have a master's in social cognitive psychology. I did some work toward a Ph.D., but I never finished it."

"I love social psychology." For the first time, he was sure her pleasant smile did not hold an ulterior meaning. "What did you study for your dissertation?"

"Diffusion of responsibility."

"An oldie but a goodie. Well, you seem like you're a pretty busy guy, so I won't bother you by asking questions about your postgrad. Winter wasn't too specific, but she said you're here to ask me about my doctor from seventeen years ago. Dr. Schmidt."

"Right." He nodded and reached into a pocket to retrieve his phone. After a couple taps, he slid the picture of Robert Ladwig over to her side of the table. "Do you recognize him?"

She paused to study the photo before she shook her head. "No, I've never seen him before."

"What about Dr. Schmidt? What can you tell me about her?"

Shrugging, she crossed her arms over her chest. "She was a good doctor. One of the best neurosurgeons in the country, if I remember right. People would fly their kids in from all over the place to see her, but I guess I was lucky enough to live in Minnesota."

"Did you stay in touch with her afterwards?"

He hadn't even finished the question before she shook her head. "No."

There was more to her succinct response, and he could tell he was getting close to a nerve.

"Honestly?" she started before he could speak. "She gave me the creeps. She was a good doctor, but she was fucking weird."

"Fucking weird how?" he pressed.

"The kind of weird that makes an eleven-year-old kid nervous. There are a lot of types of weird that can fit that bill. Maybe she collected something weird like Beanie Babies or those creepy porcelain dolls. But it seemed just as likely that she had a collection of moose heads on the walls of her rec room. It's hard to say. She was just *off.*"

"Did she ever mention any of her other patients, or say anything that might have indicated she was doing work that was unethical?"

At first, she looked like she was about to shake her head, but she stopped short. "No, she didn't," she finally answered. "But she did ask me some weird questions. At the time I figured they were just specific to brain surgeries, the type of questions that only made sense to neuro-surgeons."

The chill of adrenaline crept along the back of his neck as he leaned forward. "Like what?"

Lips pursed, she shifted her green eyes over to meet his intent stare. At the lessened distance, he could see the faint flecks of gold that ringed her pupils.

"The questions aren't what weirded me out," she prefaced. "But she'd ask me about how well my senses were, whether or not they'd been dulled by the head injury. Which doesn't make any sense to me now because the injury was to the frontal lobe, not the temporal or occipital lobes, but who knows. For all I know, it might've just been a standard question they had to ask everyone with a TBI."

"How did that happen? Your head, I mean."

Her mouth twitched with the first hint of a scowl. "I don't see how that's relevant to Catherine Schmidt."

There it was, he thought. The nerve he had brushed only moments earlier. "Did your parents know her, or was she recommended by anyone they know? I'm just trying to find out if you or your family had any connection to her, anything we could follow to find out where she is now, or what happened to her."

"No one recommended her, and my parents didn't know her." The response was curt, almost hostile.

"Did they meet her? Is there any chance we could ask them if they know anything about her?" Though he had looked over the scant information Winter and Noah had given him about Autumn's history, there had been no mention of her parents' fate—only that her mother's ex-husband had won full custody of Autumn's younger half-sister, Sarah.

"They're dead. They've been dead," she advised flatly.

"Oh." He grated his teeth as he pushed through the split-second of awkward shame. "Agent Black and Agent Dalton didn't mention that. I'm sorry."

"What *did* they mention?" she asked. "How did any of you even know that I was a patient of Dr. Schmidt? Shouldn't all that be protected by HIPAA? Is there something you aren't telling me, Mr. Parrish?"

His pulse rushed in his ears as he shook his head, and the cold touch of adrenaline had become a stranglehold. "They found her when they were looking through records on Dr. Robert Ladwig, and they found an academic journal article that Dr. Schmidt co-authored with Dr. Ladwig."

Hands folded atop the table, she leaned forward as she

narrowed her eyes. "You didn't answer a single one of my questions, Mr. Parrish."

This wasn't the first time he'd confronted a clever witness, but there was a glint in her stare that suggested she already knew the answers to her questions.

Even as the laughter built up in his throat, he didn't know what the hell was so funny. Based on her unimpressed expression, she didn't either.

"You're good at that," he offered. "Attention to detail and persistence, two hallmarks of a good interrogation. I don't suppose you're looking for a career in law enforcement?"

Rolling her eyes, she crossed her arms and straightened. "No. I doubt you'd pay me enough."

"This is the FBI, and federal agents make quite a bit more than a city cop." With a smirk, he shrugged. "Just something to consider."

"I doubt they make as much as a forensic psychologist," she shot back. "But thanks. You going to answer my questions, or nah?"

He let a good fifteen ticks of the clock pass. "An article on a news website that caters to the scientific community. I know that the surgery was part of a hot streak for Dr. Schmidt and that a lot of other surgeons were really impressed with her. And no, there's not anything I'm holding back from you."

With a mirthless chuckle, she fixed her eyes on his. "You're full of shit. There's no way the head of the behavioral analysis department at the FBI would personally sit down to ask me about my doctor from seventeen years ago just because you guys found a *news article* about how successful the surgery was. I know you don't know me, so I won't give you the spiel I save for when people insult my intelligence. But I will say this, Mr. Parrish. Don't insult my intelligence. I didn't study business law or real estate law. I studied *criminal law.*"

"I'm not holding back any more than I need to in order to avoid compromising this investigation," he returned. The moment of surprise had passed. "And *I* didn't find any of this shit. If you want to know more about it, you'll have to ask the people who did. The reason you're here talking to me is because you're friends with two federal agents, and I wanted to make sure this interview was impartial. I don't doubt that you've got a great deal of respect for impartiality, right?"

"Of course." The sweet smile laced with cunning was back. The look was as sexy as it was infuriating. "Did you have any other questions for me, or am I free to go?"

"You've been free to go this whole time." Before she could retort, he held up an index finger. "And yes, I know you knew that. Forgive me for not knowing the proper etiquette here. The only people with law degrees I'm used to talking to are lawyers. I'm not used to witnesses with Juris Doctorates. So, I'm not insulting your intelligence because, believe me, it's not lost on me."

When she laughed, the hostility dissipated. "Fair enough. Well, I hope that was useful, but I sort of doubt it. If that's all you had, then I think it's time for me to go get that giant coffee Winter's bringing me."

In the short walk back to the lobby, he thought to ask her about the subject of her dissertation research, but he decided not to press his luck.

Aiden didn't normally have a problem burning bridges with people he'd never see again, but in addition to the fact that she was Winter's friend, Autumn Trent was different.

The job offer he'd made to her hadn't entirely been sarcastic.

As soon as they stepped through the set of double doors

and into the hall, Winter leapt up from the wooden bench. He didn't miss the scrutiny in her eyes as she glanced at him.

"Here," he said, holding out a business card as he looked back to Autumn. "If you think of anything else, just let me know. Or if you change your mind about working in law enforcement…" He raised an eyebrow.

With a chuckle, she accepted the card and nodded. "You'll be the first person I call if I decide I want to be a Fed."

❄

AUTUMN HELD her cool visage together until she flicked the deadbolt of her apartment door into place. As soon as the pressure to maintain a cool façade dissipated, her stomach lurched. She hardly managed a greeting to her pets as she hastened down the short hallway to the bathroom.

Up came the last third of the salted caramel mocha Winter had bought for her, but aside from the latte, there was no food for her to throw up. She had spent the previous night waking in fits and starts as her sleeping brain dragged her through one nightmare after another, and the lingering anxiety made the idea of a meal laughable.

What happened when her friends learned about her past? Would they look at her with the same expression of pity as any other friend in whom she'd confided over the years?

Or would they decide that she was not one of them, that her messy upbringing, that the *real* Autumn Trent was not fit for their company? When they found out she was trailer trash from just another broken home, what then?

When.

There was no doubt that they *would* find out. The only question that remained was when.

For god's sake, they were federal agents. Just because all the records of her juvenile experiences were sealed didn't mean they would *stay* that way. Especially not now that Dr. Catherine Schmidt had become the subject of an ongoing investigation.

Hell, they probably knew already.

Her ability to tune into another person's emotions and motivations tended to lessen as she got to know them, though she had no idea why. Maybe as she honed her perception of them, the bizarre, lizard part of her brain grew less keen.

But as soon as she'd clasped Aiden Parrish's hand, she knew their proposed reason for questioning her was bullshit. They might have been in search of information about Catherine Schmidt, but they had not come across the surgeon's name during a review of Robert Ladwig.

She wasn't sure of the real method of the discovery, but she was sure it involved her past.

24

For six weeks, Winter, Bree, Noah, and even Aiden chased their collective tails as they tried to make sense of Catherine Schmidt and Robert Ladwig's connection. And for almost the entirety of those six weeks, a law enforcement agent had followed Dr. Ladwig's every waking move.

Winter was sick of thinking about the psychiatrist, sick of looking at pictures of a fifty-five-gallon drum, even sick of looking at the forensic anthropologist's rendition of their two victims.

They'd searched through Virginia's missing persons reports but hadn't found a victim that matched the picture of John or Jane Doe. Though none of them had said it, they all knew they would have to shelve the case if they didn't uncover a lead soon.

No matter how many times she reassured herself there was nothing she could do at work, she still felt guilty for her decision to take the weekend off.

In a show of solidarity, and in an attempt to alleviate some of her guilt, Noah had even decided to follow suit. When she asked what he planned to do with his time off, he had suggested he use the entire weekend to catch up to her and Autumn in *Game of Thrones*.

Winter knew that the man held no love for science fiction —no matter how many times Autumn tried to explain *Star Wars* to him, he merely shrugged and said he didn't *get* it. She expected the same would ring true for medieval fantasy, but she had been sorely mistaken.

Though Grampa Jack would give Noah an endless stream of grief for his unwillingness to immerse himself in the world of *Star Trek* and Jean-Luc Picard, Winter knew Noah's newfound affinity for *Lord of the Rings* style fantasy would only endear him more.

Pulling herself from the reverie, Winter glanced up to offer her grandmother a wide smile as she set a steaming mug of coffee atop the polished table. "Thanks, Gramma."

"Of course, honey. So, what brings you to our neck of the woods on this lovely Friday morning?"

With a sigh, Winter rubbed her eyes. "I needed to get out of the city, away from work for a few days. We're working on this case, and it's...it's just a mess. Well, maybe it isn't really, but that's because we don't have any information about anything."

"You've got to step away sometimes," Beth replied with a dismissive wave. "You're not doing anyone any good if you're running yourself ragged, honey. You've got to regroup and come back with a fresh perspective."

Winter paused as she took a sip of the coffee-hot chocolate mixture. "You know, you're right."

"I know I am," her grandma laughed. "You don't get to be my age without learning a few things about how to manage stress."

Before Winter could open her mouth to reply, her phone buzzed against the tabletop. Though she hadn't saved the number to her contacts list, the area code was local to Richmond.

"I think it might be work." As she scooped up the device, she glanced to her grandma.

"Don't look at me," Beth chuckled. "It might be important. Don't ignore it on my account."

"Thanks, Gramma." Winter flashed her grandmother a grateful smile as she rose to stand. Swiping the green answer key, she stepped around the table to let herself out into the warm summer morning. The sliding glass door hissed along the metal track as she eased it closed.

"This is Agent Black." Though she used her phone for private calls, she preferred a formal greeting for unsaved numbers.

"Agent Black," a familiar man replied. His tone was cheerful, almost excited.

Dan Nguyen wasn't what an average person pictured when they thought of a medical examiner. The man was tall, in good shape, and was always prepared with a lighthearted joke or comment. For the duration of her time with the Bureau, Winter didn't think she had ever seen Dr. Nguyen in poor spirits.

"Dr. Nguyen." Winter felt the corner of her mouth turn up in the start of a smile. Noah was right, the weekend away *had* been a good idea. Even after only a couple hours, her mood was better than it had been for most of the past month and a half. "You sound like you've got some good news."

"You're right," he said. "I do. You know, I had a whole preamble planned to explain how much work we put into this, but I think you're already aware of it, so I'll just start with the good part. We've got John Doe's identity."

"What?" The response was reflexive, and she almost laughed at how awestruck she sounded.

"I know, right?" He chuckled. "I'd taken marrow from his

femur, and we ran it through the system. No surprise, there wasn't a match, but I had our tech run it again every couple days to see if the states might have finally uploaded to the system."

Winter held her breath. Like everything, CODIS was only as good as the information uploaded to it, and as understaffed as many sheriff and police departments were, it sometimes took a while for all evidence to be filtered into the Combined DNA Index System.

"Your tech got a hit." Winter's hand hurt from grasping her phone so hard.

He laughed. "Damned right we did."

"You are my favorite person on the entire planet right now."

The observation only elicited more laughter. "I didn't do the analysis, I just dug out the DNA and gave it to one of the ladies in forensics. She did the rest."

"Then text me her name when we're done, and I'll send her a fruit basket."

The identity of one victim might not have been a guarantee that they would find the killer soon, or even at all, but Winter liked their odds a lot better now. Based on the lengths the perpetrator had gone to conceal their victim's identity, chances seemed good that they would be able to discover a link between John Doe and the killer.

"Vic's name is Jenson Leary," Dan started. "The reason you guys didn't find him when you looked through missing persons is because he didn't live in Virginia. He lived in North Carolina. His wife reported him missing about nine months ago, right around Thanksgiving. Turns out, the forensic anthropologist did a damn fine job. The picture they came up with matched Jenson almost exactly."

"Holy shit," she breathed. "Send whatever you've got on

him to me. I'm a couple hours away right now, but I'm about to head back."

"Already done. I sent it to you and the other agents working the case."

"Perfect. Okay, I'll stop short of writing you a sonnet here and let you get back to work. Let me know if you find anything else."

"Sounds good." He chuckled. "Safe travels, Agent Black."

"Talk to you later."

As soon as she ended the call, she pulled up Noah's number and dialed. Apparently, she hadn't needed a full vacation in order to stumble upon a viable lead.

❄️

"I STILL DON'T KNOW why you needed me here." Hands on her hips, Autumn glanced away from the sleek dining set to flash him one of her patented, knowing looks.

"Because," Noah started, sweeping an arm to the host of tastefully decorated clusters of tables and chairs. "Your place looks good, and mine, well. You've seen it. It sucks. Figured if there was anyone I'd want with me furniture shopping, it'd be the person who knows how to put a room together without it looking like a college dorm. Which is how Winter's place looks. She's got a mini fridge in her room, for the love of god."

He left off the part about how he and Winter had scarcely seen her over the past six weeks.

Supposedly, Autumn had been dedicating the majority of her waking moments to her dissertation. In less than two weeks, she was scheduled to defend the extensive research project, but Noah and Winter suspected that wasn't the only reason.

Noah had been the first to bring up the timeline, and he

was sure that Autumn's conversation with Aiden Parrish was behind her recent absence. He had come close to confronting the man about it a couple times that week, but Winter had encouraged him to talk to Autumn instead.

And today, that was what he intended to do.

Both he and Winter had taken the day off to give themselves a three-day weekend, and as luck would have it, Autumn had given herself the day off for a doctor's appointment that afternoon.

With a faint smile and a chuckle, she shook her head. "All right, all right." She rolled her eyes. "Well, what do you want your place to look like? Like mine?"

"Like a place where an adult human being lives." He flashed her a grin. "Like the person who lives there is capable of cooking something more than boxed mac and cheese, you know? Which I am, thank you. I taught myself to cook at the beginning of the year. And now, I've got all kinds of shit in my kitchen, but every other room looks like someone put it together with furniture they found lying on the side of the road."

"So, that's *not* the look you're going for? Furniture roadkill?"

"Hey, it might not be coordinated or even really nice at all, but it's functional, dammit." He crossed his arms and huffed.

"Noah, you use a file cabinet as an end table. A file cabinet you got when the FBI decided to do some remodeling," she reminded him. Finally, there was a familiar flicker of amusement in her green eyes.

"But it's functional." Raising his eyebrows, he offered her an expectant smile.

"I mean, I guess. If you need to do some filing while you're watching TV."

"See? I knew you'd understand."

"In that case, do you want to go buy all your furniture from the office supply part of the store?" She was biting back laughter, which made him laugh too. "Instead of a dining room table, we could just put four file cabinets together in a square, and then get shorter file cabinets for the chairs."

"You're getting a little extreme now, darlin'," he snickered. "I don't do *that* much filing, all right?"

"Okay." She waved a dismissive hand. "We'll find a balance, then. Balance your need for filing with your need for style."

"There we go." Before he could add to their sarcastic conversation, he felt a buzz against his leg. Raising a hand, he retrieved the smartphone from the pocket of his worn jeans. "It's Winter."

"Tell her I said hi."

"Will do," he replied, swiping the screen. "Hey," he greeted as he raised the phone to his ear.

"Noah," Winter said, her cadence hurried. "I just got a call from Dr. Nguyen. Forensics identified John Doe. He already sent you all the information about the guy. Listen, I'm in Fredericksburg right now, but I'm about to head back to town."

"Holy shit," he managed, eyes wide. "All right, yeah. I'll meet you at the office. I'll see what else I can dig up before you get back."

As he bade Winter goodbye, Autumn's expression turned curious, and he was struck by an unexpected pang of guilt.

So much for reconnecting with his friend.

25

As Aiden rapped his knuckles against the wooden door, he grated his teeth. He'd never been to the apartment complex before today, and the GPS on his phone had directed him in circles twice before he found the damn parking lot. The building wasn't in poor shape, but neither could it be classified as upscale.

Based on the whiff of must and stale cigarettes in the hall-way, the monthly rent for a one-bedroom was right in line with the income of a graduate student.

Just before the door creaked inward, he thought he heard a resigned sigh. Leaning one shoulder against the wall, Autumn Trent eased the door open with her other hand. As the opening widened, he spotted a little pointy-eared dog tucked against her chest. The pup's eyes followed his move-ments, but it didn't bark.

"Can I help you?" There was more than a little suspicion in her tone, or maybe it was impatience. Either way, his hopes for an easy dialogue were dashed.

"Yeah, actually." Brows raised, he gestured to the hallway at her back. "You mind if I come in?"

Green eyes narrowed, she stepped aside to give him room to enter.

"Shoes off," she ordered. "This complex might be a shit-hole, but that doesn't mean my place has to be."

The light scent of pineapple and vanilla was a far cry from the sour odor they left behind in the dim hall. As he glanced around the spacious living room, he could almost trick himself into believing the complex catered to well-off hipsters instead of debt-ridden college students.

A rustic, stone surfaced coffee table sat in front of an expansive sectional couch, and the television on the matching stand was at least as large as his. Rather than a table and chairs, the dining area off to the side of the open kitchen had been set up like an office.

"I've got a doctor's appointment in an hour." Her voice snapped him out of the intent observation. "And my car's in the shop, so I've got to take the bus or an Uber. So, make it quick, Mr. Parrish."

Paws clattered against the hardwood floor as the little dog trotted over to sniff Aiden's legs. Dropping down to a crouch, he held out a hand before he looked back up to where Autumn leaned against the breakfast bar. "Give me a half hour, and I'll drive you to your appointment myself."

Her olive-green shorts ended just above mid-thigh, and the start of a tattoo was visible from beneath the hem. Printed on her loose, black t-shirt were the letters NIN—the logo of a band he knew well from his days in high school and college.

Maybe he'd finally found a piece of common ground that would alleviate some of her suspicions.

Scratching one of the dog's fluffy ears, he gestured to her shirt with his free hand. "When I was in my undergrad, I saw them in Chicago. They played *Hurt*, and Johnny Cash walked out onto the stage at the start of it. Easily the best show I've ever seen."

Though he half-expected her to brush off the recollection and ask him to hurry up and get to the point, the impatience dissipated from her pretty face. She now looked incredulous. "Really?"

"What does *that* mean?" Despite the pointed question, he felt the start of a smile on his lips.

"It means I didn't pick you for a Nine Inch Nails fan," she answered with a slight shake of her head. "I don't know what the hell I thought you listened to, but it wasn't Trent Reznor or Johnny Cash."

"First, who *doesn't* like Johnny Cash? And second, you didn't know what you thought I listened to, or you don't want to tell me?" Now, the touch of amusement had turned into a full-blown smirk.

"Little of both, honestly."

"All right. I'm curious now." With one last pat on the dog's head, he rose to his full height. "What *did* you think I listened to?"

She shrugged as if the answer should have been obvious. "Shit. Either shit, or some indie stuff I've never heard of."

"You think I'm a hipster?" he pressed, eyebrows raised as he offered her an expectant look.

"Your words, not mine." She shook her head again, but he could see the first trace of amusement in her eyes. "All right. Well, if you're going to chauffeur me to my doctor's office, then I guess I've got a little time. I'm not going to turn down a chance to ditch the bus. What was it you wanted to ask me?"

With a nod, he retrieved his phone as he made his way to the breakfast bar that separated the kitchen from the living room. "Jenson Leary," he said. He watched her expression as he raised the device for her to view the screen. "Do you know him?"

She squinted and leaned closer, but there was no flicker of recognition on her face.

"No," she finally answered, shaking her head. "Sorry. I've never seen him. The name doesn't sound familiar, either."

"Here." He held out the phone for her to take. "There are some older pictures of him there too. Look through them, maybe you knew him when you were younger."

"Yeah, all right." As she accepted the phone, her fingertips brushed against the back of his hand.

The touch was feathery light, and based on the focused look she wore, the gesture had not been intentional. Now, why that disappointed him, he wasn't so sure he wanted to know.

What was important, he reminded himself, was that the borderline hostility with which she had greeted him had finally worn away. All it had taken was the mention of a concert from seventeen years ago.

White light glinted off her eyes as she sighed and shook her head. "No, I'm sorry. He doesn't look familiar. Who is he?"

"Well, he was born and raised in Minneapolis and Minnetonka."

Based on their interaction six weeks earlier, if he wanted to delve into her past, he would have to be careful in his choice of words.

She shrugged and passed the smartphone back to him. "Minneapolis is a big city, and Minnetonka is decent sized too."

"He had a traumatic brain injury when he was twelve years old. He had to have surgery, and his surgeon was Dr. Catherine Schmidt."

She stiffened minutely. "And?" she prodded.

"He was found dead in a fifty-five-gallon drum a little over a month and a half ago."

Though the look was fleeting, her eyes widened. "Oh."

"We believe that whoever killed him also killed a woman we found about thirteen years ago. We still haven't identified her, but she had a healed injury on her skull too. We were able to retain a partial list of Dr. Schmidt's surgical patients from one particular hospital, and we're getting a court order for a list of patients in other hospitals in which she had surgical privileges. After that, I'm already pretty sure that we'll find Jane Doe in that list."

Autumn crossed her arms over her chest, and Aiden noticed goose bumps raise on her skin. She just stared at him, saying nothing, the blood draining from her pretty face as he spoke.

"Whoever she was," he went on, "the medical examiner says that both she and Jenson Leary underwent brain surgery shortly before they were killed. And whoever performed the surgery knew what they were doing, because both of them stayed alive long enough for the surgical wounds to start to heal."

"And you think Dr. Schmidt killed them?" Her green eyes flicked back to his, and he saw a hint of anxiety beneath the calm demeanor.

"We aren't sure. Dr. Schmidt dropped off the face of the planet fifteen years ago. No death certificate, no obituary, no nothing. One day she was there, and then the next day, she was gone."

"But whoever they are, they're targeting Dr. Schmidt's patients. Is that what I'm picking up here?"

"We think so."

As they lapsed into silence, she tapped her fingers against the back of the tall chair at her side. "This is going to sound really weird," she started, shifting her attention to him.

"I can deal with weird. Try me."

"It was just a weird feeling I got when she'd come check up on me after the surgery. After I came out of the coma, it was like, like I was just better at socializing, I guess. I could get a read on people like I hadn't been able to before. That sort of reaction isn't unheard of with frontal lobe injuries."

Aiden nodded. "That's the part of the brain that's essentially responsible for your personality."

Autumn nodded in return. "Exactly. I was shy and quiet before, but after." She sighed and shook her head. "It's like I wasn't beholden to any of the doubts that had been holding me back before, and that, being able to read people, that was a big part of it. But like I told you, she just creeped me out. There was something off whenever she talked to me, like she had an ulterior motive for everything she asked. I didn't know what it was, I *still* don't know what it was. But, you want my honest opinion?"

He nodded. "Absolutely."

"And don't put too much weight on it. Memory, it's not as reliable as people like to think it is. We learn new information, and that biases the way we look at our memories. Memories aren't static, they're subject to change just like everything else in our brain."

The corner of his mouth turned up in the start of a smirk. "I know."

She flushed a little. "Right, master's in social cognitive, my bad."

"You remembered."

"Of course I remembered." She rolled her eyes, but the amusement in her tone was unmistakable. "Meeting the dude who runs the behavioral analysis section of the FBI is a pretty memorable experience to us plebeians, Mr. Parrish."

"Oh, okay. The woman who'll have a Ph.D. and a Juris

Doctorate by the end of the month calls herself a plebeian. Whatever you say, *Doctor* Trent."

With a matter-of-fact smile, she held up an index finger. "Not Dr. Trent yet. I've still got to defend my dissertation, and that's all provided I don't keel over between now and then. Or I guess now it's all provided I don't get nabbed by a serial killer and murdered into an oil drum, huh?"

"It's a very real concern for all of us." He offered her a shrug and a knowing smile.

"Okay." The word was a cross between a snort and a laugh. "Well, thanks for the moment of levity. That's probably the best way to tell someone you think they might be the target of a mad scientist murderer."

"I do what I can."

"You're doing a great job."

"That's nice of you to say," he chuckled. "What was it you were saying about memory?"

As the mirth behind her eyes gave way to unease, he was taken aback by a rush of disappointment.

"Right. Sorry. Memories, they're unreliable, even flash-bulb memories. But in my honest opinion," she shivered again, "based on my interactions with Dr. Schmidt and the knowledge I've got now, I think she was a sociopath."

26

B y the time he saw Winter stride into the cluster of cubicles reserved for the violent crimes division, Noah had unearthed just about every imaginable piece of information about Jenson Leary

And, as best as he could tell, Jenson was a regular guy who had lived a regular life before he was kidnapped and murdered by a deranged killer.

"Hey," he greeted, pushing himself out of the office chair to stand. "How was the drive?"

"Slow." The word was practically a groan as she readjusted the aviator sunglasses atop her head. "Any luck? What did you find about our victim?"

With a sigh, he dropped down to sit. "Pull up a chair."

"That good, huh?" She nodded as she shoved the other office chair to rest beside his. "What did you find?" As she sat, her blue eyes flicked over to take in the spread of pictures and documents on top of his desk.

"Jenson Leary was a normal dude. He was thirty-one, married, no kids, no record. Former military with a bachelor's degree in mechanical engineering from Old Dominion.

He was working on his master's when he disappeared. His wife, Faith Leary, is a supervisor in a call center for a cell phone carrier. She's got a degree, too, but hers is in chemistry. It's from Old Dominion as well, which was how they met."

Winter picked up a picture, studying the man's face. "Sad."

Noah had to agree. "A month or two before he disappeared, the local cops in Fayetteville were looking for a serial rapist around the neighborhood where Jenson and Faith lived. Jenson gave them a DNA sample to rule him out as a suspect, but they found their man before it was entered into the database, and no one thought to enter the info after the fact. A new chief came onboard and began whipping the department into shape. Had them update records, and the DNA was finally entered."

"Way to go, chief," Winter muttered, thinking of how much time that could have been saved had the information been available weeks ago.

"Since learning of Jenson's identification, we also learned that his head injury occurred when he was twelve. He was riding a bike without a helmet, and he wrecked it. Nothing suspicious, no foul play, just a legitimate accident."

"But?"

"But he lived in Sioux City, Iowa at the time, and they life flighted him to a hospital in Minneapolis. The same hospital where Autumn had her surgery, and I'll give you one guess who his surgeon was."

"Catherine Schmidt," Winter breathed. "What about Ladwig? Did this guy have any connection to him?"

"He saw a psychiatrist while he was at Old Dominion, something to do with recurring migraines. He went to a shrink because he thought it might've had to do with stress. At least that's what his wife said, so that's what he told her. It wasn't Ladwig, but…" he paused to hold up an index finger,

"I looked them up, and surprise, surprise. Guess who was at the same conference as them?"

"Ladwig."

"Right. Now, conferences about psychiatric topics don't necessarily mean that everyone there knows one another, but I think it's enough."

She wrinkled her nose. "Enough for what?"

"Enough to go have a chat with our favorite psychiatrist," he answered, closing the folder with a slap. "See what he knows about Catherine Schmidt and Jenson Leary."

"What about Jane Doe?" she wondered after a brief moment of quiet.

"Nothing yet, but Bree just finished getting a court order from a judge. We should have a list of all Dr. Schmidt's patients by the end of the day. Then, it's just a matter of matching up the one who fits the forensic anthropologist's picture of Jane Doe. We match that, plus the type of head injury and the approximate time she went missing, and we should have a tentative ID. Enough to dig around some more to find a connection between her and Ladwig too."

Propping an elbow atop the desk, she met his gaze as she leaned in closer. "What if it's not Ladwig? I didn't see him, so what if he's not who we're looking for?"

"You saw his name, though. When you were looking for information about Catherine Schmidt. That's something, right?"

"I suppose," she sighed.

"'I suppose is just about as good as we've got right now, darlin'. We've had someone following Ladwig every day for the last month and a half, but he hasn't given us anything. We don't have probable cause to arrest him, but now that we've got a victim's name, we can ask him what he knows and get a feel for whether or not we're headed in the right direction."

Winter rubbed her temple but didn't seem in any distress as she answered, "True."

"If not, if we still think Catherine Schmidt is our primary suspect, we can get ahold of someone in white collar crimes and see if they can help us track down something that'll tell us where in the hell she went." As he offered her a reassuring smile, he hoped the look was convincing.

Victim identification or not, they were grasping at straws, and they all knew it. Unless Ladwig gave them something, their trail would go cold again.

It would go cold until they found the next man or woman dissolving in a fifty-five-gallon drum.

Lips pursed, Winter finally nodded her agreement. "All right. Yeah. We should go talk to Ladwig."

"Let's do a little more digging around in Jenson's history first. Find out everything we can about him, and then see what we can find out about the conference Ladwig and Catherine Schmidt attended. The more we know, the more likely we are to get something out of him."

"Right, yeah. He's a weird guy, but he's smart. We need to make sure we've got all our bases covered."

His smile felt a little more genuine as Winter's skepticism gave way to cool determination. "The more we know about Jenson, the harder it will be for Ladwig to pull the wool over our eyes."

27

Hands folded in her lap, Autumn sat at the edge of an exam chair as she stared absently at a poster affixed to the back of the closed door. The infographic gave a rundown of the benefits of vaccines, and at the bottom-right corner was a list of sources used for the data.

After an ultrasound of her abdomen had revealed a foreign object pressing on the side of her stomach, the doctor had ordered an x-ray. If the images still didn't reveal specifics about the anomaly, then she would send Autumn to a different part of the hospital for a CT scan.

The whole process was familiar, but the familiarity was as much the reason for her unease as anything.

As the door creaked open, Autumn pulled herself from the moment of contemplation to offer a slight smile to the woman who stepped into the room. Her thoughts threatened to spiral into a mass of anxiety, but she pushed past the rush of worry.

"Well, I've got some good news," the doctor announced as she tucked a translucent, black and white print into a lighted fixture on the wall. Her blue eyes flicked over to Autumn as she tapped the circular shape of the unknown object. "It's not any sort of cancer or infection or anything of that nature. Now, you said you had surgery when you were younger, could you elaborate on that? Is there any way some piece of a medical tool could have broken off and lodged itself somewhere in your body?"

Autumn was already shaking her head before the woman finished. "No." She blinked rapidly. Was that a possibility? "Surely not."

"Have you ever had any other surgery? Anything even close to the abdominal area?" There was skepticism in her visage, and the adrenaline that hit her system made her muscles feel like they had turned to stone.

"No." Her response was flat, her stare unwavering.

"I only ask because, as best as I can tell, this isn't organic."

"Meaning?"

"Meaning someone had to put it there."

"Beg pardon?" Autumn found herself continuing to blink repeatedly as if the gesture would change the doctor's assessment.

"There's no other way it could have gotten there. Interestingly enough, I don't believe it's the source of your stomach pain. That's something we'll have to wait on a few test results for."

Autumn opened and closed her mouth, but all she could do was shake her head. What the hell did that even mean, *someone had put it there*?

If the discussion with Aiden Parrish wasn't so fresh in her mind, she doubted she would have made the sudden connection.

After all, it was the stuff of fiction. Real neurosurgeons didn't implant strange medical devices in their young patients, but real neurosurgeons also didn't perform brain surgery on unwilling victims before they killed them and disposed of their bodies in an oil drum.

"Shit," she spat. She could feel the color drain from her cheeks. "Shit, shit."

"Autumn," the doctor said, a shadow of concern in her pale eyes, "what is it?"

"I don't know." She paused to take in a deep breath. "I don't know what it is, but I think I know who might've put it there, and when. We're in a wing of a hospital, right?" She held up a hand, hating how her fingers trembled. "Don't answer that, I know we are, sorry. How soon can I get scheduled for someone to take this thing out of me?"

"I'm not sure." Brows furrowed, the woman tapped a finger against the clipboard in her arms. "If you think it might be dangerous, we can get you over to the ER."

"Yeah," Autumn replied without hesitation. "Yeah, the ER. Let's do it."

❋

As the haze of unconsciousness slipped away, the air smelled...sterile.

The scent of bleach was faint, but it was enough to tell Autumn that the room in which she lay was clean. But what room *was* she in? Was she at home?

No, Autumn told herself. She wasn't at home. With a groan, she raised a hand to rub her eyes as she yawned. There was a light tug against the inside of her elbow at the motion, and suddenly, the cobwebs in her brain made sense.

Though it was minimally invasive, laparoscopic surgery still required anesthesia, and the first few minutes of consciousness afterward were always fuzzy. Details drifted back one by one as she blinked to clear the film of sleep from her vision.

Aside from the quiet drone of the heartbeat monitor, the room was silent, the din of the hospital muffled by the heavy wooden door at the other end of the dim room.

Along with her wits, her senses returned, and she froze in place as she realized she wasn't the only occupant of the small space. Before the whirlwind of paranoia could rise up to drown her, she glanced over to the solitary chair beside the bed.

Pale eyes fixed on the glowing screen of his smartphone, caramel colored hair neatly styled, tailored suit just as sharp as she remembered, Aiden was the last person she expected to see upon her return to the waking world.

"What are you doing here?" She meant for the question to sound pointed, but her voice was still thick with sleep.

Snapping his gaze away from the device, Aiden Parrish straightened in his seat as his eyes met hers. "You sent me a text."

Autumn drew her brows together. "I did?"

With the faintest smile on his face, he glanced to the phone, tapped the screen a couple times, and held it out for her to see.

The words were blurry at first, but after she blinked a few times and squinted, she could make out the text.

Hey, this is Autumn Trent. You told me to get ahold of you if anything else came up, and even though I'm not 100% sure yet, I think something just came up. I tried to call Noah Dalton, but he didn't answer.

The message then went on to list the address of the hospital as well as the details of her upcoming surgery. As the lingering fog from the anesthesia rolled away, she could begin to recall when she had sent the message.

"Shit," she muttered, pushing herself to sit. A deep sting on her stomach marked the location the surgeon had made for the laparoscopic procedure. At the reminder of the reason for the impromptu surgery, her breath caught in her throat.

"Agent Dalton is following up on a lead right now," Aiden said, pushing up from his chair. "Agent Black is with him. That's probably why they didn't answer your calls."

"A lead?" Autumn echoed as she returned her attention to him.

He nodded. "One of our two suspects, and the only one we can follow-up on right now considering the other one's been missing for fifteen years."

"So, do you have any idea what the hell they pulled out of my stomach just now?" All manner of possibilities had crossed her mind—everything from a literal nickel she could have swallowed as a child to an alien monitoring device.

When he nodded again, his expression turned grave. "It's in the FBI's forensics department now. It's…" He hesitated. As his blue eyes flicked away from hers, he raised one hand to scratch the side of his face. A nervous tic, she noted. She'd have to remember that. "It's a GPS tracking device."

She gaped at him. "A *what*?"

"It's designed for the long-term. It's the same type of technology that biologists use to track animals in the wild, to study their migration and mating patterns. Instead of an ear tag, it's just a little disk, about the size of a watch battery. Our tech people will try to see what they can get from it, but chances are, they won't find much. Those things don't store detailed data, just approximate locations."

Eyes wide, she continued to gape at him as they were blanketed by silence. "What the *fuck*?" she finally managed.

He shook his head. "I think it's safe to say that you just went from *possibly* being the target of a serial killer to *definitely* being the target of a serial killer."

"But you said that Winter and Noah are following up on a lead, right?" she pressed, pain and exhaustion warring with worry and deep fear. And anger. So much anger. "I don't have time for this shit. I defend my dissertation in less than two weeks, and I've still got another week of teaching. Why in the hell couldn't this have happened during my undergrad? Or three weeks from now when I was done with all this shit?"

With an exaggerated shrug, he held out his hands with a hapless look Autumn had never expected to see from the man. "I've never met a killer who's conscientious about their victim's schedule, and I've met a lot of killers. I'm not saying they don't exist. I'm just saying they *probably* don't exist."

At the matter-of-fact tone and the accompanying expression, she couldn't help the laughter from bubbling up her throat. The sound was strained, a bit panicked, but her muscles felt a little less taut afterward.

From her first introduction to the tall, well-dressed man, she had been willingly able to admit to herself how physically attractive he was. In fact, Autumn figured that if she could build a man, he would look a lot like Aiden Parrish.

But until today, she had been sure he was an uptight prick.

To her chagrin, the more she interacted with him, the more attractive he became. The sentiment should have brought her a sense of giddiness, but instead, all she felt was unease. She'd picked up on enough clues to determine he was single, but she could tell he was grappling with a conflicted sense of affection for someone else. Then again, if she was honest with herself, wasn't she doing the same thing?

Black Friday—the day she and her *fiancé* split up—might have been over eight months ago, but the loss still stung when she let her thoughts dwell on the man. Clenching one hand into a fist, she pulled herself away from the moment of solipsism and back to the dim hospital room.

There was a brain surgeon turned serial killer after her,

and she had to defend a lengthy research project in less than two weeks. She didn't have time to think about the man on whom she'd wasted over four years of her life, nor did she have time to contemplate the emotional nuances of her dealings with Aiden Parrish.

I don't have time for any of this shit.

"All right," she said instead. "What now?"

28

As they made their way up the short set of stairs, Winter shot a quick glance to Noah. Neither of them had bothered to change into attire more suited for their profession, and between Noah's plaid button-down shirt and Winter's ripped jeans, they looked like a couple college students who had made off with a pair of FBI jackets.

At least she'd been able to exchange her gladiator sandals for a pair of riding boots stashed away in her trunk. They were far from the most comfortable footwear she owned, but they beat walking up to a suspect's house in open-toed black and silver sandals.

One hand rested casually on the grip of his holstered service weapon, Noah raised the other to rap his knuckles against the rich wooden door.

"Open up," he called. His second knock was more forceful than the first. "Robert Ladwig, this is the Federal Bureau of Investigation. We know you're in there, so open the damn door."

Just as Noah arced his hand back to knock again, Winter heard the metallic lock disengage. Though a crack at first, the door creaked open to reveal a familiar set of green eyes ringed with amber.

Dr. Ladwig had abandoned his glasses in favor of contacts, and the man was still better dressed on his day off than either she or Noah.

"Mr. Lomond," the psychiatrist offered. Each syllable dripped with condescension and sarcasm, and she didn't think his tone could have been any flatter if it had been run over by a steamroller.

As Noah flashed him a disarming smile in response, Winter almost laughed aloud. More than once, she'd been on the receiving end of Noah's aggravating charm.

"Howdy, Dr. Ladwig." His native Texan drawl was thicker, his voice bright and folksy.

Unless his goal was to irritate someone or throw them off guard, she could count on both hands the number of times she'd heard Noah say "howdy."

"What can I do for you, agents?" Leaning against the doorframe, Ladwig crossed both arms over his pale blue dress shirt. His hazel eyes flitted up and down as he took in her and Noah's attire. "Is it casual Friday at the FBI?"

"Sure is," she replied.

"It's part of the bureau's effort to maintain a friendly work environment," Noah explained. "It's the little things, you know?"

"Whatever you say, Agent *Lomond.*"

Noah replied to the skepticism with a wide smile. "You mind if we come in?"

"Tell me what you want, and I'll think about it."

Well, Winter would give credit where it was due. Robert Ladwig didn't display so much as a hint of apprehension at the unexpected visit from two FBI agents.

"We're here to talk to you about one of your colleagues,"

Winter advised. "We think they're involved in a case we've been investigating."

"With all due respect, Agent Black, that doesn't tell me much. I have many *colleagues*. Maybe you and Mr. Lomond here could be a little more specific?"

"All right." Noah chuckled as he pushed his sunglasses to the top of his head. "You can cut the shit, Ladwig. You know who I am, don't you?"

"Nope." The word might as well have been acid, and Dr. Ladwig might as well have been a lizard.

Reaching into the back pocket of his dark jeans, Noah offered him a sarcastic smile. When he flipped open his badge, Dr. Ladwig's countenance changed little.

"Special Agent Noah Dalton. Sorry for any confusion."

Ladwig rolled his eyes.

If she let them, Winter assumed Dr. Ladwig and Noah would have stood on the covered porch and exchanged verbal blows with one another until the sun went down.

"Catherine Schmidt," she said.

Noah and the doctor both snapped their heads to regard her with puzzled stares.

"Who?" the psychiatrist asked, his brows furrowed. As best as Winter could tell, the confusion was genuine.

What in the *hell* was going on?

"A pediatric neurosurgeon." She kept her intent stare on him. "Blonde hair, light brown eyes. About five-five. Mid-fifties by now. We've got a picture if you think that'd help. And, just real quick, it's supposed to get up to about ninety degrees today, so it'd be great if we could have this discussion indoors."

Long minutes passed before Ladwig responded with, "I'm perfectly comfortable here."

Winter shrugged. "It's still up to you, but if you want to let us bake out here on your porch, then I'll have to make some calls and get a warrant to search your place a little later today. I might just do it out of spite, to be honest. These jackets don't do much to keep us cool."

Stepping to the side, Dr. Ladwig pulled open the door. "Come on in, agents." He waved a hand to the foyer, his attempt to hide a scowl unsuccessful.

From the entrance, through the spacious kitchen and to the dining room, the place was spotless.

Golden rays from the midafternoon sun caught the polished granite of the breakfast bar, and just beyond the French doors, the turquoise waters of an in-ground pool glittered.

"Nice place," Noah remarked.

"Thanks." The irritability had not so much as lessened from Dr. Ladwig's voice.

As Winter leaned forward to peer around the arched doorway that separated the dining room from the living area, she could feel Ladwig's stare on her. She hated how much he knew about her history.

Splayed open at one end of a gray sectional was a carry-on travel bag.

"Going somewhere?" She didn't bother to look over to him as she posed the question.

Atop a coffee table was a laptop, and though she couldn't be sure from the distance, she thought she spotted a red glow on the side of the computer.

"I am," Ladwig answered. From her periphery, she saw him glance back and forth between her and Noah.

"Where're you headed?" Noah asked.

When her eyes met his, she inclined her chin in the direction of the computer.

"Maine." The doctor's response was crisp and curt.

"Where in Maine?"

"The southern part," he replied. "Agent Black, is there something I can help you with?"

She shrugged as she stepped beneath the arch. "Any particular reason you're headed to southern Maine, Dr. Ladwig?"

"I grew up there."

"That laptop." She waved a hand at the coffee table. "That's an ASUS touchscreen, right? Sorry, I'm looking into getting a new laptop, and Best Buy sold its floor model, so I haven't been able to take a look at it. Would you mind if I?" She pointed from the computer to herself and back as she edged her way past Noah and into the high-ceilinged room.

"I'd really rather you didn't." But he made no move to stop her. "It's the computer I use for work, so I'd just as soon you didn't poke around on it." He narrowed his eyes as she continued in the laptop's direction. "But it doesn't look like you're going to listen to me, so go right ahead. Yes, it's an ASUS touchscreen. I bought it at Costco, not Best Buy."

"Costco?" Noah echoed. "I wouldn't have guessed. I've been looking for some new furniture, so I'll have to keep it in mind."

As Winter neared the couch and the open laptop, the red glow was unmistakable.

There was something on the flash drive plugged into the side.

Though she was sure Ladwig's attention was still fixed on her, she tuned out his and Noah's one-sided conversation as she dropped to sit.

In the center of the standard issued Windows background was a box, and in that box was a progress bar. As she leaned closer to read the text, she took in a sharp breath.

Deleting files, 77% complete.

"Shit," she spat.

Tapping a finger against the trackpad, she pressed the

"cancel" button at least six times, though the progress bar stopped after the first frenzied click. Her pulse rushed in her ears as she pulled up the contents of the flash drive—the same contents Ladwig had been more than three-quarters of the way through deleting.

Each file was labeled with a series of numbers and letters, and while some of them corresponded to recent dates, there was plenty that made little sense. Less than halfway down the page, she saw a red glow manifest around the edges of an icon labeled "bl0715192145."

She felt the rush of ice water through her veins as the document lit up the screen. At the top, each photograph was marked with a timestamp. The first was July fifteenth at quarter 'til ten at night.

Keys in one hand, green eyes fixed on the distance, was Noah. Though no buildings were in the shot, Winter could tell that the picture had been taken in the parking lot of their apartment complex.

The next photo was stamped a minute later as Noah pulled open the driver's side door of his pickup.

Winter remembered that night. They had been awake since five in the morning, and as they combed through the case file for the seven-hundredth time, Noah offered to go pick up some late dinner.

"What the *fuck*," she murmured to herself.

"What?" Noah asked.

"He's been stalking you." With one hand on the textured grip of the Glock at her side, she rose to her feet.

"He's been stalking *me*?" Noah echoed, his voice incredulous.

"Yes. Seventy-seven percent of the information on that flash drive was deleted, but there are a whole lot of pictures still left. Pictures taken *at our complex*."

Noah snapped his wide-eyed stare from her to Dr. Ladwig. "What? Dude, why? What the hell?"

"Am I under arrest?" Dr. Ladwig grated. There was an unmistakable glint of indignation in his green and amber eyes, but behind the anger was a sentiment Winter had expected less.

Fear. Genuine, unabashed fright.

"You've been stalking a federal agent." Silver flashed as Noah produced a pair of stainless-steel handcuffs.

When Dr. Ladwig spoke again, the word came from between clenched teeth.

"Lawyer."

❄

WEEKS HAD PASSED since I performed Jensen Leary's autopsy. Weeks without so much as a new hypothesis. Robert had done a piss poor job of locating the second patient he'd seen with the same brain abnormality as Patient Zero, and I was back to the starting line.

I'd decided to let some time pass after the body of Jenson Leary was unearthed at the edge of the city, but the monotony of the last month and a half had finally ground away my last nerve.

If they'd figured out anything from Jenson's body, I'd have heard about it by now.

After all, thirteen years had passed since they discovered Megan Helfer, and they were no closer to uncovering her identity.

I did my due diligence to ensure the bodies wouldn't be traced back to me. Even if they *were* identified, the trail would lead back to Catherine Schmidt, not Sandra Evans. The change in identity had been a spur-of-the-moment decision, but not a day went by when I wasn't glad I'd done it.

Catherine had been slapped with a hefty malpractice suit after one of my patient's parents found the little tracking device I left in their son's abdomen.

The slip-up was entirely on me. I had decided to try a new spot for the implant in hopes that there would be less risk of discovery. As it turned out, the complete opposite was true.

But I owned my mistakes. I learned from them, and I never made the same error twice.

With a sip from a glass of homemade iced tea, I refreshed the webpage. There were two of them nearby, one within a two hour drive, and the other right here in the city of Richmond.

It seemed convenient to go for the young woman in town, but I'd learned long ago that convenience was rarely, if ever, *convenient*. If it was too good to be true, then it wasn't true.

Though I never truly forgot any of the children on whom I performed surgeries, this young woman occupied a special part of my memory.

She had been handed over to the state while in a medically induced coma, and not long after she was discharged from the hospital, her mother had overdosed on heroin and died.

But despite the turbulence of her upbringing, there had been a spark in Autumn Nichols' eyes that I seldom saw in someone her age.

She was resilient, and someday, she'd make it out of her little corner of hell.

I knew it then, and now, seventeen years later, she'd proven me right. She was a Ph.D. student in a track of study that was one of the most competitive graduate programs in any school. Forensic psychology.

No, I didn't want Autumn.

Not yet.

I still hadn't progressed far enough in my research, and I didn't want Autumn to die. I wanted her to be a success story, to present her to academic circles as a prime example of how brilliance could shine through the gray sludge of adversity.

I could make the drive.

As I set my glass of tea on a cloth coaster, the front screen of an archaic flip-phone lit up. The device buzzed an annoying dance on the glass table, but I scooped it up and opened it before the second ring.

"Yes," I answered.

"It's me," replied a familiar, gruff voice.

"Mr. Parker."

I kept my response as cool and composed as always, but the truth was that the man set my teeth on edge. He was a pretentious asshole, and every time I was forced to deal with him, I liked him a little less.

"They've got the psychiatrist in custody," the man started. "You're going to want to lay low, Sandra. I just got a call from Ladwig. He hasn't said anything to the Feds, not yet."

My tongue felt thick in my mouth as I echoed, "Not yet?"

"They've got something. I don't know what it is, but they've got something solid, something they can hang their hat on. We need to get their eyes off you, and we need to do it *permanently*."

"You're going to have him take the fall for it?" she surmised, her voice flat. "He's got the information I need, Mr. Parker."

"And he'll still be able to get it to you when he's in a prison cell." Parker's response left no room for debate.

"A prison cell? That's not like you, Mr. Parker."

"For now." His response was cryptic, but its meaning wasn't lost on me.

Robert Ladwig was about to confess to the murder of

Jensen Leary. And then, after he'd given us all the useful information he possessed, he would die.

❄

"WHY AM I STILL WITH YOU?" Autumn asked.

Locking the screen of his phone, Aiden turned to regard her.

The shadows beneath her green eyes had become more prominent as the evening wore on, but she had gone through some effort to keep the disheveled look at bay. Her ponytail was neat, and her subtle cat-eye eyeliner had not so much as smudged.

"You're still with me because there was a serial killer tracking you for seventeen years," he answered after a brief spell of quiet. "Sorry to say, Ms. Trent, but you're going to be seeing a lot more of us from now on."

"Motherfucker," she muttered under her breath. "I just got out of the hospital. I just had *surgery* a few hours ago. Isn't there some kind of law against keeping me in the waiting room at the FBI building for an unspecified amount of time?"

He flashed her a sarcastic smile. "You're the one with the Juris Doctorate. You tell me."

She rolled her eyes. "You've got the tracking device now, don't you? I don't really see what else you need me for."

"We've got it," he confirmed with a nod. "But that doesn't mean you're in the clear. They've been watching you for a long time, and they not only know where you live, but your daily routine, probably down to the minute. The plan is to leave it on in hopes we'll draw them to us. Not you. But still…" He left the statement unfinished and glanced back to her.

With a resigned sigh, she leaned back in her chair and stretched her legs. "But still, they're a serial killer with a medical degree, and they've been stalking me for seventeen years. How long am I going to need a babysitter, then?"

Now, it was his turn to sigh. "I don't know. I'm waiting to hear back from Agent Dalton and Agent Black. Hopefully, their lead gave them something worthwhile."

"And I'm just stuck here waiting until they get back?"

"I'm here too," he reminded her, tapping an index finger against his chest for emphasis.

"This is your job. You're getting paid for this." She crossed her arms over her zip-up hoodie.

"Well, yes and no. I'm salary, so, not really. It's not like I'm getting overtime for staying past four."

"Then why are you just hanging out in the waiting room with me? Don't you have some super secret FBI stuff you ought to be doing right now instead of babysitting a witness? I figured this would be above your paygrade, *SSA* Parrish."

"This case..." He waited until she met his gaze. "It started thirteen years ago. A colleague and I worked it, and we couldn't even figure out who our victim was. It got shelved until Jenson Leary turned up outside town. I don't think there's any way that Jane Doe and Jenson are the only two people this person has killed. Based on the precision and how damn thorough they were, they aren't new to this."

Autumn lifted her chin. "I think that's pretty clear."

"We might have that tracking device now, but I'm not willing to bet that'll be enough to stop them from searching for you. That's not to say I doubt another agent could do this, but I'm here to see this through. And right now, it looks like that means 'babysitting a witness.'"

In the silence that followed, her green eyes remained fixed on his. For the most part, he had been truthful in his explanation. Her dry sense of humor and her good looks were just an added bonus.

There was no doubt that Autumn Trent was a beautiful

woman, but he had to wonder if he felt so drawn to her because she reminded him of someone else. Someone who, with each passing day, seemed to drift farther and farther away.

"Okay," she finally said. "But, just a fair warning, I'm probably going to keep pissing and moaning until I get some food. I haven't eaten at all today."

He pushed aside the doubts about Winter—doubts about himself—to offer her a slight smile. "Then, while we wait for them to get back, let's go get some food."

29

Aside from asking Robert Ladwig if he wanted something to drink, neither Noah nor Winter had spoken a word to the man since his arrival in the FBI building. For two hours, Ladwig was alone in an interview room while he waited for his lawyer. And for most of those two hours, Noah and Winter had watched the man from behind a pane of one-way mirrored glass.

They'd stepped away after the pricey defense attorney arrived, and at least another twenty minutes passed before the man indicated that his client was ready to talk to them. Their case was almost entirely circumstantial, and the successful interrogation of Robert Ladwig was the only way to lend weight to the evidence they did have.

The interview had to be flawless.

In an effort to maintain impartiality, Winter had suggested that Noah and Bree take over. She and Aiden Parrish would watch the exchange to provide backup and ensure no aspect of Ladwig's dialogue was overlooked.

As soon as the SSA came to mind, a flicker of movement

from the open doorway snapped Noah's attention away from the one-way glass.

Fluorescence from the hallway caught the silver band of the man's pricey watch as he raised a plastic baggie for them to see. Though Noah's first inclination was to mentally berate Parrish for the absurd amount of money he'd undoubtedly spent on the timepiece, he stopped himself. Watches had never caught Noah's interest, but his granddad had a whole collection, and any one of them could rival the value of Parrish's.

"What's that?" Bree's query drew him back to the dim room.

"A GPS tracking device," Aiden answered as he set the bag on top of a wooden table. "It's what our perp used to keep tabs on their victims."

"Shit," Noah muttered. "Where'd you get it?"

Parrish's blue eyes flitted from him to Winter and then Bree before he answered. "From your friend, Autumn."

"What?" he and Winter asked simultaneously.

Aiden ignored their outburst. "There's only one person who could've put it there, and that person wasn't Robert Ladwig. That means that at the least, Catherine Schmidt is or was a co-conspirator. Your theory still holds. He might have worked with her and then killed her after she lost her usefulness."

A determined glint in her dark eyes, Bree pushed herself to stand and glanced over to Noah.

Wordlessly, he nodded.

Showtime.

Rolling up the sleeves of his white dress shirt, Noah followed Bree to the interrogation room. She rapped her knuckles against the metal surface as she pushed open the heavy door. With a wide smile that was mostly feigned, Noah nodded a greeting to the psychiatrist and his lawyer.

For the first time since they'd seen him that afternoon, the man looked worried. Until now, his visage had been cold and steely, and he hadn't so much as twitched when he was handcuffed.

Maybe his attorney had gone over the situation, and he'd realized he was cornered. But was he cornered?

Not even close, Noah thought.

They had found barely enough to arrest him, much less press charges. Sure, he had hired a private investigator to follow Noah around for the better part of six weeks, but that was hardly illegal. After all, Noah had provided false contact information, false insurance information, and false medical information to Dr. Ladwig.

Hiring a PI to figure out why Brady Lomond had falsified all those records was well within the realm of possibility.

But Noah knew there was more to the story. He knew there was something they'd missed, a detail that would put all the little pieces together like a damn puzzle, and he knew that Robert Ladwig was involved.

When he turned his attention to the lawyer, the feigned amiability vanished from Noah's face. The man was well-dressed—his tailored suit had likely cost as much as Parrish's—but that was where any resemblance to a white-collar professional ended.

Though he was seated, Noah could tell the man stood close to his six-four. His lean frame filled out enough of the expensive suit to show that he kept in peak physical shape. Jet-black hair was brushed straight away from his face, and then there were his eyes.

They were dark brown, and they brimmed with the same malicious cunning he would have expected from Charles Manson or Jim Jones. Even as he looked away from the unnerving sight, he tensed at the cold caress of a shiver that threatened.

"Evening, Dr. Ladwig." He forced the agreeable expression back to his face. "I know we've already met, but I'm Agent Dalton. This…" he paused to gesture to where Bree stood in one shadowy corner, "is Agent Stafford."

"Agents," the lawyer said. "Pleasure to meet you. I'm Chase Parker, and I'll be representing Dr. Ladwig."

"Then you know why we're here, right?" Bree's voice was as sweet as her smile was condescending.

Chase nodded. "I do." He turned to Robert Ladwig with an expectant look. "We've discussed it, and my client and I would like to make a deal."

Noah could hardly keep the stupefied look at bay. "A deal?" he echoed after the stunned silence. "What kind of deal?"

"A plea deal." The lawyer's smile was full of teeth. "A full confession in exchange for a guarantee that the death penalty is off the table."

This didn't make any sense. There wasn't enough evidence to frighten a competent lawyer into a full confession, not unless…

The flash drive. Ladwig might have made a valiant effort to erase the data, but the Bureau's tech department would be able to restore the majority of the information.

"All right." The clatter of the chair legs against tile followed Bree's laconic agreement.

As Bree sat at Noah's side, he still couldn't shake the feeling that there was an important aspect of the case they were missing. Something with the lawyer was wrong, something with Ladwig was wrong, something with this whole damn investigation was wrong.

"Let's hear it." Bree's composure hadn't faltered.

Coughing into one hand to clear his throat, metal clattered against metal as Ladwig rested his arms atop the table.

"Jenson Leary." His green and amber eyes shifted from Noah to Bree and back. "And Megan Helfer."

He could almost hear Winter and Aiden scramble to check Ladwig's statement for accuracy.

And sure enough, as Ladwig continued on, there were aspects of his story that hadn't been released to the public. Information only the killer could have known, such as both victims' history of head trauma, the missing brains, and the precision with which they had been cut apart.

His alleged motive was straightforward enough: scientific curiosity.

Though he'd hesitated when they brought up his relationship with Catherine Schmidt, he admitted that her work as a neurosurgeon had been behind the need to know more about the inner workings of human brains. He'd listened to her talk about changes in personality after damages to different lobes, and Ladwig had become obsessed with the idea that he could correct deviant behavior with the right surgical procedure.

Noah pointed out that scientists at the beginning of the 1900s had already come up with a specific surgery to alleviate criminality. A lobotomy.

At the mention of the draconian method, Ladwig only scoffed.

He hadn't wanted to give his patients a lobotomy. He wanted them to come out of the procedure as functioning members of society, not drooling messes. When the psychiatrist speculated on the barbarity of a lobotomy, Noah almost laughed aloud.

As the recount drew to a close, he and Bree exchanged glances. He didn't miss the wariness behind her dark eyes.

"All right, gentlemen," Noah said, tapping his palm against the stainless-steel table as he stood. "This is quite a bit of information, so if you'll excuse us for just a second."

Ladwig followed their movements with his eyes, and try as he might, Noah couldn't get a read on the man's emotional state.

Robert Ladwig was like a brick wall. Maybe he *was* a sociopath.

Noah had no substantive reason to doubt him, especially when he considered all the details Ladwig had revealed about the two murders.

Before he and Bree even stepped into the adjoining room, Parrish was already shaking his head. Winter sat at the table in front of the one-way mirror, her lips pursed, blue eyes fixed on the psychiatrist and his lawyer.

"What?" Noah asked.

"I don't believe him." Parrish reached out to grab the baggie with the coin-sized tracking device. "He didn't say a single word about this. Not even a vague mention of it when you two asked him how he found his victims. Seems like an important piece to leave out, don't you think?"

"A little," Noah said through gritted teeth. As much as he was loath to admit, the man was right. He usually was.

"We'll ask him about it," Bree decided. "You said that's from Autumn, right?"

"Right." Parrish nodded. "Ask him about the tracking devices he planted in his patients' heads."

"That was in Autumn's *head*?" Noah's eyes widened as he looked back up to Parrish.

"No." Aiden's voice was flat. "It was in her abdomen. Which is why you're going to say it was in her head. Then if he agrees with it, or goes along with it, we know he's not the one who put it there."

Jaw clenched, Noah nodded, looked to Bree, and tilted his chin in the direction of the doorway.

He pushed past the sudden wave of concern for Autumn. Though he and Winter had each missed a call and a text from her earlier that afternoon, the messages were vague. They sure as hell hadn't alluded to a tracking device that was surgically implanted in her body.

First, he had been pulled away from their outing, and then he'd failed to answer an urgent call.

And since he and Winter hadn't picked up, Autumn had been forced to resort to Aiden Parrish, of all people. He wouldn't be surprised if she hated all three of them by the time this debacle was over.

But he would have to deal with the pang of guilt later. Right now, he had a series of lies to peel away from a messy truth that was not even guaranteed to get them closer to the killer.

"Sorry about that." He flashed a quick smile to Ladwig and his lawyer.

"So, Dr. Ladwig," Bree started as she took her seat. "These 'patients' of yours, you said you kept track of them from when they were patients of Dr. Schmidt. How did you do that, exactly? I mean, did you actively follow them throughout their lives? That seems like a hell of a lot of work."

The dark-haired lawyer leaned forward, and as he spoke to Ladwig in hushed tones, the psychiatrist's grim countenance didn't change.

"I tracked them," Ladwig said.

"How?" Noah pressed.

"With a GPS tracking device."

"In their head?" he asked.

This time, Ladwig merely nodded.

"Why would you put it in their head? And *how'd* you put it in their head?" Bree's voice was as tense as Noah's muscles felt.

"That's where they had surgery," Ladwig replied as if the answer should have been obvious. "I went to med school, too, agents. Implanting a tracking device in someone's head after they had surgery wasn't hard."

Bree pursed her lips and tapped an index finger against her cheek. "Why their head, though? You had to know that after a traumatic head injury they'd have MRIs, PET scans, CT scans of their head. Wouldn't one of those find it? Not to mention, if it's metal and they went through an MRI." With a cluck of her tongue, she shook her head. "Well, you've got a medical degree. I'm sure I don't need to elaborate, do I?"

Aside from a flicker of wariness in the man's green and amber eyes, he didn't balk.

"Are you covering for someone, Ladwig?" Propping both elbows atop the table, Noah leaned forward and narrowed his eyes at the man. "Why would you give us a false confession?"

"False?" the lawyer echoed. "You heard what my client said."

"We did." Noah offered the man a wry smile as he nodded. "And maybe it seems like an easy open and shut case, but that's not how we operate around here. See, we like to put away the people who actually *did* the crime. And your client is full of shit. We've got one of your tracking devices."

Ladwig gasped. "How?"

Even the attorney looked stunned.

"Pulled it out of a woman's stomach earlier today. And I mean, honestly, Ladwig, can you even *do* brain surgery? Much less keep someone alive after you cut into their head? It was a stretch, I'll be honest. Pinning you as the mastermind mad scientist here." Noah laughed, and Ladwig's face turned just the shade of purple he'd been hoping for.

"That's quite—"

The doctor let out a whoosh of air as his lawyer elbowed him in the ribs.

A part of Noah smirked, but the other part couldn't stop staring at the attorney. What the hell was going on?

He looked at Ladwig again. "Now, I'll tell you what, gentlemen. When we do find the killer, and we *will* find them, this can go one of two ways."

Chase Parker regained his composure first. "Do tell." He looked bored, but his pupils were still dilated, Noah noted.

"First," he held up one finger, "your client can tell us who he's covering for and we'll go easy on him when it comes time for sentencing. Or," he raised a second finger, "you can keep your mouth shut, and then when the *real* killer's case goes to trial, you'll go on trial right along with them. And I'm afraid our 'no death penalty' deal won't extend that far."

For what felt like an eternity, Ladwig's intent stare was on Noah. The silence was so complete, so pervasive, that they could have heard a pin drop in the next room over.

"You've got twenty-four hours." Bree's voice broke through the quiet like a thunderclap.

Twenty-four hours or twenty-four minutes, Noah thought. It wouldn't make a difference. Ladwig's stare told him everything he needed to know about the level of cooperation they could expect.

They were on their own.

He just didn't understand why the man was offering himself up as the scapegoat.

30

Autumn leapt from her seat as soon as Aiden Parrish stepped through the doorway, then immediately regretted the movement. Her stomach hurt like a son of a bitch, but she'd be damned if she let the BAU chief witness it.

She had been seated in the same waiting area for the past forty-five minutes, and she was about to lose her mind. There were only so many games of solitaire a person could play before their sanity slipped away.

Despite the target a serial killer had painted on her back, she had decided to leave if no one came to update her in the next fifteen minutes.

There was more to Aiden Parrish's motivation to keep her around than he let on, but she couldn't be sure of the precise reason for the man's sudden interest in her. All she knew was that his motive was less than professional.

Maybe the attention should have made her giddy. Maybe the idea that such a smart, handsome man had taken an interest in her should have made her cheeks flush, her stomach flutter, and her mind wander. And maybe it would have if Autumn was a normal twenty-eight-year-old woman.

She was far from naïve, and she suspected that even without the sixth sense that gave her insight into other people's behavior, she would still have been suspicious.

When Winter rounded the corner after Aiden, she was so surprised by the wave of relief that she had to keep herself from stalking over to wrap the woman in a bear hug.

As she made note of Winter's stony expression, however, the cold claw around her stomach kept her rooted in place. Winter looked like she had come from a funeral to discover that someone had wrecked her car.

"What?" Autumn blurted, glancing back and forth between her and Aiden.

"He's not our guy." Even though Autumn's attention was fixed on Winter, Aiden was the first to respond.

Furrowing her brows, she turned to meet the man's steely gaze. "Wait, what? Who the hell did you bring in, then?"

"He is only an accomplice," he answered. "Whoever did the actual killings is still out there."

With a sigh, Winter rubbed her eyes. "I'm sorry, Autumn," she offered.

As the implication became clearer, Autumn only opened and closed her mouth.

So, there was *still* a serial killer out there who had painted a target on her back. Whether or not the Bureau had the tracking device, the killer had watched her movements for long enough to have a detailed outline of her routine, of her address, of her whole damn life.

She cleared her throat. "Then what does that mean for me?"

"For now, it means we're going to make sure there's an agent or a local cop keeping an eye out for you." Though Winter's tone was reassuring and kind, Autumn's stomach dropped.

"For now?" she echoed.

Aiden crossed his arms as he shook his head. "It's not a permanent solution. It's expensive, and it's not a joyous experience for you or anyone else involved."

"But we'll find them," Winter added quickly. She shot an irritable look at the taller man, but Aiden either didn't notice or didn't care. "Catherine Schmidt is our prime suspect now. We just have to find her. Bree has a couple contacts in White Collar Crimes who can expedite the investigation to find out where she went, since it looks like we're dealing with a person who's using a stolen identity."

"Mother*fucker*," Autumn spat. "Well, can I go home now, or do I get a sleeping bag so I can stay in the FBI waiting room?" She knew Aiden and Winter both wanted to keep her safe, but she couldn't help the petulance. She was exhausted and hurting. She'd just had surgery, for heaven's sake.

"No," Aiden started, "I can take you home. We'll get ahold of the local PD and have someone post up outside your apartment building."

Though Winter's glance to Aiden was fleeting, Autumn thought there was enough venom behind her eyes to kill a regiment of soldiers.

She didn't have to touch them to recognize the tension in their dynamic. There were as many unresolved issues between them as there were between Autumn and her most recent ex.

Was that it? Had Winter and Aiden dated?

No, the man would have come up in conversation between either her and Noah or her and Winter. Autumn could tell Noah's affection for Winter went beyond platonic, but he was respectful of her boundaries and valued her friendship.

As Autumn turned her attention back to Aiden, the picture became clearer. *Aiden's* affection for Winter went beyond platonic too. Unlike Noah, however, he was still at war with himself over the feelings. She could see it in the way he looked at her, could hear it in his voice when he addressed her.

But what about Winter? Was she at war with herself over her feelings for Aiden Parrish?

When the corner of Winter's mouth twitched in a faint scowl, she thought she had her answer.

"It's fine." Autumn waved a dismissive hand. "I'll take an Uber. I need to check my stitches, and I'm so sick of this building I don't think I ever want to see it again."

"I was about to leave." Winter took a step toward her. "I'll take you home. If it's alright with you, I'll stay at your place so you don't have to deal with a stranger outside your door all night."

Autumn bit off a weary sigh and nodded. "Yeah, that's fine. Sorry, Mr. Parrish. I'm going to have to go with my friend on this one, even if it means riding in a Civic instead of a Mercedes."

At first, the man looked like he might protest. Why in the hell were he and Winter fighting over her? Were they *really* fighting over her, or was this some sort of pissing match that went with their ill-perceived affections for one another?

She fought against a groan. She had never wanted to be at home as much as she did right now.

"Okay," Aiden finally replied.

Propelled by a sick sense of curiosity, Autumn extended a hand to him and feigned an amiable smile. "Thanks again for the food."

As he accepted the handshake, she wanted to release her grip and sprint out the door, but she held the agreeable expression together until she and Winter turned to leave.

Aiden Parrish might have had an ulterior motive for his actions toward Autumn, but mixed in was a sense of intrigue she hadn't expected. She could only assume that the draw he felt to her was the basis for the conflict that raged in his mind.

Still, she couldn't fault him for the sentiment. The inner turmoil was just one more thing she and Aiden Parrish had in common.

Only, in her case, the bridge had already been burned. Aiden still had a chance to pursue the woman who captivated him so, and Autumn did not have such a luxury.

Neither she nor Winter spoke on their trek out to the familiar little Honda. As Winter turned the key over in the ignition, Autumn fastened her seatbelt and rolled down the window.

"So," she started, her tone as casual as she could manage. "How long have you and Parrish known one another? Seems like you guys must go way back."

A less keen observer might not have noticed how Winter stiffened at the question. "Yeah," she answered. "Um, I've known him since I was about thirteen. So, thirteen years, give or take a couple months."

"Really? How'd you meet an FBI agent when you were thirteen?"

Shadows from the ruddy streetlights shifted along Winter's face as she clenched and unclenched her jaw, and Autumn felt a twinge of guilt. She was prying, and she *hated* when people pried into her past.

"I told you that my parents died when I was younger, right?" Winter's blue eyes flicked over to Autumn as they pulled up to a red light.

"Yeah, I'm sorry. I didn't mean to bring that up. I guess I just thought it might've been a funny story or something."

As Winter shook her head, a faint smile passed over her face. "No, it's all right. Part of being friends is sharing stuff, right?"

Autumn returned the smile and nodded.

"Well, that's how I met Aiden. My parents were both killed when I was thirteen and he, the guy who killed them, he hit me in the back of the head really hard. I think he was trying to kill me, but I woke up from a coma after three months."

"No way." Autumn kept her tone light in hopes it would alleviate some of the wistfulness she saw on Winter's face. "You had a traumatic brain injury too?" Before the light could turn green, Autumn pushed aside some of her auburn hair to point at a jagged scar on the side of her forehead. "I was in a medically induced coma for two weeks."

"Really?" Winter gawked, her eyes wide. "Holy shit. How'd it happen? Did you get smacked in the head by a serial killer too?"

With a snort of laughter, Autumn shook her head. "No. I tripped and fell into the edge of a coffee table."

The lie was so practiced that, these days, it rolled off her lips like it was the truth. But in that moment, she suspected she wasn't the only one of them withholding something.

Winter's moment of wide-eyed disbelief hadn't been the level of surprise Autumn expected. She'd expected a string of four-letter words, repeated utterances of sympathy, or a stunned silence. Instead, Winter reacted the same way Autumn would have expected if she'd announced they had the same favorite flavor of ice cream.

"Well, still." Winter flashed her a smile. "TBIs suck. It sucks that you had one too."

"They do suck." Autumn chuckled, pushing her friend's demeanor out of her thoughts. "Sorry, I didn't mean to interrupt you."

Winter shook her head. "No, I appreciate the levity. It's been a long time since it happened, but it can still be hard to talk about. My parents, they were both killed by a serial killer named Douglas Kilroy. His moniker was The Preacher."

Though Autumn wanted to gawk at her friend, to vocalize her awe, she swallowed the sentiment down and merely nodded instead. Douglas Kilroy might have been fascinating from a psychological perspective, but the man had killed the parents of Autumn's good friend.

"I followed that case," she replied. "That guy was a serious piece of work. I'm sorry you had to go through that."

"It was hard," Winter said, her voice lowered. "I won't lie about that. But my grandparents raised me, and they're both wonderful. They took me in like I was their own kid. That's why I wanted to be an FBI agent, though. So I could track down Kilroy and put him away."

Autumn could tell the recollection had become more difficult. "Maybe someday you can tell me about it."

With a wistful smile, Winter nodded. "Yeah, someday."

Autumn hesitated before she spoke again.

She wanted her friend to know she wasn't alone, but at the same time, she didn't want to reveal all the messy details of her relationship with her biological parents. Maybe she should have been proud of how far she'd come, but when she thought back to her childhood, all she felt was shame and isolation.

"My parents are gone too." She was sure at least a full minute of silence had passed before she broke the spell.

At the last possible second, she'd decided she didn't want Winter to feel like she was alone.

Autumn knew the feeling well, and as long as she could help it, none of her friends would be forced to contend with that level of isolation when she was around them. She might have felt like Winter was holding something back, but she didn't know what that *something* was.

For all she knew, it could have been a case detail kept

secret for her safety, or to avoid compromising the integrity of their investigation.

"I'm sorry," Winter murmured.

"It's okay." Autumn's tone was just as quiet. "I was eleven at the time. Honestly, they weren't great parents. Mom overdosed on heroin, and I don't even know what happened to my dad. He just up and disappeared. Probably got killed and buried in the woods somewhere for ripping off a dealer or something. But, like you said about your grandparents, my adopted parents took me in like I was theirs."

Winter's smile was tiny. "I'm glad they were good to you."

"They were my foster parents to begin with, and they were just like those foster parents you see in feel-good movies. They'd never had any kids of their own, and they took their duties as fosters really seriously. I remember them getting a steady flow of thank-you letters from kids who were the first in their families to graduate high school or get accepted into college."

"Wow," Winter said, her voice a bit thick. She cleared her throat. "That sucks, but it's amazing all at the same time. They sound like great people."

"Probably the type of people who would be friends with your grandparents." Autumn grinned as Winter looked over to her.

"Probably," Winter laughed.

The only person with whom Autumn had ever discussed details of her parents was her ex, and they had been in a committed relationship for close to a year before she offered up as much as she had told Winter. Though she told herself she should be nervous about confiding in another person, she was relieved.

❄

With my back propped against a pile of pillows, I'd just opened my newest, hefty paperback novel when I heard the obnoxious clatter of my burner phone. I couldn't remember the last time it had received so many calls in a single day, and I felt the corner of my mouth turn down at the thought.

As I scooped up the device to glance at the screen, my scowl deepened. The number was the same that had called me earlier.

"Yes," I greeted, my voice as flat as I could manage.

"We need to talk," the man replied.

"About what, Mr. Parker?"

"They know about the tracking devices. They recovered one from a woman, and they brought it up during the interrogation. How many of those things do you have out there?"

My heart picked up speed, and I willed it down to its normal rate. "Only a few." I'd only been willing to take the risk with the patients who were most auspicious. Jensen had been one, and now there were only three left. One was an hour north of the city, one was *in* the city, and the other was still in Minnesota.

Which meant if the FBI had discovered one, there was only one likely source.

"Did they say who?" I didn't want it to be Autumn. She was so resilient, so *promising*.

"No, but everything I gathered from them indicates that whoever it is, they're local. They had the device in their possession, and it'd have to be someone near here for them to have gotten ahold of it so fast." There was a rare note of foreboding in Mr. Parker's words, and I didn't like the implications of his tone.

But if I lied, if I kept Autumn's name to myself, he would know. Parker *always* knew. I didn't know the first thing about the man, but he knew everything about almost anyone with whom he worked. It was a one-sided relationship, and it always had been, but what choice did I have? As much as I disliked him, I knew well enough how dangerous Parker was.

"I need their name, Sandra. I need their name, and I need to know how well they knew you so I can figure out how much we've got to worry about." The chill was back in his voice, and honestly, I thought I preferred that to the menace.

Autumn might have been promising, but she wasn't nearly enough for me to compromise my own wellbeing.

"Don't kill her if you can manage it." I closed my eyes. "Her name is Autumn Nichol. She's in Richmond. She was a patient of mine seventeen years ago. I doubt she has a better recollection of me than anyone else."

"You're going to need to lay low. Even lower than you are now. Take some time off work, and I'll call you back when it's clear."

I clenched my jaw. How was I supposed to manage *that*? Maybe Parker could take time off work whenever *he* wanted, but that wasn't how hospital jobs worked.

"I can't just 'take some time off,'" I grated.

"You're smart, Sandra. You'll figure it out."

31

Winter's sore muscles protested with each step she took toward her couch. In part to offer security and in part because she was interested, Winter had gone with Autumn to her Krav Maga classes over the past few days. Even though her friend was still healing from surgery, Autumn still pushed herself further than most post-op patients should.

Despite Winter's disciplined workout routine, the hand-to-hand combat technique employed muscles she didn't normally utilize during her morning run. She didn't care. Part of her enjoyed the pain. Needed it, even. It helped with the frustration building through her system.

In the eight days since the arrest of Robert Ladwig, the man hadn't offered another word. The majority of their communication with the psychiatrist had been conducted through his lawyer, Chase Parker.

Neither Ladwig nor Parker's adamancy of Ladwig's guilt had so much as waivered in the last week. Any time one of them poked a hole in his statement, he put up a brick wall.

Aiden had been the first to propose that the disgraced psychiatrist was frightened. According to Aiden, there was no other reason a person would take the fall for a crime they hadn't committed.

While Winter agreed with his assessment to some extent, she also thought the story was more complicated than Robert Ladwig being scared.

Besides, she reasoned, Ladwig had spent ten years of his adult life in the armed forces. The details of his combat record were still a mystery to them—the military was loath to release such sensitive information, even when it was associated with a murder suspect—but there was no doubt that the man had seen combat.

With ten years of military experience, what exactly would scare Dr. Ladwig so much that he would willingly submit himself to a life sentence in a federal prison?

Winter's theory held that Ladwig was just as guilty of the murders as his co-conspirator, and he had decided not to give them up due to some twisted sense of honor. Though Bree agreed, Noah was reluctant.

For how often he and Aiden wound up on the same side of an argument, she was surprised they hadn't become friends. Then again, maybe the commonalities were as much the reason for their dislike of one another than anything.

According to Autumn, Aiden had a "thing" for Winter. She was unwilling to elaborate beyond the cryptic remark, and Winter had merely laughed off the suggestion.

As the week progressed, she became even more certain that Autumn's observation was inaccurate. The thought frustrated her, but she wasn't sure it *should* have been so frustrating.

Why would she *want* Aiden to have a "thing" for her?

Sure, her attraction to the tall, dark, and handsome Aiden

Parrish had been inexorable during her high school years, but since then, she'd learned the necessary components for a good relationship. Trust, common ground, shared values, all were part of the foundation for a relationship that was lasting.

If she pictured herself with Aiden, could she tick off a single item on that short list?

She'd been given no reason to doubt his motives since after the Douglas Kilroy investigation, but the Machiavellian tactics they'd both employed in those months was not easy to forget.

And did she even know any of Aiden's interests outside his professional life, much less share them with him? Even though she'd known him for thirteen years, the majority of their discussions had revolved around work, or at least around topics related to the criminal justice system.

But she couldn't shake the recollection of their first interaction after she returned from her three-month hiatus. When he'd made a sarcastic remark about his secret love of Mountain Dew Code Red, it was like no time had passed between them at all.

That was always how it felt with Aiden. No matter how long they were apart, they could always pick up where they'd left off, and the transition was seamless. Still, that was hardly enough to form the basis for a lasting relationship.

Then, there was Noah.

She *knew* Noah. She knew he adored cats, that he didn't care for big dogs, that his favorite music genre was country but he held a lesser known love for alternative and grunge rock from the 1990s. She knew he had a special place in his heart for Italian food, and she had watched him tear up at the end of the third *Lord of the Rings* movie.

He didn't hide his emotions like Aiden. If Noah was angry, sad, or a combination of both, she knew about it. She didn't have to drag an emotional response out of him like she did with Aiden. In fact, most of the time, it was the other way around with her and Noah.

Maybe Aiden's interest in Autumn was for the best. If anyone could understand what was running through that man's head, it would be the soon-to-be doctor.

Still, Aiden's excuses and logic for his routine visits to Winter's friend did not sit well.

Shit.

Was she jealous?

And if she was, who was the object of her envy?

Was she jealous because she had hardly seen Autumn over the last week and Aiden had? Or was she jealous because she suspected Aiden had a "thing" for her friend? Or did she just *want* him to have a thing for Autumn and not her?

With a groan, she leaned back and covered her face with both hands. She wanted to run the thoughts by someone, but she couldn't bring the topic up to Noah or Autumn.

When the knock sounded out from the front door, she heaved a sigh of relief.

Her tired muscles ached as she pushed herself to stand, and she almost chuckled at how ridiculous she must have looked. She looked like a ninety-year-old as she hobbled toward the entryway. The pain was always worse the day *after* the workout.

"Hold on," she called to the person on the other side of the front door. Hopefully, that person was Noah, and hopefully, he'd already stopped to pick up the Thai food he had promised earlier in the day.

When she spotted his green eyes through the peephole, she couldn't help the smile that crept to her lips. Flicking back the deadbolt, she pulled open the door and stepped aside.

After another day of dead ends in the search for

Catherine Schmidt, Winter had departed the FBI office on time. Based on the suit and tie Noah still wore, he had stayed at work several hours past the typical five o'clock end time. The scent of garlic and curry wafted from him, and she felt her stomach grumble.

"You look as tired as I feel," she remarked as he stepped out of his shoes.

"I feel as tired as I look." With a disarming smile, he held up the brown paper bag. "I'm going to eat all this food I bought for myself then lapse into a food coma while we watch some TV. But I'll be completely honest with you, darlin', I need a break from this damn case. If I keep staring at shit about Catherine Schmidt, I'm going to start to think I *am* Catherine Schmidt."

"Hey." She held up her hands as they made their way to the galley kitchen. "You're preaching to the choir. I could use a break too. We'll eat this delicious food while we work on getting you caught up to where Autumn and I are in *Game of Thrones*."

"Oh, perfect." He rolled his eyes in feigned exasperation. "So instead of being stressed about finding Catherine Schmidt, I get to be stressed about which one of my favorite characters is going to die next."

Winter laughed. "Pretty much."

"I'll let you get the food figured out." He loosened the black tie around his neck. "I'm going to go change."

Winter flashed him a thumbs-up as she retrieved a couple plates and forks. By the time she returned to the kitchen to retrieve a bottle of beer for each of them, she heard a knock at the door before Noah announced he had returned.

Though she had almost hoped to see another one of his surprising band shirts, he wore a plain gray t-shirt and gym shorts instead.

Her appetite seldom matched his, but repeated attempts

to disarm a seasoned hand-to-hand combat student like Autumn Trent had made her hungrier than any other workout she'd tried so far. Now, she thought she understood how Autumn was able to match Noah in a chimichanga eating contest.

Even with the stomach pain she'd been fighting since before Winter met her, Autumn's ability to put away food was impressive.

As Noah watched the end of the second season unfold, her mind wandered back to Autumn's assertion that Aiden had feelings for her.

Part of her wanted the observation to be accurate, but now, with the warmth of Noah's body so close to hers, she doubted the knee-jerk reaction. Did she want Aiden to have a "thing" for her, or was that just a leftover part of the high school girl who had been convinced she was in love with the dashing federal agent?

Maybe that was why she didn't want Autumn to be right.

Whenever she thought of any sense of romantic affection for Aiden, she felt like she was a naïve kid all over again. Like she was that starry-eyed teenager who revered the same man with whom she'd exchanged verbal blows on a regular basis.

Sure, Aiden was smart, handsome, and capable, but he was human. He was flawed, just like any other human being, and she hated that thoughts of his alleged feelings for her transported her back to a place where she had been unable to see those flaws.

There was no hope when she imagined herself with Aiden Parrish.

No matter the lingering sense of affection she felt for him, any sort of relationship would be doomed to failure. She cared for him, but he was a reminder of her past, a reminder of a place to which she never wanted to return.

But what if Autumn was right? What if he wanted more than a platonic relationship, and she didn't?

As polished as Aiden was, she found it hard to believe that he took rejection gracefully. If Autumn was right, did that mean Winter and Aiden's *friendship* was at stake?

The realization made her stomach turn. Even though she didn't want to risk that friendship, she wouldn't lie to herself or him to maintain an amiable air.

A pronounced groan at her side snapped her out of the solipsism. As the television darkened and the credits rolled, Noah glanced away from the screen and over to her.

"Tell me that asshole dies," he groused.

Despite the emotional quandary she had just departed, she laughed. "Which one?"

"There are a lot of them, aren't there?"

"Oh, you don't even know the half of it yet. That wasn't even the season two finale. Come on, Dalton. Get your head in the game."

"Sometimes, watching this show feels like an exercise in masochism," he muttered as he leaned back in his seat.

She waved a dismissive hand and flashed him a grin. "That's every good show, isn't it?"

"I guess so, yeah." As his green eyes flicked back to her, the start of a smile worked its way to his face. In the silence that followed, she held the tentative gaze.

Even as she fought against the urge to lean forward, to close the distance between them and breathe in the familiar, comforting scent of peppermint and fabric softener, she suspected her affinity for Noah had far surpassed platonic.

But no matter her suspicions, she was determined not to create another awkward hiccup in their friendship. Noah was a good friend, a loyal friend, and a damn lifesaver. Until she was one-hundred-percent sure any lingering fondness for Aiden had vanished, she refused to risk her and Noah's friendship.

No matter how much her heart pitter-pattered at the thought of the taste of his kiss, no matter how keenly aware she was of his close presence, she would refrain. Noah deserved that, she thought.

He deserved certainty.

32

On seven of the last eight days, Autumn had been visited by none other than Aiden Parrish himself.

The excuses he used to stop by in person were half-assed at best, but she still hadn't summoned up the mental fortitude to call out his less than professional curiosity.

She'd asked him about it on a couple occasions, but his response was much the same as what he'd told her in the FBI waiting room more than a week earlier. This was an old case of his, and he intended to personally see it through, blah, blah, blah.

By now, she had turned the rationalization into a joke between the two of them. The fact that she had an inside joke with Aiden Parrish felt strange, but she used it as an outlet for the mounting frustration that came with being shadowed by a law enforcement agent whenever she so much as breathed.

Though, considering her car was out of commission until she could drum up the cash to fix the transmission, maybe the constant presence of a cop or a Federal Agent had a silver lining: reliable transportation.

As she glanced to the man in the driver's side of the black sedan, she tucked her messenger bag beside her feet and fastened her seatbelt.

Only a couple years older than Autumn, Agent Bobby Weyrick was a six-year veteran of the United States Army and a self-proclaimed nerd. He was also her second favorite federal bodyguard. Her favorite, whether or not she liked to admit it, was still Aiden Parrish.

At the beginning of the year, Bobby and his wife—an EMT named Kara—had closed on a house. They'd adopted two German Shepherd puppies from a shelter a few weeks earlier, and each time she saw him, he had new pictures of the growing dogs. According to Bobby, his two cats were "teaching the pups to cat."

The man was also a habitual smoker, and even though Autumn had rid herself of the nasty habit a few years ago, the frustration of the past week, coupled with the tantalizing scent of second-hand smoke in the car, had pushed her to her breaking point.

"Hey, Bobby." She flashed him a guilty grin.

Turning the key over in the ignition, he glanced up to her. "What's up?"

"Do you think you could swing by a gas station on the way back to my place? I need some damn nicotine."

"You can just have one of mine." He held out a cardboard pack of smokes.

Autumn wrinkled her nose and shook her head. "You smoke menthols, man. I want nicotine, not to feel like I've got the flu."

"Yeah, yeah." With a slight smile, he shook his head. "That's fine. I could use some coffee and a taquito, anyway."

"So," she started as they pulled out of the student parking garage, "you've been at the FBI for a few years now, right?"

"Yep." He nodded. "Since I got out of the military four years ago."

"What do you know about Aiden Parrish?" She blurted out the question before she could consider why she even wanted to know.

He flashed her a curious look. "Head of BAU? Not much. I've been in Violent Crimes since I started, stuck on the damn night shift. But it's what Kara works, too, so I don't complain. This is like my morning right now, hence my need for coffee. I don't hardly ever run across any of those weird day shift people." Bobby's native Tennessee twang was different from Noah's drawl, but until recently, Autumn had been unable to tell one southern accent from another.

"Huh, all right. Fair enough. Night shift, though? That sounds rough."

"It's not all that bad." Shrugging, he flicked on the signal to turn into a bustling gas station. "Plus, it keeps me and Kara on the same schedule."

"True. Okay, well, I've been drinking coffee all day, and I need to run to the bathroom so I'm not doing a weird dance while we're waiting in line."

With a chuckle, Bobby nodded his understanding as they stepped out of the car. Autumn made a beeline back to the ladies' room, and her federal agent shadow posted up at the opening of the hallway where he pretended to look interested in the selection of coffee.

As far as any outsiders were concerned, she and Bobby were just two friends at a quick pit stop on their way home from class. Though Aiden Parrish was perpetually well-dressed, Bobby opted for inconspicuous attire.

A couple days ago, Aiden had accompanied her to the night class she taught. She'd been quick to point out that his tailored suit, expensive watch, and equally pricey shoes would make him stick out like, well, like a federal agent on a college campus.

"You look like such a Fed," she had told him. "You're going to sit in the back of the room like that and freak all my students out, so they talk even less than they usually do. They're going to think you're from the IRS or that you're a hitman or something."

"Can't you just tell them that I'm from the university to sit in on the class for some administrative reason?" he had suggested.

Autumn had offered a snort of laughter in response. "No one who works for a public University dresses as well as you. Believe me. I've been in school for a long time."

He looked down at himself. "Well, I left all my band t-shirts at home, so you'll have to figure something out." There was still a clear picture in her memory of the little self-assured smirk he'd worn. It was a look that made her knees weak, and she had started to wonder if he knew it.

If there was one thing she did *not* want him to know, it was how attracted to him she had become.

Rather than have him sit at the back of the classroom, she'd introduced him as a guest speaker at the last possible moment. He'd been startled for a split-second, but like always, his recovery was quick.

Flicking water from her hands into the bowl of the sink, she glanced up to her reflection and heaved a sigh.

At two years away from thirty, she was too damn old for a crush, but here she was. Infatuated with a man whose affections quite clearly lay with another woman.

With her friend.

Emotionally unavailable had always been her type.

As she pulled a couple paper towels free to dry her hands, she froze in place. Though the sound was muffled, she heard a shout from beyond the closed door. Balling the damp paper towels up in one hand, she held her breath and strained her hearing as the first shot of adrenaline worked its way up her back.

Something was wrong. The *air* was wrong.

She needed to grab Bobby and get the hell out of this building. She would make him coffee and taquitos, and she would smoke a menthol cigarette. The pit stop had been a mistake.

Opening the door, she stepped into the hall, fully prepared to set off in a run. Before she could take one step, an arm came around her throat just as the cold metal of a gun pressed against her temple. She tried to kick…scream… anything, but the arm tightened on her carotid arteries even harder as the man yanked her backward toward what she was certain was an exit.

Autumn felt like she was suspended in a stasis bubble, like each movement she made was forced through a vat of molasses. Worse, her vision was growing darker by degrees.

Where was Bobby? Anyone? Surely a place as large as this would have numerous people milling about, buying potato chips and sugary drinks. But no. She was being taken…alone…and…

Stop it!

Even as her body panicked, a deeper more rational voice entered her mind.

Fight!

MUCH OF HER desire to learn the hand-to-hand combat technique of Krav Maga had been based in her knowledge of the dangers of the forensic psychology profession—after all, much of her time as a forensic psychologist would be spent alone in rooms with men who'd committed heinous crimes.

But even as she was dragged backwards, she realized she

had not truly expected to use her extensive knowledge of close-quarters combat training.

She needed to use it now.

When she snapped out a hand to take hold of the assailant's wrist, the moment of trepidation vanished. She'd fought against more sparring partners than she could count. Granted, none of them had pointed a live weapon at her head, but Autumn had always been adept at handling herself under pressure.

She shoved his arm to the side until the barrel of the handgun pointed harmlessly away. As she used her grip to turn, she took a swift step forward and slammed her knee into his stomach.

A sharp exhale told her the wind had been knocked from his lungs, but she didn't stop. She tightened her grasp on his wrist until she thought her fingers would break the skin, and then she twisted until she felt the crunch of cartilage. The clatter of the weapon against the tiled floor followed, and before she could give the move a second thought, she crouched down to retrieve the handgun.

As she turned back to face him, the glint of malevolence in his gray eyes took her aback. She'd never met this man in her life, so what the hell had brought on such an obvious display of anger?

The overhead fluorescence glinted off the polished silver of a wicked hunting knife in his functional hand. Apparently, he thought that the slender, twenty-something-year-old in front of him would balk at the prospect of using his own handgun on him. He either expected to take the firearm from her grasp, or he expected to stab her.

In either case, as she glared down the sights and took aim, all she could think was that he had brought a knife to a gun fight.

She squeezed the trigger and watched his body jerk backward from the force of the first shot that hit his chest. The entire scene was surreal. She could hardly believe she was about to kill someone, and that all the physical effort required from her was a slight motion of her index finger.

The second shot spattered the wall at his back with dark splotches of blood and brain matter as crimson blossomed from the center of his forehead. As his body crumpled into a graceless heap, she realized she'd been holding her breath.

As she inhaled sharply, a flicker of movement snapped her attention back to the hallway's entrance. She leveled the handgun at the space, but as soon as she saw the newcomer's face, she dropped her hand with a sigh of relief.

"Bobby," she breathed.

33

A iden had only just dropped down to sit on the sectional couch at Autumn's side when his phone buzzed from the pocket of his slacks. With a quick glance to his hostess, he retrieved the device and swiped a key to answer the call.

"Yeah." His greeting bordered on irritable, but he didn't particularly care.

"Aiden," the caller replied. "It's Dan Nguyen at the ME's office. We got an ID on your guy, and I figured you'd want to know before anyone else."

"You figured right. Who is he?"

"Nicolas Culetti. Goes by Nico. He's a contract killer for the Russo family. Or, at least, that's what the general understanding is. The Russos are mostly based out of D.C., but they've been poking around Richmond for the last few years."

"All right. Send me what you've got on him and let me know if anything else comes up." Aiden suppressed a sigh as he lifted a hand to rub his eyes. It was barely nine at night, and already he felt like he'd been awake for a full twenty-four hours.

"Will do. Talk to you soon, I'd imagine."

"Yeah. Later." Swiping the screen, he dropped the phone to the stone surface of the coffee table with a clatter.

"What?" Autumn asked. He could feel her curious stare on the side of his face.

"The ME identified the guy who tried to kill you." Though he tried to keep his tone neutral, he heard the tinge of foreboding.

To her credit, Autumn's expression changed little. "And?" she pressed. "Who was he? One of my crazy exes?"

Did her brand of sarcasm ever completely disappear? Even as he looked over to gauge her reaction, the corner of his mouth twitched in a slight smile. "Not unless you dated a contract killer for the Russo family."

She paused to wrinkle her nose. "I've made some bad choices when it comes to men, but that was never one of them, no."

I wonder if you'd be willing to make another one tonight.

The thought came to him unbidden, and he was glad she hadn't turned on the floor lamp. When he finally dared to look back at her, the light from the flickering television glinted off the whites of her eyes.

Stifling a yawn, she scooted away from him to rest her head on an assortment of throw pillows. Both animals perked up at the movement, but they settled back onto their cushions as Autumn tucked her knees to her chest.

"Are you sure you're all right?"

She shifted in her spot until her green eyes met his. "I'm fine. Do I look like I'm not fine or something?"

"No, but you just killed someone a few hours ago. Someone who was trying to kill you, and now you know that someone was a mafia hitman."

"You just answered part of that yourself." She ran both hands through her hair. "He was trying to kill me. Should I feel bad about taking him down first? And now you're telling me he was a hitman, so, really? Should I feel bad about it?"

"No." He felt like a parrot. "But there are a lot of people who still would. Plus, guilt or not, you just went through something traumatic."

"I'm not 'a lot of people.'" She raised her hands to add the quotes as she pushed herself to sit. "And believe me, I know what just happened. But I also know how the human brain works, and I know that there are plenty of people who don't have stress reactions when shit like this happens. I get that there was a gun in my face, but there wasn't a single point where I genuinely thought I was going to die. I've been going to Krav Maga lessons for years, and everything I did was just second nature."

"You're lucky he didn't know that."

Fire flashed in her eyes. "I've been making my own luck for years."

He inclined his head. "You did good, Autumn, but the stress—"

She snorted. "The fear, the actual *stress*, that's what's at the root of adverse stress reactions. And since I didn't experience it, I'd say I'm more than likely in the clear. And if I'm not, I happen to know the names of plenty of counselors and psychiatrists around town. I'm not trying to sound like a know-it-all or a jerk, I just want to make sure you know that I know what happened and how it usually affects people. I also want you to know that I'm genuinely fine. I'm just tired." As if to emphasize her point, she stifled a yawn.

With a slight smile, he nodded. "All right. I believe you. You're resilient. That's the technical term, right?"

"It is." She returned the expression as she leaned back into the pile of pillows.

His attraction to Autumn felt disingenuous, he realized. Sure, she was smart, witty, and stunning, but he thought he was drawn to her for all the wrong reasons. He was drawn to her because she reminded him of someone, someone he doubted he could ever have.

That someone might have been out of reach, but Autumn was right here, and Autumn wasn't associated with the emotional baggage and memories of failure that came with thoughts of Winter.

"Do you think it's a good idea for you to stay here tonight?" he asked after another spell of quiet. He didn't know what in the hell he thought to accomplish with the line of dialogue, but he knew his intent was anything but professional.

"As long as Bobby's outside." Her response was flat, and for a split-second, he wondered if she had read his damn mind.

"Wasn't Bobby with you when Nico Culetti tried to shoot you?"

She rolled her eyes. "Nico paid some heroin addict to get in a fistfight with someone else to distract Bobby so he could try to shoot me. Nico was a good hitman, I'll give him that. Just wasn't all that great in the hand-to-hand combat department."

"But you know there's a *hitman* after you, right? As in, someone paid to have you killed? Probably the same person who had that tracking device implanted in your stomach. Obviously, they know who you are and, more importantly, *where* you are if they were following you and Agent Weyrick back from your class. Nico or his people had probably been tailing you for days."

"And?" She sat up and narrowed her eyes at him. "What exactly am I supposed to do here? Every spare penny I've got is going to fixing my damn car, and now, what? Did you think I was serious when I suggested I roll a sleeping bag out in the FBI waiting area? Or am I supposed to go stay at a fucking hotel? Please, tell me how I should pay for that."

Now he knew where his suggestion had been headed. "I have a spare bedroom. And a couch. Or, we can stop at a sporting goods store to get you a sleeping bag. If that's what we're doing, we'd better hurry because I think most of those places close at ten."

Despite his attempt at levity, her eyes were slits. "Is that protocol? To invite a witness to spend the night with you?"

"It's protocol to keep you alive."

With a derisive snort, she crossed her arms. "Right. *That's* what you're trying to do right now."

Was she a fucking mind reader? He was sure he'd kept his expression neutral, his tone unassuming. But based on the dangerous glint in her eyes, he might as well have announced every little thing he wanted to do to her.

"Tell you what." Extending a hand, she scooted closer to him and tucked one leg beneath herself. "I'll make you a deal." Brows raised, she made a show of glancing to her hand, to him, and then back.

As he accepted the handshake, he made no effort to conceal his confusion. "Okay?"

"I'm going to tell you what *I* think is going on right now, and if I'm wrong, then we can swing by Dick's on the way to your place."

Nervousness wasn't a sensation in which Aiden was familiar, but as his pulse rushed through his ears, all he could manage was a nod.

The steeliness behind her eyes softened, and she rested her other hand on the back of his hand.

He didn't know how much time elapsed before she spoke again, but for all he knew, they'd spent an entire hour staring one another down. He could tell she was warring with herself, but he didn't feel authorized to give his opinion.

"You know what," she started, holding up both hands. "Never mind. Deal's off. Honestly, what the hell is it with you people?"

Furrowing his brows, he opened his mouth to respond, but she cut him off before he could form the question.

"No, Aiden. I'll tell you exactly what I told Noah about four or five months ago. No. I'm not interested in going home with you. You've clearly got some unresolved shit clattering around in your head, and I don't want anything to do with it. I've got plenty of my own unresolved shit to deal with, okay? I don't need to take on yours too!"

"Wait." He held up a hand to stave off a rebuttal. "Wait, what? What you told Noah? What the hell does *that* mean?"

"Take it at face value," she scoffed. "This shit you're doing, the same shit that he *was* doing, it's unbelievably unhealthy. You could even call it toxic. Whatever's rattling around in your head, whatever spurned lover you're avoiding thinking of, you need to deal...with...it. Talk to a counselor, talk to your friend, talk to a stranger on the bus, I don't care!"

He tried again. "I—"

She held up a hand. "But stop trying to do this, whatever the hell this is. Stop trying to take your emotional baggage out on someone else because you think it might help you in the short-term, and deal with your shit! I'm dealing with mine, all right? I'm not trying to get you to sleep with me so I can get over someone, so I'd like to kindly request that you politely knock that shit off."

He opened and closed his mouth, but he couldn't summon a coherent sentence to his lips. What in the *fuck* had just happened?

Forensic psychologist, he reminded himself. *That's what just happened. You tried to pull a move on a forensic psychologist, and it backfired.*

As he started to chuckle, he shook his head. "Wow. I guess that's what being on the other end of an interrogation must feel like. Are you sure you don't want to work for the FBI?"

To his relief, the irascibility melted away from her face as her lips curled into a smile. "I'm sure." She sighed and pushed both hands through her hair. "Like I said, I don't think you'd pay me enough. I've got a hundred grand in student loans to pay back starting in a few months."

"Speaking of." He paused to gesture to her laptop. "I've been meaning to ask you if I could look at your dissertation. Maybe I can help you with it."

She offered him a thoughtful glance as she reached for the computer. "Maybe, yeah. I defend it next week."

"Then if you don't want to sleep on my couch, I'll sleep on yours."

34

Winter wasn't sure when the sounds from the television had turned into dreams, but she could distinctly recall the warmth of Noah's arm around her as she rested her head on his shoulder.

By the time she drifted back toward the waking world, the television was quiet. Noah had reclined in his seat, and now her cheek rested on his chest. She could feel the rhythmic cadence of his breathing along with the faint beat of his heart.

Nestling her face into his shirt, she let the calm sounds lull her back to sleep.

She thought maybe she should have been surprised or even disconcerted by the physical contact, but to her surprise, she felt the opposite. The warmth of his body was a comfort, not a source of unease.

As sleep crept back to the edge of her consciousness, she wondered what it would be like to wake up beside him every day.

When a jagged pulse of pain blossomed from her temples, she thought at first that the sensation was part of a dream.

She'd dreamt about headaches before, and more often than not, she awoke from them with a headache.

But when the image in her mind came into focus, she realized she wasn't in a dream. She was in a vision.

Aside from the red tinge to the light fixture over the table, the entire scene was exactly as it had been little more than a week earlier. Dr. Ladwig's handcuffed wrists rested atop the scratched, metal surface, and to his side, a familiar dark-haired man with eyes that brimmed with the sort of cunning that was more suited to a cult leader than an attorney.

As she approached the two men, neither so much as cast a sideways glance in her direction. She was in a memory, just like she had been when she watched Autumn's head injury.

"They have something," the lawyer said, his tone quiet but hurried. "We don't know what it is, but we know they have something, or else you wouldn't be here."

Robert Ladwig shook his head. "I don't know what it is. There wasn't anything on the flash drive I took, aside from pictures and files about a guy who tried to use false information on his insurance forms. Last I checked, hiring a legitimate PI to track down someone who tried to screw me over isn't illegal."

"No, it's not illegal," Chase confirmed. "But that's not what we're worried about. It's good that there wasn't anything on that flash drive, but that just means that we're back to square one. We don't know what they have, but based on the fact that you're still here, it's something solid."

"So, what then?" Ladwig's hazel eyes snapped over to the well-dressed man at his side. "How do we handle this?"

"We can't let them get to her. She knows too much."

At the mention of *her*, the color drained from Ladwig's cheeks. After an uneasy pause, he nodded. "Okay. What do you need from me, then?"

"A confession." Chase Parker's expression was grave as he

leaned in closer to Dr. Ladwig. "We take the death penalty off the table. Look, I know it isn't ideal, but you have to trust me on this, Robert. We'll make sure you're taken care of when you're on the inside."

She saw the shadows move along Ladwig's face as he clenched and unclenched his jaw. What was the attorney holding over the doctor to make him even consider such a deal?

"Fine," Ladwig finally said on a breath of released air. "Tell me what I need to do."

The attorney seemed pleased and more than a little relieved. "Jenson Leary and Megan Helfer. Those are the names of the two victims they've found."

As the man rattled off the rest of the details—such as where each body was found, when the person disappeared, how they had been killed—Winter was dumbfounded.

How the hell did Chase Parker know so much about the victims if he wasn't the person who had killed them? And what did he mean when he said *we'll* make sure you're taken care of in prison? Who the hell was *we*?

With a sharp intake of breath, she sat bolt upright as she was whipped through time and space to the shadowy living room of her apartment.

The air felt cooler beneath her nose, and when she dabbed at the spot, she was unsurprised to see a splotch of crimson on her fingertips.

As she reached out for a tissue, she caught a glimpse of movement in the corner of her eye.

"Are you all right?" Noah's voice was still thick with sleep, and she could feel the warmth of his hand on the small of her back. The touch was a comfort, and she offered him a slight .smile as she nodded.

"I'm fine." She knew that recalling her vision would drag him fully out of his slumber, and from there, the countdown to his departure would begin. But as much as she wanted him to stay, she didn't think she could keep the realization about Ladwig's lawyer to herself.

"You have a nightmare or something?" he asked when she didn't elaborate.

"No, not a nightmare. A...a headache. A vision." She wiggled her fingers to add the air quotes. Naming the vivid recollections still felt too sci-fi, but she didn't know a better term.

Blinking repeatedly, he shifted to sit upright. "About the case?"

"Yeah. I think I know why Ladwig confessed."

"You do?"

"Yeah. It's that lawyer, Chase Parker. Parker told him to confess." Her frown deepened. "And we have no way to prove it."

❄

MY PARENTS HAD BEEN wealthy and educated, and as long as I have lived, I've never wanted for anything. Deb and Tim Schmidt, my mother and father, made their living in the financial industry as hedge fund managers. Even to this day, I wasn't entirely sure they had even liked one another. In my opinion, the only reason they stayed together was to keep up appearances in their circle of well-to-do friends.

I thought my mother had tried to be a parent in those first few years of my life, but even at that tender age, I could tell her actions toward me were always forced. Eventually, as I grew older, I stopped caring about the lack of attention.

Deb had been close to forty when she had me, and it was only a matter of time until the drinking and the drugs caught up to her. When they were gone, I'd inherit their veritable fortune, and that would be the end of it. I tried to care about them, tried to care *for* them, but I'd never been successful.

When my father got drunk and drove them off the side of a ravine, I swear I tried to grieve. I tried to summon up memories of the good times to make myself sad, but the only good memories I had were of the housekeepers and me.

My father screwed around with at least two of the women, but the infidelity didn't change the fondness I had for my surrogate family.

After all, what in the hell were those women supposed to do when Tim Schmidt made an advance toward them? Were they supposed to rebuff him? Go to the police?

Considering almost all the women were undocumented Russian and Ukrainian immigrants who hardly spoke a word of English, such defiance seemed unlikely. And when I learned of his string of adultery, it only put more distance between me, him, and my mother.

When I was sixteen, my mother caught my father with one of the cooks, and afterward, he fired the woman. By then, I had a healthy understanding of all the twisted shit that went on under our roof.

My father didn't know it, but I also knew the combination to the safe in which he stored a hefty sum of cash. One night while he and my mother were asleep—in separate rooms, of course—I unlocked the stash and pulled out close to a quarter-million to give to Svetlana, the cook.

To make sure they noticed the missing cash, I cleaned out the entire safe.

When they awoke the next day, I waited for them to come to where I sat beside the fire pit in the backyard. There had been no snow on the ground at the time, but the air was crisp with the first of the season's chill.

Before either of them could protest, I lit a book of

matches and dropped it down to the cash I'd soaked with lighter fluid.

I could still remember the way the heat from the flames had distorted their faces as I watched them from the other side of the blaze.

There was only one thing Tim and Deb understood, and that was money. As much as I'd wanted to give the rest of the stash to the other housekeepers, I'd wanted to hit my father in a way he couldn't get it back.

They threatened me, but I had expected the bluster. It wouldn't make a difference.

I was untouchable. All my schoolmates and my teachers adored me, our housekeepers adored me, everyone except for *them* adored me. If they tried to ship me off to a boarding school like they assured me they would, I would drag them down into a spiral of darkness and shame they'd never escape.

We reached an understanding that day, and my father never touched any of the staff again.

My mother sponsored Svetlana for her work visa, and she and my father paid for all the other workers to obtain their citizenship.

After I left for college, the only reason I came back home was to ensure that my parents had not slipped back into their abusive ways.

When they died, I sold the house and divided up the profits among all the men and women who had worked on the grounds over the years. I kept a small percentage of the estate for myself, but the sum was more than enough for me to live comfortably, even if I hadn't gone to medical school.

Money had never been a draw for me. That wasn't why I conducted my research—I conducted it in hopes of achieving a scientific breakthrough. Fame. Accolades. That was a reward.

Should have been my reward, anyway.

Without ever actually meeting the man in person, however, I knew Mr. Parker was motivated by the same greed, the same lust for wealth as my parents.

When I received the call from him to tell me that the hit he had ordered on Autumn had failed, I could hear the same ire in his voice that I'd heard in my father's so many years before. But as much as I loathed the man, I knew that the order to kill Autumn had not come from Parker.

Even now, after more than twenty years of this work, I wasn't entirely sure the extent of the hierarchy, nor was I so sure I *wanted* to know.

As glad as I was to hear that Autumn hadn't been killed, I knew the failed hit meant that there was a storm on the horizon. And if I stayed to weather it out, I knew without a doubt I'd be swept away by the storm surge.

35

As Autumn made her way back to the living room, she passed off an unopened toothbrush to Aiden Parrish like it was a baton. He had accompanied her for Toad's evening walk around the block, and now, after almost three hours of discussion about her dissertation, Autumn had announced that it was her bedtime.

The only bathroom in the apartment was through her bedroom, so she had told him he could brush his teeth now, or forever hold his peace.

When she glanced away from the rerun of *Supernatural* to where he reappeared from the shadowy hallway, she stifled a yawn.

As far as Autumn was concerned, the past twenty-four hours had lasted for an entire week.

Between the failed hit and Aiden's constant presence afterward, she thought for sure she was about to crack. After all the trouble she went through to stop at that damn gas station, she hadn't even been able to buy a pack of cigarettes.

She inhaled deeply through her clean lungs. Not getting the cancer sticks was probably for the damn best.

"How much longer will I need a babysitter?" She hadn't wanted the query to sound accusatory or irritable, but at this point, she was too tired to care.

As he dropped down to sit at her side, Aiden's blue eyes met hers. "Until the moment after we catch whoever ordered that hit on you."

"And if you don't?"

He kept his intent stare on her in the silence that followed. Shaking his head, he combed a hand through his hair and sighed. "Honestly?"

"Yeah," she replied. "Honestly."

"Witness protection, more than likely. Nico was the real deal, Autumn. He was a seasoned contract killer for one of the larger Italian crime families in the D.C. area. Whoever hired him had resources, because I can't imagine his rates are affordable. He was connected, and that means whoever paid him to kill you is just as connected. You don't get in touch with a Mafia hitman unless you were already into some shady shit to begin with."

Her eyes widened, and she made no effort to conceal the shock from her face.

After everything she'd dealt with in her life, after all the suffering she'd experienced at the hands of her parents and the foster care system alike, she was about to be forced into witness protection because some unknown goon or some elusive serial killer wanted her dead?

"Witness...witness protection?" she echoed. "Did I hear you right?"

Expression grave, he nodded. "Yeah, you did. It's the only way you're guaranteed safety. Otherwise, if we don't find out who sent Nico after you, who knows what else they might try."

She shook her head. "No, I can't do that."

As the look on his face softened, he held up an index finger. "That's only if we don't find them."

"Even if you don't, I can't just run away and hide from my problems. Look, without going into all the details, I'll just tell you that I've been through a lot to get where I am right now. None of it was handed to me. I worked for *everything* I have, and I'll be damned if I'll throw it away so I can move to the middle of nowhere in Nebraska to manage a fucking fast food restaurant."

She could feel her heart as it hammered in her chest, and she fought against the sting in the corners of her eyes. She'd be damned if she shed a tear in front of someone like him. Someone so polished, someone whose life was so orderly and accomplished, someone who had no idea the type of struggle she'd endured.

But as a shadow of hesitation passed behind his eyes, she wondered about the accuracy of her assumption.

Aside from the fact that he was from Chicago, she knew little of Aiden Parrish's upbringing. Apparently, he was about as forthcoming with his background as she was with hers.

"You know," her voice was softer now, "when I was still in my undergrad in Minnesota, I went to a Q & A session with a forensic psychologist from the University of California out in Irvine. It's one of the schools I applied to, and honestly, I was a little disappointed that I didn't get in. That lady, the psychologist, she was a really interesting person. She'd been working in the field for something like thirty years, and she had a lot of stories to tell."

His gaze was focused on her. "I'm sure."

"But one thing she really stressed was what a dangerous job it could be. Not all convicts will be glad to see a shrink, that's the basis of what she told us. She had been married, and she had a couple kids, but she never changed her last name. Her kids used her husband's last name. You know why? It was so it'd be harder for people to track her family down if they found her on social media."

"Good thinking."

Autumn rubbed at her tired eyes. "She'd been physically present when one of her colleagues was killed, and she'd personally known two others who were murdered. She received death threats on a regular basis, and plenty of them were credible. I've known since I was twenty-two what a dangerous line of work I was getting into, and I don't really see what difference a couple hitmen here and there are going to make."

A silence descended on them in the wake of her tirade, and she studied the change in his expression as the seconds dragged on.

She was acutely aware of his closeness, but she wasn't overcome by the uncertainty she knew she should have felt. As he reached a hand toward her, the motion was tentative, almost like he sought permission for the physical contact.

Though she should have backed away or leaped to her feet, she didn't so much as shift in her spot on the couch. The tips of his fingers felt feathery light as he brushed a piece of auburn hair from her face, but even the slight touch was enough to remind her of the same uncertainty she'd called him out on earlier.

All she had to do was lean forward. She could satiate the bizarre attraction she felt to him, and at the same time, she could distract herself.

Wasn't he using her as a distraction, anyway? She wasn't sure.

She'd spent enough time around him that the sharpness of her ability to read him had begun to dull. And with Aiden Parrish, she didn't think it would be wise to let down that part of her guard.

He wasn't a bad person, to be sure, but his motive in that

moment—in every interaction since they'd *met*—was questionable. Maybe he didn't realize the ignoble intent himself, but to Autumn, it had been clear from the start.

Rather than put into motion a series of events she was almost certain she would regret, she took hold of his wrist. Her grip was gentle but resolute as she guided his hand back to his lap.

Rising to stand, she pointed to a microfiber blanket draped over the cushion at his side. "If that's not enough, there are more in the linen closet in the hallway."

"It's still warm outside," he replied. The disheartened look in his eyes was fleeting. "I'm sure I'll be fine."

"Peach, my cat, she likes to sleep on the couch. She's persistent, so I hope you don't mind cats."

"I don't. Cats are fine." There was a wistful tinge to his slight smile as she made her way over to the hall. "Sleep well, Autumn. I'll see you in the morning."

She forced a smile to her lips, though all she wanted to do was swear at him. If she wasn't drawn to him, rejecting an advance, even one as innocuous as what had just happened, would be easy. She could tell him she wasn't interested, that he was acting like a creep, or both.

"You too. Thanks again for, you know, being my babysitter."

With a quiet chuckle, he nodded. "Any time."

36

The last time Autumn remembered catching a glimpse of her alarm clock, the glowing numbers had advised her that it was after two in the morning. When her eyes snapped open at quarter 'til six, she flopped an arm over her face and groaned. For another hour, she tossed and turned as she tried to fall back to sleep, but the effort was for naught.

As she muttered a string of four-letter words under her breath, she shrugged into a zip-up hoodie. Toad's little feet clattered against the hardwood as he followed her down the hall to the coat hooks.

If the person lying on her couch had been Winter or Noah, she would have made a concerted effort to keep any noise to a minimum. She would have carried Toad to his leash to avoid the sound of his steps, and she would have eased the door shut as she let herself out into the musty corridor.

Even when the attempt on her life from the night before popped to mind, she trudged out to the grassy courtyard by herself.

She shouldn't have been outside alone, but she was sure she had closed the door with enough force to wake both Aiden and her cat. For the duration of the short trip, she glanced around the surrounding area, one hand easily within reach of the folded knife she'd tucked into the pocket of her running shorts.

When she returned to the foyer and unclipped Toad's leash, she caught a glimpse of movement in her periphery.

Though she entertained the idea of stomping across the wooden floor, her steps were little more than a whisper of sound as she padded to the kitchen.

But what she missed out on while walking, she made up for as she retrieved a red container of coffee from a cabinet. The wooden door fell closed with a clatter, and she made sure to smack the serving spoon against the side of the canister when she was done.

"Jesus Christ," Aiden spat.

At the muffled outburst, she felt the corner of her mouth turn up in satisfaction. "Sorry, did I wake you? One of the detriments of having an open floorplan, I guess."

Propped up with both elbows, Aiden narrowed his eyes. His caramel brown hair was disheveled, and she realized it was the first time she had seen him look like anything other than an attendee at a black-tie event.

In response, she offered him a sugary sweet smile.

"My sister used to do this shit all the time," he muttered. "She was ten years older than me, and when I was eight and she was a senior in high school, my mom made her take me to school. Instead of just waking me up, half the time, she'd stomp around and slam kitchen cabinets, much like you're doing right now."

She chuckled at the dry sarcasm as she made her way back to the living room. "I never had to worry about that."

"Must've been nice having a *younger* sister."

Autumn froze mid-step.

She knew she'd never mentioned Sarah to him.

She'd never mentioned Sarah to *anyone*.

Part of the reason she kept her past records sealed so tightly was to *avoid* the mention of Sarah or her stepfather. Unlike Autumn's biological dad, Ryan Petzke had beaten the scourge of addiction. The last time Autumn ever saw Ryan or her little sister, the man had been determined to make a better life for his daughter. He'd even gone so far as to tell Autumn that he would try to sue for custody of her too.

Whether he never tried or was simply unsuccessful, she still didn't know.

The mirth on Aiden's face turned grave, but he didn't speak.

She didn't know what expression she wore, probably a combination of ire and outright terror, she figured. Enough to tell him he'd fucked up.

No matter how many times she swallowed, she couldn't will away the tightness in her throat or the sting of bile as her stomach turned.

She shouldn't have been surprised. Aiden Parrish was a Supervisory Special Agent at the damn FBI. It was his *job* to know anything and everything about a witness or a suspect's background.

But if he knew, then who else? Who else had dug around in her past? Who had dug so deep they'd come across *Sarah*?

As much as she wanted to shout the questions at him, the edges of her vision started to blur as a sudden twinge of pain speared through her stomach. Clutching the site of the pang with one hand, she grimaced as she dropped down to sit at the edge of the couch.

"Are you…" In a rush of movement, he pushed away the plush blanket as he straightened. "Are you okay?"

"Yeah." She managed a nod. "It's just my stomach. That's why I was in the doctor's office a week ago when they found that GPS tracker."

"Did you find out what was causing it?" His tone was quiet and gentle enough to displace some of her anger, and she was left with only fear.

She nodded again. It was endometriosis, but she didn't want to discuss her uterus with a federal agent. As it stood, he already knew far more about her than she was comfortable.

"How much do you know?" she asked instead.

"Everything." The response was just as hushed as his question had been.

"Who else knows?" she pressed.

When he didn't reply right away, she pried her attention away from the floor to fix her stare on him. The early morning sunlight made the pale blue color of his eyes look almost iridescent as he finally met her gaze.

"You know you can't lie to me, right?" As much as she wanted the statement to sound like a threat, she just sounded tired. Defeated.

"I've gathered as much." He sighed, long and deep. "They're the ones who told me."

Her stomach turned again, and she thought for sure she was about to throw up.

❄

THE SUN HAD BARELY CRESTED the horizon by the time Noah and Winter walked through the doors of the city jail. They handed their weapons and badges to the corrections officer behind the glass at the entrance, and then a different man led them to the windowless room where Robert Ladwig waited.

Even in the harsh fluorescence overhead, the dark circles

beneath Ladwig's eyes were pronounced. As Noah took a seat beside Winter, the psychiatrist crossed both arms over his bright orange shirt.

"Where's my lawyer?" he asked. Despite his unshaven cheeks and haggard appearance, there was still a defiant glint in his green and amber eyes.

"We're not here to talk to you as a suspect," Noah advised.

Though he normally would have been inclined to add a wide smile to the statement just to set the man on edge, he maintained his grave expression.

If Winter's vision was accurate—and so far, none of them had been wrong—then Ladwig was innocent, and even their theory that he had led Catherine Schmidt to her victims was inaccurate. From what Winter saw, Ladwig hadn't even known the victims' *names*. Chase Parker had provided them so Robert Ladwig could craft a believable confession.

"Really?" Ladwig scoffed. "I find that hard to believe. Right now, it just looks like you're here to violate the Sixth Amendment."

"No, we're not," Winter replied, folding both her hands atop the tarnished metal table. "We're here to talk to you as a *witness*, and you don't need to have an attorney present for that unless you feel it's necessary. The Sixth Amendment doesn't apply here. And before you cut me off and tell me you want your lawyer, I want you to hear me out." She waited until he met her gaze before adding, "Will you?"

In the silence that blanketed the cramped space, Ladwig kept his petulant stare fixed on Winter.

On the drive over, Noah and Winter had agreed that Ladwig would be more receptive to her suggestions than to his. They had a history, and Noah's only history with the doctor was his half-assed attempt to goad the man into elaborating on Winter's visions.

"Fine," Ladwig grated. "I'll listen, but that's *all* I'm doing."

"That's all I'm asking."

"Then, by all means." He gestured to her with one hand.

"We know you're innocent," Winter started. "And personally, I don't like to see innocent people go to prison. I don't know why you're willing to take the fall for something you didn't do, but I'll tell you what I think. I think you know who actually did it, and you're copping to these murders so you don't have to risk ratting them out."

She paused, giving him a moment to respond. He didn't. The only sign of his anxiety was the rapid flutter of his pulse beating overtime in his throat.

After half a minute, she went on. "And I'm here to tell you today that I get it. If she's in on it, and if your lawyer is in on it, that doesn't leave you with a lot of options, does it? If you dismiss your lawyer, then she'll find out about it, and if you give her up, then Parker will know about it. You're stuck between a rock and a hard place."

The doctor mumbled something that sounded like "no shit" but didn't elaborate.

"But here's a third alternative, Dr. Ladwig." For emphasis, Winter held up three fingers. "You tell us who she is right now, we make a call, and then one of us waits here with you until the US Marshals arrive. We're offering you witness protection. No trial, no nothing. All we want is a name, and then you can disappear."

As Ladwig clenched and unclenched his jaw, they lapsed into a spell of eerie quiet.

"When you say disappear...?" He left the question unfinished as he glanced to Noah and then back to Winter.

"We mean disappear," Noah put in. "As in no trace left behind. The Marshals handle it, so even *we* don't know where you are. They give you a new name, a new identity. It might not be as glamorous as what you're doing right now, but you'll be safe."

When Ladwig's eyes broke away from Noah's, the man heaved a sigh. "You were in the military, weren't you, Dalton?"

Noah pushed aside his surprise at the unexpected query. "Yeah," he answered. "Marine Corps for six years. You were Army, right?"

"I was." There was a distant look in Ladwig's eyes, and he kept his vacant stare fixed on the door as he spoke. "Ten years, but you knew that. You probably knew that I was a medic too. The Army was the only reason I wasn't flat broke by the time I finished med school. You were in the Corps, so you've heard about the Battle of Fallujah, right?"

Noah's face was grim. "Yeah," he answered.

"I wasn't there for the First Battle of Fallujah, but I was there for the second. They said it was the bloodiest battle since Vietnam."

Noah leaned forward, memories churning in his gut. "Urban warfare is brutal."

Ladwig nodded, finally looking at the other man for longer than a second. "It's fucking excruciating, it's exhausting, and you're right, it's brutal. While I was there stitching up gunshot wounds and trying to save twenty-some-year-old kids from dying, it didn't occur to me that I was part of a historical battle." He paused, seeming to be expecting a response.

"The movies make it more glamorous than it is," Noah said, his face tight.

Ladwig's nostrils flared. "Damned right. There wasn't anything even remotely glamorous about it. I was just there to pay for my damn med school, and there sure as hell isn't anything valiant or heroic about that, is there? That fight lasted for a month and a half, and I was there for every damn day of it."

"That's where you met them," Winter said, speaking so softly that Noah almost missed it.

Ladwig looked startled. "Yes." Surprise turned to chagrin, then anger. "None of this shit was supposed to go like this. When I met these people, I thought they were after the greater good too." With a mirthless chuckle, Ladwig shook his head.

"What do you mean?" Noah asked. "What greater good?"

"I know you know about it too, Dalton." The psychiatrist inclined his chin in Winter's direction. "Agent Black's..." He studied her more closely, eyes narrowed. "How do you say it? Agent Black's brain abnormality. The same thing you tried to tell me had happened to you when you pretended you were Brady Lomond. The visions, the heightened senses, the way your mind directs you to important items."

Winter shifted in her seat, looking uncomfortable.

Ladwig barked out a sound that resembled a laugh. "Yeah, HIPAA, I know. But, look at me." He gestured to the orange shirt and matching pants. "You think I give a shit about HIPAA right now? I'm staring down the barrel of a death sentence, for god's sake. But that's it, agents. That's what they wanted to find. They wanted to find out what made that happen. And I was the dumbass who confirmed that the abnormality existed. Before me, all they had to go on were rumors from some shady medical circles."

A hallowed shadow passed behind Winter's blue eyes, and her fair face looked even paler.

"I wanted them to figure it out." Ladwig shifted his gaze back to Noah, and there was a hint of defeat in his expression that hadn't been there during any of their meetings. "I wanted them to replicate it so they could pass it over to the military. I didn't give a shit what kind of edge it'd give them in combat. All I could think of was how many of those kids *wouldn't* have died in Fallujah."

In the art of interrogation, silence was golden. Noah held his tongue and kept his face carefully neutral while he waited for the doctor to go on with his story. Thankfully, Winter was quiet too.

"But I can't even use that as an excuse anymore, can I?" Another bark of sound. "This has gone so damn far from what I thought it was, I can't even recognize it anymore. I just kept clinging to the fucking greater good, like it gave me an out. You know how the saying goes, right? The road to hell is paved with good intentions."

Noah didn't even bother to try to process the admission that the killer was in pursuit of Winter's so-called brain abnormality. Even if he tried, he was sure the effort would only give him a headache.

No matter the motive, they still had a serial killer to find.

"Then make it right." Noah's voice was soft. Supportive. Agreeable. Urging. "Tell us who she is, and if you can, tell us where she is. We put her away, and you go put all this shit behind you."

Minutes passed, and the only sound Noah heard was the beating of his own heart.

Tell us, tell us, tell us, his heartbeat seemed to say. As another minute passed, he thought he'd begin screaming out the words.

"I wish it was as easy as you make it sound, agent. But even if it isn't, yeah, I'll do it." Ladwig dropped his hands to rest atop the table. "I don't know who in the hell Chase Parker is, or if Chase Parker is even his real name, so you're on your own for that one. But I also know that he's not the one who's been killing these people."

More minutes passed, and this time, Noah knew the

silence needed to be filled. The doctor needed just a bit more encouragement. Winter seemed to sense this too.

"Who's the killer, Dr. Ladwig?" she asked in a gentle voice.

Ladwig sighed, then inhaled deeply again. As that breath released, he exhaled the words they needed to hear. "Sandra Evans."

37

Aiden had tried to explain to Autumn that Winter and Noah had only dug around in her history so they could try to keep her safe, but he walked a dangerous line. One wrong word and he would give away Winter's secret, just like he'd blurted out the comment about Autumn's younger sister.

He was still pissed at himself for that. He hardly ever made such stupid mistakes.

But no matter what he told her, he already knew he couldn't lessen the sting of betrayal. Unless he could tell her the fucking truth, any endeavor to assuage her unease was pointless.

Elbows propped on her knees, Autumn kept her unseeing stare fixed on the black screen of the television. He had watched the clock, and before she spoke again, a full three minutes had passed.

"I can't do this," she finally managed. As she shook her head, she still didn't return her gaze to him.

"What do you mean, can't do what?" he pressed.

"I can't be friends with people who thought it was fine to

dig around in my fucking past without so much as a heads-up! Is there anything you don't want people to know about you, Aiden? Anything about your past that you're not all that proud to share with other people? Now, what if someone you trusted went snooping around without your permission?"

"That's not the same thing, and you know it," he returned. Though the affection he'd fostered for her over the last week and a half had acted as a buffer for his usual mantra of brutal honesty, he had hit a dead end. He couldn't tell her the truth, and he had no other route to take. "They were investigating a *serial killer*."

"You know what they say about the road to hell, right?" she shot back. Green eyes narrowed, she turned her glare to him. "Paved with good intentions and all that bullshit."

Before he launched into a rebuttal, he told himself the harsh words were as much to distance himself from her as anything. She was right, after all. He had plenty of inner turmoil of his own. He didn't need to make another stupid decision so he could spend years regretting it too.

"Is it just because you actually *were* a victim that you've gotten so damn good at *playing* the victim?" he snapped. At least if she was pissed at him, Winter's secret would be safe. "Because there are at least two dead people, people whose bodies were dissolving in a fifty-five-gallon drum of lye for who knows how long before we found them. Those poor souls might take exception to your delicate sensibilities right now!"

Her eyes widened as she took in a sudden breath, but the shock was replaced in short order by malice.

Before either of them could speak another word, his phone buzzed against his leg. "Just in case you forgot, Ms. Trent, that's what your friends were doing. They were chasing a fucking *serial killer*!"

As he rose to stand, he pulled the phone from his pocket

and swiped the screen to answer the call. He hadn't even bothered to pay attention to the caller ID.

"SSA Parrish," he grated.

"Aiden, it's me," Winter replied, her voice breathless. "We've got a name and a location for Catherine Schmidt."

Based on the venomous glint in Autumn's eyes, he would have better odds of survival at the takedown of a serial killer than he would if he stayed.

✳

THE SOFT DIRT and moss beneath the cover of the cluster of trees muffled Winter's footsteps as she and Aiden circled around to cover the back exit of a rustic cabin. Just as Robert Ladwig had promised, Catherine Schmidt, also known as Sandra Evans, had absconded to an isolated patch of land in the neighboring Henrico County.

Ladwig had been clear that he had never been to the property, and he had prefaced the information by saying he shouldn't have even known about the location. But in the years he had known Sandra, he had connected a series of dots to gauge an approximation of the hiding place.

Though Noah had offered to stay behind to brief the US Marshals who would take on the task of ensuring Robert Ladwig's safety, they had assembled a full tactical team to accompany them to the Virginia woodland.

Then again, as she glanced over to make note of Aiden's persistent scowl, she wasn't so sure they *needed* the tactical team. At any point, she fully expected the BAU director's skin to turn green as he transformed into the Incredible Hulk.

Aiden wasn't a chipper person on an average day, but ever since his arrival at the FBI office that morning, Winter had been keenly aware of the air of petulance that surrounded him. Even if they didn't have a task, she knew better than to ask the reason for his ire.

She felt a tickle on the side of her face as another droplet of sweat rolled down her cheek.

The black jackets emblazoned with bright block print were necessary to distinguish friendly counterparties from foes, but the temperature that day was slated to reach ninety-four.

The sooner they cuffed Catherine Schmidt, the sooner they could return to air-conditioning.

"We're in place at the southern and eastern edges." The man's voice in her ear was tinny, like someone had spoken through an old radio.

As she flattened her back against the trunk of an old oak, she glanced over to where Aiden stood behind another tree. His pale eyes were fixed on the cabin as he raised a hand to cover his mouth.

"The north exit is covered," he advised.

"The west side of the house is covered too," Bree chimed in.

"Roger that," the first man replied. "We breach the front door in five."

Winter tucked the stock of her M4 Carbine against her shoulder, the barrel still pointed at the ground. As the seconds ticked away, she held her breath to strain her hearing for the telltale clatter of splintering wood. She had expected the disturbance to be muffled by the distance, but the battering ram smashed into the front door with the same force as a gunshot.

A handful of shouts identified the intruders as FBI agents, and then two different men shouted for the occupants to drop their weapons. Abruptly after the second request, a series of raucous pops sounded out in rapid succession. *Those* were gunshots, she knew. She could only hope they had been fired by the team that had breached the door.

In tandem, her and Aiden's gazes snapped over to a flicker of movement. The wooden door at the back of the cabin flew open in a blur of movement.

A woman emerged, shrugging on a backpack as her panicked eyes darted around to take stock of the tree line. With one last glance over her shoulder, she sprinted across the lush grass. The afternoon sunlight caught the lustrous shine of her golden hair, and even from a distance, Winter immediately knew who she was.

When Winter glanced to Aiden, he raised a hand before he jabbed a finger into the Kevlar over his chest.

To her chagrin, the malevolent glint in his pale eyes had not so much as lessened. Where she would have normally protested, she nodded instead.

As Catherine Schmidt closed the distance, the sound of her labored breathing became clearer. Once she crossed over into the shade beneath the canopy of leaves, she paused for a fervent look back to the property. She set off into the wooded area at a jog.

But before she reached safety, she had to pass by Winter and Aiden's post.

A twig snapped beneath one of the woman's booted feet, and even the quiet disturbance rose above the drone of the summer wildlife.

Aiden flipped the matte black rifle over in his hands, stepped out from behind the tree, and swung the M4 in a single, fluid arc. The wet crack of the weapon's stock against Catherine's skull stood out in such stark contrast from the breaking twig that Winter thought it was almost poetic.

With a muffled clump, the woman's stainless-steel handgun fell to the damp earth as she crumpled into an unceremonious heap.

"We've got her," Winter announced. "At the north exit. She's unconscious."

"Roger that," a man replied. "Two hostiles killed inside, but the rest of the house is clear."

"Shed out back is clear, but it looks like we've got a cellar door out here." Winter recognized the speaker as Miguel Vasquez.

"That might be where they kept the victims," Bree suggested. "Wait to open it until we get some forensics people out here."

"Roger that," Miguel responded. "In that case, we're all clear, ladies and gents."

"Holy shit," Winter murmured to herself. She glanced to Catherine's unconscious form and then to Aiden. "We got her."

For the first time that day, some of his irascibility dissipated as he nodded.

They got her.

The main spider of this dangerous web.

But what about all the flies?

38

After four days without a single word from Autumn, Winter finally badgered Aiden into telling her what had happened. She had been in his office at the time, and her first thought was to snatch up the nearest item and hurl it at his head.

A stapler, a little jar of paperclips, a pen, a damn handgun, whatever she grabbed first. She didn't care, and he'd deserve worse.

She wasn't upset that he had told Autumn the truth—Autumn deserved that. Winter could have lived with *that*. But why he felt the need to hurl a slew of inflammatory remarks, remarks that were far from accurate, Winter had no idea.

He assured her his intent was only to ensure that Winter's secret wasn't revealed, but Winter brushed aside the rationalization like the veiled excuse it was.

She didn't pretend to know what went through the director of the BAU's head on most days, but she knew without a doubt that there was more to his knee-jerk hostility toward her friend than he let on.

The confrontation ended with Winter throwing her

hands into the air as she let out a laugh that sounded closer to a cough.

"I can't believe you." The words were low and deadly calm, but she refused to lose her cool and be some emotional female.

Without waiting for a rebuttal, she had flung open the glass and metal door and stalked through the series of cubicles that housed the BAU. Okay…maybe a little emotional.

Rather than puzzle over Aiden's motives, she spent her drive to Autumn's apartment contemplating how to approach her explanation.

As she pulled into the pockmarked lot and parked, she felt like she stood at a crossroads, a point in her life on which she could either look back proudly or look back with shame.

Aside from Aiden and Noah, she didn't have any other friends. Hell, she didn't even *like* many people, much less count them as friends. Who even *was* there for her to befriend? Sun Ming?

At the thought, Winter rolled her eyes.

Yeah. Right.

Pushing open the car door to step out into the abundant sunshine, she realized the only way she could avoid the loss of her friend was by telling the truth. Not the version of the truth that Aiden had tried to convey, but the *real* truth.

Maybe revealing her "ability," her "woo-woo," or her "sixth sense" would lead Autumn to look at her with the same disdain as her old friend Sam. That was the worst-case scenario, wasn't it?

But if that was Autumn's reaction, then Winter would know she had never been friend material in the first place.

With a sigh, she made her way to Autumn's building, climbed a set of stairs, and knocked on the familiar door before she could second-guess herself.

"Hold on," a muffled voice called.

There was a moment of hesitancy before the deadbolt clicked and the door creaked inward. Fluffy dog beneath one arm, Autumn offered Winter a wary glance before she moved aside to give her room to enter.

The apartment was as presentable as it always was, and today, the air smelled like citrus and coconut.

"I was hoping you'd have a minute to talk," Winter said as she followed Autumn to the living room.

"Sure," she replied, shrugging. "Have a seat."

"I need to tell you something," Winter blurted.

Before her thoughts could spiral into a flurry of doubt, she glanced up to meet her friend's weary gaze. "Okay." Autumn's quiet voice gave her the last little push she needed.

"I'm going to tell you this, and it's going to sound insane. It'll sound like I've lost my damn mind, but I swear, it's the truth."

There was a flicker of curiosity behind Autumn's green eyes as she nodded her understanding.

"When I got hit in the head by the Preach..." She cleared her throat. "I mean, by Douglas Kilroy, the man who killed my parents, he was trying to kill me. He left me there for dead, but I didn't die. I was in a coma for three months, and when I woke up, it was like I was on a different planet."

Autumn crossed her arms over her chest. "I'm sorry."

Winter nodded. "I was just overwhelmed with every single thing, my senses were completely overloaded all the time. And now, I see things. Things like..." She ran a hand through her hair.

Compassion mixed with the curiosity in Autumn's eyes. "Things like what? You can tell me."

Their gazes met, and Winter knew it was true.

"At this burial site on the first homicide case I worked with Noah, I could see a red haze on certain parts of the ground. No one else could see them, but I knew what it was."

Autumn shivered and crossed her arms tighter over her chest. "Graves?"

Winter blew out a breath. "Yes. The graves glowed red for me. And that...that's not it."

She took in a measured breath to calm her nerves before she dared another glance at Autumn. Though she expected to see disbelief, mocking amusement, or even fear, she was relieved by the belief that had brightened her friend's face.

"Sometimes, I get these weird headaches out of nowhere. It'll feel like someone put my head in a vice, and there are still times when I'll get them, and I'll be convinced I'm about to die. But then I'll lose consciousness, and I'll *see* things. Sometimes things that are real, things that really happened, and sometimes things that point me in the direction of something that hasn't happened yet."

Autumn blinked. "That's—"

"Insane," Winter finished for her. "I know it sounds insane, but I swear, this is the God's honest truth. That's how I knew that Catherine Schmidt had something to do with this case. I just, I woke up one day, had this massive migraine, and then it was like I was walking through these points in your life. I saw you with an orange stuffed cat while you read a book. I can't remember what the book was, but the song was *Scar Tissue* by the Red Hot Chili Peppers."

To Winter's surprise, there was no skepticism on Autumn's face as she averted her gaze. "That song still makes me sad. It makes me think of my mom. She played that album all the damn time after it came out. When she was high, she'd always tell me about how she was going to take me to see them at Red Rocks in Colorado."

"You," Winter inhaled a deep breath, "you believe me?"

In response, Autumn nodded, but her countenance didn't change. "Yeah," she murmured. "Yeah, I believe you. I get it, as well as I can without being a Fed, anyway. And for the record, I was going to say remarkable, not insane."

"But you're still upset with us." Winter made sure to keep her tone gentle and non-accusatory. "With me."

"You all know," Autumn started as her green eyes flicked up to the blank screen of the television. "You all know everything. Everything I've worked my ass off to keep hidden from everyone I've ever been friends with. You saw my dad, then, right? Saw how I got this?" She brushed aside her auburn hair and pointed to the faint scar.

"Yeah. I saw it."

With a wistful smile, she shrugged. "Then I guess you all know that I'm not one of you. That none of you are broken like I am. You've all got families, you all had parents that didn't scare the shit out of you and let you down at every feasible fucking opportunity."

"Maybe we didn't go through the same thing, but we've all got our battle scars. We've all got stuff we don't want other people to know about, but as luck would have it, you found yourself friends with FBI agents and then you found yourself the target for a crazy woman. It was that combination that forced us to dig through your past."

Autumn snorted, but she didn't add anything to it.

"But one thing we do all know, or at least that *I* know is what it feels like to be all alone. To feel like there isn't a single person on the face of the planet who knows what you're dealing with. Douglas Kilroy shot my dad in the head, and then he raped and mutilated my mom. He literally painted the walls with her blood, and I *still* can't get that image out of my head. And maybe your family are a bunch of colossal assholes, and mine are gone, but come on. We ought to know better than anyone that family means more than a genetic similarity."

Autumn covered her eyes with one hand, and for one

horrifying second, Winter thought her friend would cry. Instead, she chuckled quietly.

Winter had no idea what could be funny. "What?"

"You." She scrubbed her face with her hands before dropping them to her sides. "You're ruining my pity party, you know that?"

39

When Winter suggested he visit Autumn to apologize, Aiden wondered at first if the woman was trying to trick him. Was Autumn going to open her door to immediately put him in a headlock? Or would she just skip the wrestling move and punch him straight in the face?

Honestly, he thought there was a real possibility that he deserved a violent greeting. And honestly, he was glad Winter had made the request. Otherwise, he wasn't sure he would have ever initiated the conversation himself.

As the wooden door creaked open to reveal the woman who was the object of so much of his recent contemplation, he had to force a neutral expression to his face. Though Autumn's eyes glinted with suspicion, the dog in her arms perked up his ears and cocked his head.

With a sigh, she waved a hand at the hall as she stepped to the side.

"What do you want?" she asked as she set Toad on the hardwood floor. Straightening to her full height, she brushed off the front of her gray t-shirt and crossed her arms.

"Did Winter not tell you?"

She rolled her eyes. "She said she was going to say something to you. Not that she was going to bribe you to come over here to, well, whatever in the hell you're here for."

"I'm here to apologize, and no, Winter didn't *bribe* me." Admissions of wrongdoing were not Aiden's strong suit, but as much as he was tempted to turn around to leave, he met her expectant stare instead.

"Okay." She shrugged. "Apology accepted. Thanks for stopping by. Have a good night. Don't let the door hit you. Drive safe. Sweet dreams."

He held out a hand to block the door from closing. "You were right."

She opened it back up a couple of inches, a lone eyebrow raised to her hairline. "Nice beginning. Go on."

He actually felt his face grow a bit warm, which startled him a little. Refusing to be sidetracked from his embarrassment, he barreled on, "When you said that I had unresolved shit I had to deal with. You were right. And I took some of that shit out on you, and I shouldn't have. Look, I always thought my childhood was garbage, and I always thought there couldn't be a lot of people who had it worse than I did. We were dirt poor, my mom dated a series of serious douchebags while I was growing up, and then my sister started doing meth, and it, it was just a shitshow."

The cynical eyebrow lowered, and Autumn's expression transformed into compassion. "I'm sorry."

He waved the apology away. "I'm not trying to make this about me and my problems. I don't know, maybe that and the unresolved shit in my head made me defensive, I'm not sure. Winter told me that she filled you in on everything, but at the time, I didn't want to say anything about it. I didn't think it was my place to tell anyone about it, but that's still not an excuse. And if it's worth anything now, it was all bull-shit. I was just being an asshole to be an asshole."

She dropped down to sit at the end of the couch as she heaved a sigh. "You *were* an asshole. But I get it. She means a lot to you, and you were trying to keep her confidence."

"Yeah, but you know what they say about the road to hell." He stepped past her to take a seat at her side.

"Maybe, but intentions are also what separate premeditated murders from accidental deaths."

He narrowed his eyes. "Funny how you didn't mention that the other day."

With a sweet smile, she shrugged. "It didn't suit me the other day. It suits me now."

"Wow, you know, I can definitely see why you and Winter get along so well." He feigned a look of exasperation and shook his head. "I've also got some news for you about the Schmidt case."

"Did she escape from prison or something?" Autumn muttered.

"No, at least not in the traditional sense."

Her brows drew together. "Then what?"

"She's dead. She hung herself in her cell after she was remanded."

Autumn's lips formed a perfect circle. "Well, I say justice was served."

Aiden shook his head. "Not really. I feel certain that there were more than two victims. Many more. And with her dead, we'll—"

"Never know the extent of her evil," Autumn finished for him. When he only nodded, she studied him even closer. "There's something more, isn't there?" she prodded.

There it was again, he thought. The mind reading.

"If you ask me, based on the case file I saw and what I know about her, I don't think it was a suicide. That lawyer, the guy who represented Robert Ladwig, Chase Parker. I looked to see what I could find on him, and it turned up a whole lot of nothing. As far as our records are concerned, the guy never existed. And he wasn't at the cabin where we found Schmidt."

"Shit," she breathed. "I'm still not going into witness protection, if that's what you're hinting at."

"It's not." He chuckled then decided to change the subject. The other would only end in an argument. "There's something else I wanted to ask you, though. If you've got a minute. Something psychology related."

"All right, shoot."

"There's this kid, a missing person of sorts. When he was a kid, five or six years old, he was taken in by a sociopath. And I mean that literally, not just that the man who took him in was an asshole. He was a bona fide sociopath with signs of paranoid schizophrenia to boot.

"As best as I can tell, when the kid was in high school, he blended in with a few distinctly different social groups. He'd tell one group of friends all the crazy shit he'd done and all the fights he'd gotten into in his old schools, and then he'd turn around and attend Wednesday evening youth group with another group. And they were all completely convinced that this kid was one of them. *That's* how well he blended in."

Autumn tapped a finger against her lips as she paused, looking thoughtful. "He moved around a lot, then?"

"He did."

"Well," her eyes flicked back to his, "based on what you've told me, I'd say you were reciting a textbook case of antisocial personality disorder. Also referred to as psychopathy or sociopathy."

"No, this is a real case," he assured her.

"Then, still based on what you've told me, it sounds like you might well be looking at a sociopath. Now, I can't say for sure without talking to the kid in a clinical setting. Just so we're clear on that, all right?"

"Absolutely. Thank you."

The fact that a forensic psychologist had reached the same conclusion he had drawn about Justin Black was validating, but at the same time, he had almost hoped she would tell him that the young man's development was completely normal.

Wish in one hand, shit in the other.

❄

WHEN WINTER TOOK in a sharp breath, Noah snapped his attention to where she sat beside him in their favored booth. He felt like an entire lifetime had elapsed since the last time they spent a lighthearted night at The Lift with their friends. Though he and Winter had beaten their companions to the bar, Bree and Autumn had both sent text messages to advise that they weren't far behind.

But when he noticed the haunted look in Winter's blue eyes, he wondered how lighthearted the night would be.

"What is it?" he asked.

In response, she merely turned her phone for him to see. On the screen was an email, the title of which was "no subject." As he looked down to the body of the message, he felt his eyes widen.

Hey, sis. Heard you've been looking for me.

"Holy shit." Noah's mouth gaped open at the same time a duo of familiar women came into view. The amusement vanished from Bree and Autumn's faces as they spotted him and Winter.

"Everything all right?" Bree scooted into the booth, Autumn close behind.

"It's Justin, my brother," Winter managed to say past the

emotion in her throat. "He knows we're looking for him. He sent me an email."

The fleeting surprise on Bree's face gave way to a reassuring smile. "Hey, we just closed the Schmidt case, right? Why don't we take a look at Justin's case while we've got downtime? We can send that email to the tech people, and I'll touch base with my contact in White Collar Crimes to see if they can give us some help looking into a stolen identity. That type of thing is their bread and butter."

When Winter's pang of worry slowly dissipated, Noah thought he could have reached across the table to give Bree a bear hug. "Then let's order a round and watch some preseason football," he said. "Or whatever other sport they're playing in here tonight. I don't really care."

"I can ask my aunt for the remote," Autumn replied with a chuckle.

Noah winked at her. "You *can?*"

"Dude, yes." She pushed herself out of the booth with an amused smirk. True to her word, when she returned, she held a sleek television remote. "So, what do you want to watch, Noah? A cooking show? Some SpongeBob?"

"Honestly? Either one's preferable to professional football. I like college ball, but when you get to the professional league, they just suck all the fun out of it."

Bree leveled an appreciative finger at him. "Couldn't have said it better myself."

"I don't mind professional football," Winter put in with a hapless shrug, glad for the distraction from her baby brother. "They're playing the game at the absolute highest level. It's impressive."

"I've got to back Winter on this one," Autumn added, her green eyes fixed on the nearest television as she flicked through channels. "It's not something I go out of my way to watch, but it is impressive."

"Whoa, Autumn, go back." Bree leaned forward to get a better view of the flickering screen mounted above the bar. "One more. There."

"CNN?" Autumn arched an eyebrow.

Beside the news anchor, the mugshot of a twenty-some-year-old man switched over to a photo of the same man taken from social media. Though Noah couldn't place him, he knew the face was familiar.

"Oh my god," Bree managed. Her dark eyes flicked over to him and then to Winter. "You remember the two guys who held a bunch of people hostage the night we found Kilroy?"

Even before she went on, he realized where he'd seen the man's face.

"That's one of them." She raised an arm to gesture to the television. "He's dead, murdered."

When Noah's phone buzzed in his pocket, he wondered if the word "murder" held an ancient power to summon a call from someone at the FBI. "Shit," he spat, "it's Osbourne."

Three sets of eyes were trained intently on him as he raised the device to his ear.

"Agent Dalton," he answered.

"Dalton," Max started. "One of the suspects we had in custody for the mass shooting earlier in the year was just killed. The guy was in federal custody, so it's federal juris-diction."

Noah bit back a derogatory comment about expending valuable federal budget to investigate the killing of a mass murderer. "He had to have been surrounded by cops. Do they have someone in custody?"

"No." Max hesitated. "They've got no leads, no nothing."

"How?"

"Because whoever killed him was a sniper."

The End

To be continued...

Want to Read More About Winter?

The next book in the series, *Winter's Ghost*, is now available! Some ghosts still live and breathe... Find it on Amazon Now!

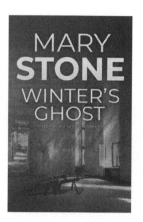

ACKNOWLEDGMENTS

How does one properly thank everyone involved in taking a dream and making it a reality? Let me try.

In addition to my family, whose unending support provided the foundation for me to find the time and energy to put these thoughts on paper, I want to thank the editors who polished my words and made them shine.

Many thanks to my publisher for risking taking on a newbie and giving me the confidence to become a bona fide author.

More than anyone, I want to thank you, my reader, for clicking on a nobody and sharing your most important asset, your time, with this book. I hope with all my heart I made it worthwhile.

Much love,
Mary

ABOUT THE AUTHOR

Mary Stone lives among the majestic Blue Ridge Mountains of East Tennessee with her two dogs, four cats, a couple of energetic boys, and a very patient husband.

As a young girl, she would go to bed every night, wondering what type of creature might be lurking underneath. It wasn't until she was older that she learned that the creatures she needed to most fear were human.

Today, she creates vivid stories with courageous, strong heroines and dastardly villains. She invites you to enter her world of serial killers, FBI agents but never damsels in distress. Her female characters can handle themselves, going toe-to-toe with any male character, protagonist or antagonist.

Discover more about Mary Stone on her website.
www.authormarystone.com

 facebook.com/authormarystone

 goodreads.com/AuthorMaryStone

BB bookbub.com/profile/3378576590

P pinterest.com/MaryStoneAuthor

O instagram.com/marystone_author

Printed in Great Britain
by Amazon

55449906R00183